BLUM BMC

12/96

MYSTERY

WITHDRAWN

Cold Hearts and Gentle People

Also by John R. Riggs
in Thorndike Large Print ®

A Dragon Lives Forever
One Man's Poison

Cold Hearts and Gentle People

John R. Riggs

A Garth Ryland Mystery

Thorndike Press • Thorndike, Maine

Published in 1995 by arrangement with Barricade Books.

Thorndike Large Print ® Americana Series.

The tree indicium is a trademark of Thorndike Press.

The text of this Large Print edition is unabridged.
Other aspects of the book may vary from the original edition.

Set in 16 pt. News Plantin.

Printed in the United States on permanent paper.

Library of Congress Cataloging in Publication Data

Riggs, John R., 1945–
    Cold hearts and gentle people / John R. Riggs.
        p.   cm. — (A Garth Ryland mystery)
    ISBN 0-7862-0317-X (lg. print : hc)
    1. Large type books. I. Title. II. Series:
Riggs, John R., 1945– Garth Ryland mystery.
PS3568.I372C65 1994b
813'.54—dc20   94-39558

T O   C A R O L E

who gave me the idea.

Special thanks to Ken Hirt, Denny Bridges, Edith Welliver, and Matt Huber.

I love those dear hearts
And gentle people
Who live in my hometown.
Yes, those dear hearts
And gentle people
Who'll never ever let me down.

— *from the song*
    "Dear Hearts and Gentle People"

CHAPTER 1

I was already awake when the phone rang.

Twenty-four hours ago, which was two A.M. Friday, I had put the *Oakalla Reporter* to bed, helped my printer and his wife put on the mailing stickers and load the newspapers into their old two-tone green Pontiac station wagon that resembled a tank and drove like one, then sat down at my desk, put my feet up, leaned back in my chair, and congratulated myself on a job well done. Had there been a cigar handy, I would have smoked it.

What pleased me most about that week's edition was that I had finally gotten around to writing the column that I had been wanting to write for years; but up until Wednesday, when I found myself in Fleenor's Drugstore, eating a hand-dipped butter pecan ice cream cone while gazing at the cover of an *Uncle Scrooge* comic, I had lacked the ammunition to make my point.

My point: small-town kids had it tough

these days. Hardly shocking news to anyone who read a newspaper or watched television or went to the movies, or who lived,
breathed, and entertained occasional
thoughts — original or otherwise. Kids ev-
erywhere had it tough these days, so aside
from the obvious — drugs, divorce, AIDS,
pregnancy, suicide, burglary, larceny, armed
robbery, rape, and murder — what was left?
Money, honey. Which is what makes the
world go round.

When I was a kid, I earned most of my
money mowing yards, carrying newspapers,
bucking bales of hay, helping my dad make
ice cream to sell in our dairy, and occasionally
helping the local veterinarian vaccinate and
castrate hogs. For mowing yards, I earned a
dollar or two a yard, depending on its size.
Five dollars a week for carrying the daily and
Sunday *Indianapolis Star*. A penny a bale for
bucking hay. Fifty cents an hour for making
ice cream. Five dollars a trip for castrating
hogs.

Most of that money I spent on ice cream
cones and comic books — nickel ice cream
cones, dime comic books. So a newspaper kid
in Oakalla today would have to earn seventy-
five dollars a week just to break even with
me. He would have to get fifteen to thirty
dollars each for yards in town and fifty to a

hundred for those in the country. He would need to bring in a hundred and fifty dollars for a thousand bales of hay, a good day's work for us, and for two hours of wrestling hogs another seventy-five. No kid in Oakalla that I knew of made that kind of money or was likely to in the near future.

What that did, then, was to put the working kid at risk. Either he had money to spend or he had time to be a kid, but he couldn't have both. So he usually gave up his time and as a result, gave up his childhood.

To my surprise, most of my readers agreed with me and had called me at the *Oakalla Reporter* on Friday to tell me so. By the end of the day, after so many pats on the back, I almost felt like a talk show host — omniscient, omnipotent, and omnificent. At least until five P.M., when I walked in the door at home.

"I see you're at it again" were Ruth's first words to me.

Ruth is a big-boned, iron-jawed Swede somewhere in her seventies, who has been my housekeeper ever since I've lived in Oakalla, which is longer than either of us care to remember. Unlike me, she has no love affair with the past.

"At it again," I said.

I took a seat at the kitchen table. Ruth stood

at the stove with her back to me. She appeared to be browning hamburger for either spaghetti or goulash. We didn't eat chili until the snow flew.

"But don't you agree that kids today are worse off than they were thirty years ago?" I said.

For the moment she didn't say anything. She had been chopping an onion to put in with the hamburger and had turned around to wipe her eyes with her apron. Onions were about the only thing that could make Ruth cry.

"I don't agree or disagree," she said. "I think you loaded the dice, that's all. Not everything has gone up like ice cream cones and comic books."

I leafed through the mail on the table, looking for something to read, and found it in my fraternity's national magazine, *Pin and Crescent*. The glow that I had brought home with me had already begun to fade.

"Wouldn't you load the dice to make a point?" I said. "Haven't you, to make a point?"

"I don't print a newspaper," she answered. "I don't always have to tell the whole truth."

"But I do?" I said, feeling the need to defend myself.

"Somebody does," she said.

"And I didn't?"

She poured the grease from the hamburger into a small bowl that would later be filled with table scraps and fed to the neighbor's dog. Since Ruth really didn't like the dog, a dachshund that, with regularity, barked at night and crapped in our yard, her plan must have been to harden its arteries to a premature death.

"No. You didn't," she said. "If you had, you would have gone back a few more years to when I was a kid, when most kids would work all day at home for nothing, and a grown man would work from sunup to sundown for a dollar a day or less just to feed his family. Those were not the 'good old days,' Garth. I know, because I lived them."

"So what's the answer?" I said, shoving the magazine aside.

She added a fresh tomato from our garden to the skillet. "The answer is not to hold too tight with either hand. To either the past or the present. Both have room for improvement. Even your own."

"Not to me, it doesn't. My past, I mean."

"That's because you were lucky. A lot of us weren't."

"I won't argue with that. I was a lucky kid.

Either that or I was too dumb to know the difference."

"Not dumb, Garth. But maybe something else."

"Such as?"

She rinsed her hands in the sink and used a paper towel to dry them. Up until the time that she began to set the table, I thought that she was going to answer me.

Supper turned out to be goulash, white bread, and butter, instead of the spaghetti, meat sauce, and garlic bread that I was hoping for. We had canned pears for dessert. Then Ruth washed the dishes, and I dried them and put them away.

Afterwards we went into the living room where she sat down in her favorite chair, I sat down in mine, and we watched the national news together. By the end of the broadcast, which featured a Neo-Nazi march and a Right-to-Life blockade, the smile that I had brought home with me on this, the fourth day of September, seemed as distant as the first robin of spring. I picked up my magazine and began to read.

"Damn," I said aloud. I had just read in the *Pin and Crescent* that one of my fraternity brothers had died.

Ruth looked over the top of her reading glasses at me and said nothing.

"Ron Richards died," I said, as if that explained everything.

"I see," she said, looking back down at her *National Geographic.* Ruth had never met a magazine that she didn't like. We had more titles in stock than some newsstands.

"Ron Richards was a fraternity brother of mine," I said. A Vietnam veteran, he had gone through medical school on the GI Bill, had become a family doctor in Mansfield, Ohio, and in the past few years had married his childhood sweetheart, whom he had loved all along but who had married someone else when he was off to war. Ron Richards was one of those funny, irreverent, sentimental, give-you-his-last-dollar guys, who I thought would always be around because the world was a better place with him in it. "Every other year since college," I continued, "I planned to go visit him. But I never did."

"Now you never will," she said without sympathy.

Ron Richards was still on my mind when the phone call came a few hours later. That was one of the reasons that I was awake. The storm that sneaked into town without so much as a gust of wind or a clap of thunder, then dropped its load of rain straight down in a hail of silver bullets, was the other.

"Is that you, Garth?"

I recognized the voice on the other end of the line. It belonged to Eugene Yuill, Oakalla's newest deputy sheriff in what lately had been a long line of deputy sheriffs.

"It's me. Is that you, Eugene?"

"Right as rain. I'm on my way over there now to pick you up." Eugene Yuill sounded out of breath, as if, like me, he had just stumbled down the stairs in the middle of the night to answer the phone. Except Eugene didn't have a stairs in his house.

"May I ask why?" I said.

I listened through the kitchen window to what was left of the rain. It had come without a rumble. It was leaving the same way.

"Luella Skiles claims that there's a prowler in Monroe Edmonds's house. Clarkie said to call you if I got into something that I thought I couldn't handle alone."

Clarkie was Sheriff Harold Clark, who had left on Sunday for a two-week police-training seminar in Milwaukee. What he hoped to learn there was how to be a more effective day-to-day police officer, which was a skill that all of us in Oakalla agreed that he needed. However, I questioned the wisdom of it all. Training Clarkie to police the town was sort of like trying to teach a seal to hunt rabbits. You either had the instinct for it or you didn't.

"You've handled it all week without any

14

problems," I said. "What makes tonight any different?"

Deputy Eugene Yuill waited a moment before answering. He seemed to be gathering his courage to tell me the truth. "Something long and hairy that's crawling right up my backbone. That's what makes tonight different," he said.

I listened as the rain dripped off of my roof into a puddle below. It alone knew what else was out there. "I'll be waiting for you on my front porch," I said.

"Trouble?" Ruth asked after I'd hung up.

I had thought that she was upstairs in bed. But apparently she had fallen asleep on the couch, since she was still wearing her clothes from earlier that night.

"I don't know. Luella Skiles thinks that someone is prowling around in Monroe Edmonds's house."

"Do you believe her?" Ruth said. "If memory serves me right, she's cried wolf before on that count."

"It could be true," I said. "Times are tough, and Monroe has a lot of antiques sitting around."

"I don't like it, Garth. More to the point, something in me doesn't like it. That's why I was still on the couch. That same something in me said there was no point in going to bed."

15

Though she didn't profess to be psychic, whenever Ruth got a feeling about something, I knew better than to ignore it.

I started upstairs to my bedroom. "Something in Eugene Yuill doesn't like it, either."

I left by the front door at the same moment that Eugene Yuill's squad car pulled up in front of the house. We drove without lights to the four-way stop at Jackson Street, then along School Street toward the south end of Oakalla.

A smokelike mist had followed the rain into town. Patches of it lay stretched between houses and along the street like giant spider webs. They glistened under the streetlights, closed in around us as we approached Monroe Edmonds's house.

"I don't see any prowler about," Eugene said.

He had parked under a giant silver maple in front of the house and shut off the engine. Intermittent drops of rain fell from the maple onto the roof of the car. Enveloped in fog, we were lucky to see as far as the sidewalk right there beside us.

I looked over at Eugene. A tall, bony, slow-talking and slow-moving not-so-free thinker, who always wore steel-tipped Redwing work boots, size fourteen, and who had driven a feed truck for the elevator for the most of his life (and still did some weekends), he didn't want to get out of the car any more than I did.

"How can we tell from here?" I said.

We eased our doors open, then closed, and stood a moment on the sidewalk, listening for any prowlerlike noises that might be coming from the house. We heard one, at the same time that we saw what appeared to be a light flash on and off inside the house.

It took Eugene a moment to find his voice. "I'll take the front door," he said in a hoarse whisper. "You take the back."

"Just give me time to get there before you go inside."

I went around to the back of the house, which I knew to be painted a rust red but in the dark looked brown. Hibiscus grew in a row right up next to the house and pressed their pink heads against its siding, as if for warmth. A thick tangle of ivy had entwined itself around and around each of the two supporting pillars of the back stoop and seemed to be about the only thing holding them together. Rhubarb and asparagus, both gone to seed, grew on either side of the stoop, and foxtail stuck up like long green feathers, through the deep cracks in the stoop itself, giving the whole place the sad aura of neglect.

Stepping up onto the stoop, I was about to

open the door when I heard hurried footsteps headed my way from inside the house. I stepped aside just in time to see the back door fly open and someone trip over my foot. He hit the ground with a loud groan, rolled over on his back, and lay there dazed, looking blindly up into the beam of my flashlight, like an owl at the unwanted sun.

"Hello, Tom," I said. "Fancy meeting you here."

"Turn that damn thing off before I shove it down your throat," he growled.

Tom Ford, the man who lay on the ground at my feet, was, when sober, Oakalla's best electrician, a decent father and husband, and for the most part, an okay guy. When he was drinking, which was a lot of the time lately, he was your basic s.o.b.

"Garth, where are you?" I heard Eugene Yuill call from inside.

"I'm out back," I yelled.

Tom Ford raised his hand to shield his eyes. "I said turn that damn thing off. I'm not going anywhere."

"You promise to stay put?" I said.

"I said I would."

I turned the flashlight off and waited for Eugene Yuill who arrived on the scene a few seconds later. In his haste to get there, he slipped on the back stoop and nearly put his size fourteen boot with its steel toe right in the middle of Tom Ford's face.

"Jesus Christ!" Tom yelled, rolling away from him. "Watch where you're going."

Tom Ford sat up. His eyes were hot, and his hands were clenched into fists. I could smell beer on him, but he didn't reek with it the way he sometimes did.

"I was lost, that's all," Tom said. "I walked into the wrong house by mistake."

Tom Ford and his family lived across the alley in the next house west of there. Had it not been for the alley, it would have been hard to tell where Monroe Edmonds's crabgrass ended and Tom Ford's crabgrass began.

Eugene holstered his gun, then glanced at me to see whether I bought that explanation or not. I shrugged. Stranger things had happened in Oakalla. And with a drunk in the middle of the night, about anything was possible.

"Why did you run, then, when you heard me come in the front door?" Eugene asked.

"Because by then I knew I was in the wrong house. And the way Old Lady Skiles keeps her eye on me, I already knew who might be at the door. It's not the first time that she's called the cops on me."

I knew that to be true if Eugene Yuill didn't. Once when Rupert Roberts was still sheriff

19

and once after Clarkie had become sheriff, Luella Skiles had called to say that Tom Ford was beating his wife. It was obvious after checking out the situation at Tom Ford's house that Luella Skiles had been right, but both times Tom Ford's wife, Tanya, refused to press charges. So the beatings went on, I assumed, as they always do.

"Miss Skiles didn't name names, if that's what you're saying," Eugene said. "She just said that there was a prowler in the house."

I looked at the trusty Timex on my left wrist. Its semifluorescent hands said that it was now two-thirty A.M. Luella Skiles's call to Eugene had come in at least thirty-five minutes ago. Tom Ford had spent an awfully long time discovering that he was in the wrong house. But then time was not something that drunks usually paid close attention to.

"Why don't you go on home for now, Tom," I said. "Deputy Yuill and I will try to sort this out between us."

Tom, however, seemed in no hurry to leave. I followed his gaze to the house next door where the silhouette of Luella Skiles was visible through her bay window. His gaze was bright eyed with malice.

"While you're at it," he said, "you might tell Old Lady Skiles to mind her own business. That is, if she has any."

After a pause of a few seconds that seemed longer than it was, he squared his shoulders and walked across the alley toward home. For someone who couldn't find his way out of his neighbor's house, he walked a remarkably straight line.

"What do you think?" Eugene asked me after Tom Ford was out of hearing.

"About what?" My gaze was still on Tom Ford, who even though he had just been granted a reprieve, seemed not to have noticed.

"About any of this," Eugene said. "Do you buy Tom's story that he got into the wrong house by mistake?"

I thought back to a confrontation that I'd witnessed less than thirty-six hours ago, when Tom Ford came into the Corner Bar and Grill where his wife, Tanya, worked as a waitress. Though I was too far away to hear all of what was said, two things were immediately apparent. One, Tom Ford was angry at his wife, angry enough to shove her up against the bar with the place full of customers; two, Monroe Edmonds was what he was angry about.

"No," I said to Eugene. "I'm not sure I buy that story."

"What do you figure he was doing in there?"

"I don't know. Maybe Monroe can tell us."

We went in the back door and began turning

on lights as we went from the utility room to the kitchen to the formal dining room to the parlor, where two pieces of Victorian furniture, a studded high-back chair and a studded high-back love seat sat facing each other across a square of hardwood floor. An oak upright piano stood against the oak staircase between a Chinese vase on a fern stand and small misshapen closet door that led under the staircase. On the plaster walls of the parlor hung three oil paintings, two rimmed in gold and one in silver, none whose work I recognized.

"What's that I smell?" I said to Eugene.

We stood at the foot of the stairs. I'd just caught a whiff of something that was old, very old, and familiar.

Eugene stuck a stick of spearmint gum into his mouth and offered me one, which I refused. "I don't know, Garth. I can't smell a thing but this stick of gum."

Neither could I by then.

I called up the stairs for Monroe to come down but got no response. "Maybe he can't hear you," Eugene said.

"Why not?"

"Maybe the fat's gone to his ears."

"You might have a point."

Monroe Edmonds was a bachelor, who weighed somewhere over four hundred pounds, and who rarely left his house anymore simply because it was too hard for him to get around. A former railroad engineer, he had dabbled in antiques all of his life and after he had retired from the railroad at an early age, had opened an antique shop there in his house. Two years ago, he had sold the bulk of his antiques at auction and retired for the second time, though the word around Oakalla was, if the price was right, he was still willing to deal.

"Monroe, are you up there?" I yelled.

No answer.

I led, as Eugene followed me up the stairs. Breathing heavily, stomping each step as if killing rats while at the same time chomping on his gum, he sounded like a horse with asthma behind me.

We stopped at the top of the stairs, and I again called out to Monroe Edmonds and again got no answer. Beside me there on the landing, a curved-glass china cabinet displayed a chocolate R. S. Prussia berry set along with several R. S. Prussia pitchers and bowls. Shelves had also been built along the top of the landing to hold an assortment of crockery and tinware, most of them unusual pieces, the likes of which I hadn't seen before.

"There's a lot of nice stuff here," I said.

Eugene picked up a whale-oil lamp from the shelf, gave it a cursory glance, and set it back down again. "You couldn't prove it by me."

Monroe Edmonds wasn't upstairs. Not in his bedroom, the spare bedroom, bathroom, junk room, or linen closet. I pulled down the stairs, climbed up into the attic, and shone my flashlight around. Neither was he up there, unless he was hiding in a trunk.

"I don't figure it," Eugene said, taking out his gum and sticking it in a wad behind his ear. "Where could the man be?"

I looked along the upstairs hallway. The only door that we hadn't tried was the one to the elevator, which Monroe used to haul himself and his four hundred plus pounds upstairs and downstairs. The reason that we hadn't tried it was that neither one of us had thought of it.

"He might be in here," I said, sliding open the elevator door.

Sure enough, he was.

CHAPTER 2

Monroe Edmonds lay, in his red-and-white striped pajamas, on his side on the floor of the elevator. He didn't appear to have died in his sleep. His right arm was outstretched in front of him as if in supplication, his hand partially open, its five fat fingers grasping nothing but air. Dark purple, almost black, his face reminded me of a swollen water balloon about to burst. He smelled bad, too. Sometime before he died, Monroe Edmonds had peed his pants.

"Whoo!" Eugene said, backing up a step. "I ain't seen nothing like that since Korea."

I wished I could have said the same.

"Is he cold?" Eugene asked, as I knelt beside Monroe's body.

"That's what I'm about to find out." I gingerly touched my hand to Monroe's face. "Cold," I said. Cold as a crick rock, Grandmother Ryland would have said.

"What do we do now?"

"You'd better call Ben Bryan." Ben Bryan was the county coroner.

Without thinking, Eugene had taken his gum from behind his ear, put it into his mouth, and started to chew it. I was beginning to think that Clarkie wasn't such a bad bargain after all.

"Can't," he said. "Ben and Faye have gone to Eau Claire to visit their kids. He told me not to expect them back before Tuesday or Wednesday."

"Call Doc Airhart, then. Tell him if he needs a ride, I'll come after him."

"Will do." But Eugene made no move in any direction.

"I think there's a phone in the kitchen," I said, believing that he needed direction. "And probably one in Monroe's bedroom."

"That's not it, Garth. Shouldn't we call somebody else?"

"Who, for instance?"

He hesitated, then said, "The law."

"We are the law in Oakalla, Eugene, like it or not." He, officially appointed by the county council. I, unofficially, with my tarnished special deputy's badge that Rupert Roberts had given me over a fifth of Wild Turkey several hundred years ago.

"I don't feel much like it," he said.

"That makes two of us."

While he went to call Doc Airhart, I examined the dents that I had discovered in the sides of the elevator. They seemed to match the bruises on the palms of Monroe's hands and the heels of his feet. I wondered if he had somehow gotten trapped in the elevator and tried to pound his way out. So I tried the elevator door several times, but it seemed to work fine.

Eugene returned from downstairs. "Well?" I said, as he stood smacking his gum while looking over my shoulder. "Did you get ahold of Doc Airhart?"

"I got ahold of him."

"And?"

I could tell by the look on Eugene's face that he didn't want to answer. "And he said he's not coming. He's getting too old for this sort of thing. But he'd send someone else."

"Who?" I couldn't think of anyone else in Oakalla who had even a passing knowledge of pathology.

"He didn't say."

"So what are we supposed to do in the meantime?"

"Wait here, Doc said."

I looked down at Monroe Edmonds, whose appearance didn't seem to be improving any. "Easy for him to say."

Five minutes later, I heard a car pull up outside. A few seconds after that, I heard someone enter the house by the front door. I looked at my Timex again. Whoever said that time went by on winged feet obviously hadn't spent too much time with Monroe Edmonds lately.

"Hello? Anyone here?" I heard someone say from the bottom of the stairs.

My heart jumped, missing a beat. She sounded exactly like someone I used to love. Not in the pitch of her voice, but in its timbre, that music to my ears that her voice had come to mean to me.

"Up here," I said, barely trusting myself to speak. "We're up here."

I wasn't disappointed when I saw her, just disheartened. I had been expecting one person and got another — one who wore a green surgical smock, her straw-yellow hair tied back with a rubber band, and who smelled faintly of cigarette smoke. She appeared to be about five-feet four-inches tall and somewhere in her mid-thirties.

"Hi," she said cheerfully, offering Eugene her hand. "I'm Abby Airhart."

Eugene nodded but didn't say anything. I didn't know if he were tongue tied, star struck, or both.

"And you must be Garth Ryland," she said,

offering her hand to me. "I've heard a lot about you."

I took her hand. As I did, I noticed her eyes for the first time. Blue-green with tiny orange flecks in them, they fairly bubbled with life. Smiling eyes. Eyes that could know sadness but never be sad for long.

For one of the few times in my life, I found myself at a loss for words. I nodded stupidly as Eugene had done, then said, "Who are you?"

She dropped my hand. The smile briefly left her face but just as quickly returned. "Abby Airhart. I thought I made that clear."

"What I mean is, what are you doing here?"

"Uncle Bill didn't tell you?"

"Apparently not."

"I'm the new surgeon in town. I started at the hospital just this week."

I scratched my head, no doubt looking as dumb as I felt. She seemed to be enjoying my discomfort and didn't try to hide it.

"Why didn't I know that?" I said.

"I thought you did. You wrote me up last week in the *Oakalla Reporter*."

Now she really had me going. If I had written her up, I would have known about it.

"Says who?" I said.

"Says me. Remember that blurb about an

A. Pence, the new surgeon at the hospital. That's me."

I barely remembered the blurb. It had been passed on to me by the hospital a couple weeks before, and I had printed it because I needed a filler for the front page the following week. What I did remember about it, though, was that her credentials were impeccable. At the time, however, I assumed that I was writing about a man. Silly me. Standing here with egg all over my face. A male chauvinist pig, to boot.

"You introduced yourself as Abby Airhart," I said, trying to salvage something out of this.

"That I did," she said, without offering an explanation. "Now, if you gentlemen will excuse me, I have work to do."

She withdrew some plastic gloves from the pocket of her smock and went into the elevator. I left Eugene standing guard over her and went outside where a black Cadillac El Dorado, a street wide and nearly a block long, was parked in front of Eugene's patrol car. Sitting in the driver's seat was none other than Uncle Bill himself.

"Thanks, Doc, for setting me up," I said.

"You don't have to thank me," he answered. "You laid all the groundwork yourself."

A small spritely come-as-you-are man with

snow-white hair and merry blue eyes, Dr. William T. Airhart was the closest thing to an icon that we had in Oakalla. Once coroner of Cuyahoga County, Ohio, and at the time one of the top-ranked surgeons in the world, he had come to Oakalla in the 1930s where he had practiced medicine until at age seventy-five he had retired several years ago.

He and I had first met over a case of chicken pox (mine) very early on in my life when he came out to Grandmother Ryland's farm and saved me from what I thought was sure death. For a few years after that, I saw him about once a summer, usually with an earache from swimming in Hidden Quarry, and then for a long period of time, until I bought the *Oakalla Reporter* with the money that Grandmother Ryland had willed me and moved to Oakalla, I didn't see him at all. Since then, we had renewed our acquaintance and become fast friends.

"Why didn't you warn me who she was and that she was coming to town," I said, "before I exposed my ignorance?"

"That's not the way she wanted it. She wanted to come here with as little hardware and fanfare as possible."

"Why? Is she ashamed of you or something?"

Doc only smiled at that. He knew I was

trying to get his goat. When he smiled and his eyes crinkled in laughter, I realized where the laughter in Abby Pence-Airhart's eyes had come from. Like with Doc, it bubbled up from somewhere deep in her soul.

"Besides," I said, "the hospital referred to her as A. A. Pence. She introduced herself to me as Abby Airhart."

Doc leaned his head out the window of the Cadillac to take a long drink of the night air. "Pence is her married name. Airhart's her unmarried name. She's in the process of changing it."

"To what?"

"Airhart, you ninny. She's in the middle of a divorce."

"Oh," I said.

"What does that mean, *oh?*"

I smiled at him. As much as I liked Doc, it was hard to explain to someone who had never been through a divorce, who in fact had married for life and buried his wife, Constance, fifty-five years later, that no matter what the court said about who went where or who got what or when by the calendar your marriage officially ended, once the process was begun, you were in the middle of a divorce for a long, long time — sometimes even longer than you had been married.

"Are there any kids involved?" I said,

avoiding his question.

"Nope."

"That's something, at least."

Eugene Yuill came outside to where Doc and I were. I heard him coming from the time he hit the stairs.

"Not much Indian blood in him, is there," Doc said to me.

"Not that I can see."

Eugene stopped and stood awkwardly a few feet away, hesitant to interrupt us, even though it was obvious that he had come on an errand. "Dr. Airhart would like to see us both upstairs," he said to me. He tipped his hat to Doc. "No offense, Doc."

"None taken," Doc said. He folded his arms, laid his head back on the seat, and closed his eyes. "Just tell that niece of mine that I'm not going to sit out here all night."

Eugene and I went back inside the house where Dr. Abby Pence-Airhart was waiting for us on the second-floor landing. She didn't look any worse for her encounter with death. But I supposed that as a surgeon, who I remembered now had done her residency in the emergency room of Detroit's Henry Ford Hospital, she had gotten used to it.

"I think he died of a heart attack," she said. "But I won't know for certain until after the autopsy."

"Which you'll perform when?" I said.

"Tonight. As soon as we can get him out of here."

I didn't ask her what her credentials as a pathologist were. I assumed that since Ben Bryan had asked her to cover for him, she had some. If not, Doc could walk her through the process.

"What about the dents in the elevator?" I said. "Those bruises on Monroe's hands and feet?"

"You don't miss much, do you?" she said. Her look was noncommittal. I didn't know whether I had just been complimented or ever so subtly reprimanded.

"Not much," I said.

"To tell the truth," she said, "that's what I wanted to talk to you about. I don't think that those bruises came as a result of a heart attack, but the other way around. What I mean is, I think Mr. Edmonds somehow got trapped in the elevator, panicked, tried to beat his way out, and had a heart attack as a result."

"The elevator was all the way to the second floor when we found him," I said.

She smiled at me. It seemed genuine. "That was going to be my next question. We seem to be thinking along the same lines here."

Two of us, anyway. The look on Eugene's face said that he didn't have a clue as to what we were thinking. "Just what are you saying, Dr. Airhart?" he said.

"Do you want to take it from here?" Abby Pence-Airhart said to me. "I've got to find a way to get Mr. Edmonds back to Uncle Bill's."

"My suggestion would be to call the volunteer fire department," I said.

"You're kidding, of course."

"It's going to take ten men and a boy to carry him out of here the way it is. We might as well get all the help we can."

She thought it over, then said, "What's their number?"

"Call Danny Palmer. He's the chief. Have him round up the rest of the guys for you."

"And what will you be doing while all of this is going on?"

"Watching, I hope."

"You don't do bodies?"

"Not if I can help it."

While she went to call Danny Palmer, I explained to Eugene why we were concerned about the assumed sequence of events that had led to Monroe Edmonds's death. If he had trapped himself in the elevator and had a fatal heart attack as a result, how then did the elevator get to the second floor where we had found it? So it was possible that he hadn't trapped himself in the elevator but had been trapped there by someone else, died as a result of it, and then been given a ride to the second floor to make it look like an accident.

"How could somebody trap Monroe in his own elevator?" Eugene asked. "I don't see any stop button on it."

"Wait here," I said.

I went downstairs. On my way through the parlor, I met Abby Pence-Airhart. "They're on their way," she said.

"Good."

"Where are you going in such a hurry?"

"Come along and I'll show you."

She followed me through the dining room and kitchen into the utility room where I finally found Monroe's fuse box under one of his old coats.

"What are you looking for?" she asked, as I opened the box.

"The master switch."

"Aren't we all?"

I didn't know how to answer that, so I didn't try. "It's going to get very dark very soon in here," I said.

"I'm not afraid of the dark."

"I am."

The instant I pulled the master switch the whole house went dark. "That's how!" I yelled at Eugene.

"I'm right here," Abby Pence-Airhart reminded me.

How could I not know that?

When I turned the lights back on, she was in the kitchen. I hadn't heard her leave, but I had surely felt it, the vacuum that followed in her wake.

"I thought you weren't afraid of the dark," I said to her on our way up the stairs.

"It's not the dark I'm afraid of."

"What then?"

She stopped ahead of me on the stairs. I almost ran over her and had to grab ahold of her to keep from knocking her down. When I held on to her a moment longer than was necessary, she made no attempt to break away.

"Being wrong," she said, resuming her climb up the stairs.

"Are you often wrong?"

She stopped again at the top of the stairs. This time I kept my distance. "No. But when I am, I make up for all the times I wasn't."

"Same here."

"Strange, isn't it," she said, "the messes we sometimes find ourselves in? Who'd have thunk it when we were kids way back when?"

"Not me," I assured her.

"Me either."

Within minutes, almost as quickly as if they had been on a fire call, several of Oakalla's volunteer firemen arrived, wrapped Monroe Edmonds in the rubber sheet that Danny Palmer had brought along for just that purpose, carried Monroe down the stairs and out the door, and loaded him into the back of Jeremy Dellinger's pickup. I watched the pickup drive away, then Abby Pence-Airhart and her Uncle Bill, then Eugene Yuill when I told him that since it was no longer raining, I'd just as soon walk home.

Behind me, Monroe Edmonds's house was dark and would likely stay that way for months to come. To the south, Luella Skiles still stood silhouetted in her bay window. I wondered how long she had been there. I wondered how long she would be there. If she were waiting for Monroe Edmonds to come home again, it would be a long time.

CHAPTER 3

About an hour after I landed in bed, I awakened to the smell of coffee perking and bacon frying. Dawn had come, bringing a new day with it. Better than the alternative, I supposed.

"Morning," I said to Ruth as I poured myself a cup of coffee and sat down at the kitchen table.

Ruth stood at the stove frying bacon. She wore the flowered pink robe that Martha Washington had willed her and the fur-lined moccasins that I had bought her for Christmas several years ago. She also wore a scowl on her face, one that meant she was at odds with herself or with me.

"Scrambled eggs or French toast?" she said.

"Both."

"I can do that."

I was hoping she could.

She continued frying bacon. I continued to sit and to sip my coffee. Outside, Oakalla was wrapped in a blanket of fog. Though, above it, I could see a hint of blue sky.

"You're awfully quiet this morning," I said.

"I've got something on my mind." Using a fork, she began to turn the bacon one piece at a time.

I yawned and stretched and felt better than I had a right to on an hour's sleep. "I figured as much," I said. "Want to tell me about it?"

"I was out of line yesterday about your column in the paper. It's just that the fifties, which you are so proud of, weren't all that good a time in my life. That's when Mary Jane died."

Mary Jane was Ruth's daughter, who had died of polio.

"Nineteen fifty-four, right?" I said.

"Yes. Nineteen fifty-four."

"You can't blame me for that."

She began to remove the strips of bacon one by one from the skillet and laid them on a platter that she then put in the oven. She broke some eggs into a bowl and using the same fork that she had on the bacon, began to scramble them. If the depression had taught Ruth anything, it was economy of thought, word, and deed. Not that she was in any way miserly. Just the opposite was true. But better than anyone else I knew, except perhaps for Grandmother Ryland, she knew the difference between need and want, and never got the two confused.

"I don't blame you, Garth," she said. "It's just that sometimes I see you in her and her in you, and I wish that she could have enjoyed her life, the way you seem to."

"It's been a long time in coming," I said. "And I'm not even sure I'm there yet."

"You're there, Garth. You might not know it yet, but you're there."

After breakfast we sat drinking a second cup of coffee, as the fog began to lift, revealing more and more of Oakalla and the sky above. Ruth took my plate from in front of me, stacked it and our silverware on hers, set both plates out of the way, settled back in her seat, and said, "Want to tell me about last night?"

"What I can of it."

When I finished, she didn't say anything for several seconds. I didn't know if she were thinking or if I had put her to sleep. "It doesn't figure, Garth," she finally said.

"What doesn't figure?"

"Any of it. In the first place, drunk or sober, Tom Ford has never had any trouble finding his way home before."

"We don't know that for sure."

Ruth gave me a stony look. She hated to be contradicted, particularly when she was building up to something. "In the second place, if Monroe Edmonds was as cold as you said he was, Tom Ford couldn't have had anything to do with it because he didn't get into the house all that long before you did."

"I thought of that," I said. "But we don't know how long Tom Ford was in the house before Luella Skiles noticed he was there."

"Not long," Ruth said with certainty. "Knowing Luella Skiles."

"Tom Ford did say that she was keeping a close eye on him."

"It's not Tom Ford that she's keeping an eye on."

"Elaborate, please."

"Think about it, Garth," she said. "Who have been next-door neighbors longer than just about anybody else in Oakalla?"

The sun burned through the fog and buried itself in our apple tree. "Let me guess. Luella Skiles and Monroe Edmonds."

"For nearly seventy years now. And both living in the same houses that their parents were married in."

"Go on."

Ruth got up and began to clear the table. She couldn't sit still for long, only when reading or sleeping or falling asleep in front of the television. "I've heard that they were once talking marriage, but something happened to put an end to that."

42

"Do you have any idea what?"

She squirted some Ivory into the sink and began running hot water for dishes. "I have an idea. But you'd do better to ask Luella Skiles herself."

It was time I left. Otherwise, I would end up drying dishes, which was not something that I wanted to do on a sunny September Saturday morning. But there was still something that I needed to talk to Ruth about.

"Ruth, I met someone last night," I said. In telling Ruth about what went on, I had omitted mentioning Abby Pence-Airhart by name. Instead, I had referred to her as the "new surgeon in town."

"Doc Airhart's niece, you mean."

"How did you know?"

"Simple. She's the new surgeon in town."

"You might have told me."

"You didn't ask."

I thought that over and decided that it wasn't worth pursuing. "Anyway," I said, "she reminds me a lot of Diana."

Ruth stiffened. Diana Baldwin was not one of Ruth's favorite people, and Ruth had never been shy about letting me know that.

"That's not what I mean," I said.

"Then why did you say it?"

"What I mean is that she has the same something that Diana had, that same giggle in her soul that makes her fully alive, and makes me attracted to her. That's all."

Ruth plunged her hands into the soapy water and began washing dishes. "So what's the problem?"

I drank the last of my coffee. Cold or not, it tasted good. "No problem. I just wanted you to know."

The phone rang. "Garth, I didn't catch you at a bad time, did I?" It was Eugene Yuill.

"No, Eugene. What's on your mind?"

He hesitated, then said, "I just wondered where I should start today?"

The sun had eaten away nearly all of the fog. Only a few stubborn patches, those in the deepest shade, remained.

"Where did you start yesterday?" I said.

"At the pump house."

"Then that's where I'd start today."

"What about . . ." Then he whispered, as if someone might overhear, "you know, what happened last night."

Since he had been sheriff, Clarkie had already gone through several deputies. One of the reasons, I felt, was that Clarkie, who hated the job but loved the position, subscribed to the same school of thought that my father had followed in teaching me how not to swim — the throw-them-in-the-deep-end-sink-or-swim school of thought. What Clarkie failed to realize, like my father before him, was that some of us, once in deep water, sank like a brick to the bottom of the pool.

"I'll take care of it, Eugene. You go ahead doing what you've always done."

"You will?" He sounded more disappointed than relieved. Maybe I had misjudged him.

"For now," I said. "But I'll stay in touch."

"Garth," he said before I could hang up. "I've been thinking about that elevator. It came to mind that Tom Ford is an electrician. A pretty darn good one, at that."

"That came to my mind, too," I said. "But it doesn't take an electrician to find and pull a master switch."

"I suppose you're right," he said. "But say somebody did trap Monroe in his own elevator and he died as a result of it, would that be murder?"

"I don't know what the state would call it, Eugene. Why don't we wait for the autopsy report before we call it anything."

"Do you suppose it's ready by now?"

"Dr. Airhart said it would be."

"Thanks, Garth." Click.

"What did Eugene want?" Ruth asked after I hung up.

"A blank check, I think."

"Did you give him one?"

"I'm not sure, Ruth. I hope not."

"God help us if you did."

I nodded but didn't say anything.

"I'll see you later, Ruth. I need to take a walk somewhere."

Ruth had finished the dishes and was rinsing the soapsuds down the drain. "We got interrupted. Was there anything else about Doc Airhart's niece that I should know?"

"She smokes. I smelled it on her clothes."

"So did Karl, for the most of his life." Karl was Ruth's late husband, who had died a few months before I moved to Oakalla.

"Karl also died from lung cancer."

Ruth shrugged. "I don't blame the cigarettes, if that's what you're thinking. His clock just ran down, that's all."

"Still, it's a concern."

She gazed into the empty sink. I would have given a lot to know what she saw there. "As it should be."

CHAPTER 4

Stripped of its fog, its shadows shrinking as the streets and lawns of Oakalla were laid bare by the sun, the day outside was starting to heat up. It had been a strange year. Spring had come too soon in late February and early March, backslid into winter, rallied briefly, and died. All summer, the coolest in my memory, it had felt like fall. Now that September was here, it finally felt like summer. But not for long, I imagined. The days grew short when they reached September.

A block from Doc Airhart's house, I saw a sheriff's car back out of his drive and head south toward the hospital. I didn't wonder who was in it.

Doc Airhart lived in a large two-story white frame house with an acre of green roof, two red brick chimneys, and a high, wide, and handsome front porch, built especially for long and lazy summer afternoons. As I knocked on the front door, I heard Doc's English setter

Daisy bark in greeting. A gift from me, Daisy would soon lead Doc and me on her first official grouse hunt. I hoped she wouldn't be too disappointed in us.

"You people must think I'm starved for company," Doc said after opening the door. Daisy came bounding up to greet me. I bent down to scratch her ears and got licked in the face for my trouble.

"There's only one of me that I can see," I said, squeezing past Daisy into the house.

"I'm referring to your partner in crime, Eugene Yuill," Doc said. I followed him down the hall and into the kitchen where Daisy went running for the corner, returning with a nearly bald tennis ball for me to throw. "He just left here not more than five minutes ago."

"I know. I saw him leave."

"Don't throw that ball!" Doc warned, just as I was about to give it a toss. "Unless you want to spend the next hour doing that. Here," he said, taking the ball away from me, "give it to me."

Doc walked to the back door, opened it, and threw the ball outside, as Daisy nearly tore a hole in the linoleum, trying to get traction to go after it. Once in motion, however, she made up for lost ground and ran the ball down before it even bounced twice. Meanwhile Doc closed the back door on her.

"That's a cruel trick," I said as Daisy came racing up to the back door with the ball in her mouth, only to find no one there.

"She's young. She'll soon get over it." Wiping his hands on his pants, Doc returned to the kitchen and poured us each a cup of coffee.

He was right. She soon got over it. The last I saw of her, Daisy was pushing the ball around the yard with her nose, having a high old time. I left my stand at the window and sat down at the table across from Doc.

"You had breakfast?" he asked.

"I just got up from it."

"Good. Because I wasn't planning on fixing another one."

Warm from the morning sun, the kitchen smelled like apples. "What was Eugene doing here?" I said.

"Don't you know? I thought you sicked him on me."

Daisy now had a squirrel treed. I could hear him barking at her as I rose to see her on point under Doc's beech tree. "Come look at this, Doc," I said. "She's pointing a squirrel."

Reluctantly Doc rose to look out the east window, then sat back down again. "Yesterday evening, it was the neighbor's cat. The day before that, a woodpecker. Be our luck it'll be a skunk when we finally get her in the woods."

I sat down as the squirrel continued to rail at Daisy. "How long will she hold her point?" I said.

"Until the squirrel breaks and runs, or hell freezes over, whichever comes first."

"Sounds like she might be a good one."

"Better than either of us have a right to expect."

I doctored my coffee with cream and sugar, then sat back in my chair to drink it. "Just what did you tell Eugene?" I said.

"I told him the same thing that I'll tell you. You want to know about Monroe Edmonds, you'll have to talk to Abby."

"And where might she be?"

"The hospital. Making her rounds."

"Which was where Eugene was headed when he left here?"

"That'd be my guess."

I studied him. There was a twinkle in his eye, so I knew he was up to something. "It's a long walk to the hospital, Doc. Are you sure that you can't tell me what Abby found out in the autopsy?"

"And if I could?"

"I'd be eternally grateful."

"What good will that do me?" he said. "You already owe me more favors than I'll ever collect on."

He had a point. I'd leaned on Doc almost

as much as I had Rupert Roberts when he was still sheriff.

"Anyway," he went on, "Abby did say before she left that if you stopped by here, I was to tell you whatever you wanted to know. So I guess that lets you off the hook."

"What did Abby have to say about Monroe Edmonds?" I asked

"Died of a heart attack, just like she thought. Somewhere between ten P.M. and midnight is her best guess. She also scraped some of his skin from those dents in the elevator, so there's no question that he was pounding around in there, trying to get out."

"No surprises, then?"

"No. No surprises."

I finally got around to taking a drink of my coffee. It tasted as if it had chicory in it, which I liked in small doses. "No chance he had the heart attack first and then tried to pound his way out?"

Doc shook his head emphatically. "Not a chance in the world. Abby showed me the heart when she was done with it. The bottom half of it was ballooned out just like a big old rubber tire from trying to pump blood that wasn't going anywhere. Once it hit, the best he could do was to lie there and take it."

"Did he suffer long?"

51

"There's no way of telling, Garth." Doc's face showed his anger. "But he suffered hard. I can tell you that."

I took another drink of coffee and rose from the table. Though the squirrel was no longer barking at her, Daisy still stood on point beneath the beech tree. A good one for sure, that dog.

"Thanks, Doc."

"Daisy still out there on point?"

"Rock solid."

He too rose from the table. "Then maybe I'd better go rescue her."

Luella Skiles lived on School Street in a faded blue two-story frame house just south of Monroe Edmonds. An L-shaped porch with faded yellow posts and railing faced School Street and then ran a short way along the west side of the house where it ended at a door. Beyond the door was a bay window and beyond that a couple smaller windows with faded yellow trim. The rest of the house was swallowed by the giant shadow of an enormous white pine, perhaps the largest still standing in Adams County, which grew right up next to the house and every year ate a little bit more of the eave. The yard was shaded by maples and oaks, and its silky-soft grass was the kind that was a pure pleasure to walk barefoot through.

I climbed the three steps to the door and knocked. A lace curtain covered the oval glass of the door, which made it hard to see inside. Then I heard footsteps. Hard heels on hardwood, they sounded like to me.

Luella Skiles pulled back the curtain to check me out, then opened the door. "Yes, Garth, what is it?"

"May I come in?"

She sighed heavily as if it were an imposition. "I guess so."

Luella Skiles and I went a long way back — all the way back to the Sunday school of Oakalla's United Methodist Church, then the Methodist Church, when Grandmother Ryland would collar me, make me put on a suit and tie, and drive us off to town. In the hour before church, Luella Skiles played the piano and ran the chapel service for us kids before we went off to our separate classes. Then once church started, she played the organ and directed the choir.

A somewhat tall, big-boned woman with large moon eyes, rust-red medium-length hair, and thick doughy skin that always looked as if it needed a shot of sunlight, Luella Skiles was one of those cheerless people who genuinely liked kids, but because of their dour nature, are rarely liked in return. I had tried to like her, had tried to like the songs that she chose for us to sing, had tried to find meaning for me in the message that she brought to us each Sunday. Obviously she was a learned woman and in her own way wise, but inspiring she was not.

To complicate matters for me, she had also taught music at Oakalla High School until she retired a couple years ago. I wondered as a kid, as I had often wondered in the years since, how anyone so dour, so utterly cheerless, could teach kids about either music or life. Unless it was to hate them.

I followed her into a surprisingly warm brightly sunlit room. A lush turquoise rug, as soft as the grass outside, covered most of its hardwood floor. An antique organ with a pale green vase and a flow-blue vase sitting on top of it stood in the southeast corner next to a bay window; a tiger-maple secretary and two hanging potted plants, both overflowing with small purple flowers, were in the bay window itself.

I sat down on the couch. Luella Skiles sat down on a platform rocker facing me. Directly to her right was a grand piano, whose presence I felt as much as hers.

"Now that you're in," she said, "what is it that you wanted?" Luella's eyes looked red and puffy, as if she had been crying.

"I need to talk to you about last night. What

54

you saw and what you might have heard."

"Why?"

"Because I'm investigating what might be a crime."

"What crime?"

I debated on what to say and finally came up with the only word that seemed to fit the crime. "Murder. Monroe Edmonds's murder, to be exact."

The word hit her hard. But then it was a harsh word.

"On whose authority?" she managed to say.

I opened my wallet and showed her my special deputy's badge. Lately I had started carrying it in the hope that I then wouldn't need it. But Murphy's Law didn't work in reverse.

"I didn't know you were a deputy," she said.

I put my wallet back in my jeans. Either my jeans were getting looser or my wallet was getting thinner. There was more room in my pocket than at the start of the summer.

"I'm not usually one," I said, "but with Sheriff Clark gone and Eugene Yuill new to the job, I am one today."

"Eugene Yuill called me earlier this morning," she said. "I don't know what I can tell you that I haven't already told him."

"Why don't we go ahead and find out."

While she gathered her thoughts, my eyes

strayed to a framed black-and-white photograph standing on the end table beside me. Five children, all girls, dark-haired and fair-skinned stairsteps from the 1930s, stood beside what looked like an old milk house. It wasn't hard to guess which one was Luella. The oldest wore a frown that would have frozen July.

"That's my sisters and I, if you were wondering," she said.

An uneasy silence followed, not unusual for the two of us. For years, most of my life really, I had wanted to ask her what made her so sober. For years, the same length of time, I never had the courage to do so. Thus, we stayed on the surface of life, where neither one of us was very comfortable.

"What time did you call Deputy Yuill last night?" I asked.

"It was nearly two A.M., I believe. I'd heard the storm coming and had gotten up to check my windows."

"The storm was nearly over when Deputy Yuill called me," I said.

Her face seemed to run a gamut of emotions, from defiance to chagrin, like a child caught in a small lie that she shouldn't have had to tell in the first place. "Well, yes, that's true," she said. "It wasn't until after the storm had passed that I saw the light next door and called Deputy Yuill."

I was tempted to ask her what she had been doing from the time that she had gotten up to close the window until the time that she had called Eugene Yuill, which was at least forty-five minutes in all, if the storm had lasted as long at her house as it had at mine. But I saw nothing to gain by it.

"What did you do then?" I asked.

"Waited for Deputy Yuill to arrive."

"In the meantime, did you see anyone enter or leave the house?"

"No one."

"You're sure."

Her pasty-white cheeks wore a rose-colored glow. "Absolutely."

"Let me ask you this, then. Why did you think it was a prowler inside Monroe's house, instead of Monroe himself?"

"Because . . ." she began, then stopped, as her voice cracked. "Because, being neighbors as we have been for all of these years, I know his habits as well as my own. Every night at ten, he turns off all of the downstairs lights and goes upstairs to bed. After that he doesn't stir again until morning."

"Not even for heartburn or diarrhea?"

She gave me a hostile look, as if I had just spit on her floor. "Monroe had a well-stocked medicine chest in the bathroom right next door to his bedroom. Had such an emergency

57

arisen, he would not have needed to go down-stairs, which," she added for effect, "he was loathe to do because he hated riding in that elevator."

"Why did he hate to ride in the elevator?"

"He was claustrophobic."

Despite the warmth of the room, I suddenly felt cold. I too was claustrophobic. The thought of being trapped on an elevator, or in any closed in space, was one of my worst fears.

"How many people in Oakalla knew that he was claustrophobic?"

"None that I know of," she said. "Besides me."

"This isn't the first time that you've called in the middle of the night to report a prowler in Monroe's house," I said.

Once, several years ago, I had come here with Rupert Roberts in the middle of the night. Then a few months ago, when Clarkie was between deputies, he and I had made the same trip. Both times we had staked out Monroe's house, but come up empty.

"No. There have been at least three times before last night that I can remember," she said. "Not coincidentally, I don't think, there had been a large sale in or around Oakalla, one in which Monroe was a principal buyer, just before the nights the prowler came."

"Principal buyer of what?" I asked.

"Anything and everything. Junk mostly, which he promptly resold at a yard sale or gave to Goodwill. But along with the junk, which he usually bought by the boxfuls, always came a few treasures that he sold for a handsome profit, or kept for himself if he couldn't bear to part with them."

There might be something to that, but I wasn't sure what. "Are you saying that Monroe was in the habit of buying large lots of things, rather than bidding on individual items?"

Luella Skiles smiled. It was definitely a smile. I would testify to that under oath. "Yes, he was. The more items that were heaped on the table, the more likely he was to bid on them. But, as I said, boxes were his specialty. He liked to buy boxes of things sight unseen just to discover what surprises might be waiting inside."

"He sounds like a kid at heart," I said.

Her smile abruptly left. "He was a child at heart. A very large and gregarious child, and sometimes a very cruel one."

"Was anything ever taken from Monroe's house on those nights you saw someone there?"

"No. Not that I recall."

"And you do know, of course, that Tom

Ford was found inside Monroe's house last night?" I said.

She was staring at her grand piano. Its presence seemed to give her strength. "Yes. Deputy Yuill told me."

"Have you been in Monroe's house since then to see if there was anything missing?"

"No. I didn't think it appropriate . . ." She momentarily lost her voice and had to look away. "Under the circumstances."

"Would you mind going over there with me now to see what we might see?"

The thought of it brought a look of panic to her face. "Yes. I'm very much afraid I would."

"Perhaps another day, then."

"Perhaps," she said.

"Do you believe Tom Ford's story, that he was drunk and got in the wrong house by mistake?"

"No."

"You're not willing to give him the benefit of the doubt?"

"Absolutely not. In the first place, he doesn't deserve it for the way he treats his wife and children. In the second place, he is a miserable, weak human being, who, if he weren't a drunk, would be something else equally as base. In the third place," she added before I could protest, "I saw Tom Ford carry something into Monroe's house by way of the back door yesterday morning. He was trying to be sly about it, but I saw him just the same."

"And you were . . . ?" I let the question hang. For just a neighbor, she seemed to know an awfully lot about what went on next door.

The question angered her. I thought it might. "I wasn't spying on him, as you might think, and as he might have told you. Neither do I spend all of my spare time at my window as if I had nothing better to do. I was out back hanging up clothes. He couldn't see me, but I could see him."

"How large was it," I asked, "whatever Tom Ford was carrying?"

"Large enough that it took both his hands."

"Do you have any idea what it was?"

"No idea whatsoever."

"Do you remember what color it was?"

"Green, I think."

"Square or round?"

She shook her head. "I wasn't paying that much attention."

"Why would Tom Ford be delivering something to Monroe at that time of day?"

"You'll have to ask Tom Ford that."

I sat for a moment longer, admiring the

grand piano, which appeared to be made out of rosewood. It outshone everything else in the room, including the room itself.

"Do you play anymore?" I asked.

"No."

"Do you miss it?"

"Not in the least."

I thanked her and left.

CHAPTER 5

Tom and Tanya Ford lived with their three girls in a small white bungalow that was slowly going to seed. Its grass was high and needed to be cut. Its roof was patched up and needed shingles. Its windows were loose and needed caulking. Dents pocked its aluminum siding, whose grey-white paint was a shadow of its former self, and its foundation, never much to begin with, seemed to be slowly dissolving into the earth.

I deliberated a moment before knocking on the back door. One good rap, and its screen might fall out. When no one answered right away, I knocked a little harder. From inside I could hear the television going, so someone must be up.

Tanya Ford came to the door. She wore a thin pink housecoat, loosely held together by a frayed pink belt, and carried a cigarette in one hand and an ashtray in the other.

"You're too late," she said through the

screen. "Eugene Yuill just came by and arrested Tom." She seemed neither pleased nor displeased by that turn of events. It was just one more shower in a life filled with rain.

"He did *what?*"

I followed her into the kitchen where she took one last drag from her cigarette and put it out in the ashtray. She then set the ashtray on the kitchen table and sat down herself. A cup of coffee sat on the table in front of her, along with an assortment of books, magazines, and dirty dishes.

"He came and arrested Tom not more than five minutes ago," she said. "For the murder of Monroe Edmonds."

I heard the soft pad of bare feet, as three girls, all with dark eyes and long brown hair, all wearing long white nighties with thin shoulder straps came into the kitchen to stand behind their mother. The two younger girls, about eight and ten, showed their fear and concern. The oldest girl, who looked twelve going on eighteen, showed a fierce resolve to survive this, no matter what.

Looking at each of them in turn and then at their mother, I could see the resemblance there. All were long, lean, and limber, and not likely to run from a fight. All had foxlike faces that, if not exactly beautiful, were close enough to turn a man's head. But unlike her daughters, Tanya Ford wore her hair short and streaked which made her seem less the playful fox and more the cunning coyote.

"Did Deputy Yuill say where he was taking Tom?" I said.

Tanya Ford picked up a package of Kools, shook out a cigarette, and lighted it. It made her mouth look small and hard, like a plastic O-ring. "To the jail, I imagine. Isn't that where murderers usually go?"

"Daddy's not a murderer," the oldest girl said with such force that it caused her mother to turn around and look at her. But Tanya Ford couldn't face her daughter's gaze for long before she turned back to me.

"He is in my book," Tanya said. "We'd all be better off without him."

Her daughter didn't disagree. She simply said, "He's still not a murderer."

Meanwhile the middle girl, who had been fighting back tears, lost the battle and started to cry. The youngest bowed her head and started to suck her thumb. Taking them both in hand, the oldest led them out of the kitchen to (I presumed) sit in front of the television again.

Tanya Ford dismissed them with a wave of her cigarette. "Kids," she said. "What do they know?"

"Only what's in their heart."

Her eyes momentarily flashed to life. She had small olive eyes that reminded me of the oh-so-sharp-clawed, alternately sweet and sly, Siamese cat that Grandmother Ryland used to have.

"You think that oldest kid of mine has a heart," she said as the cigarette bounced up and down in her mouth. "Just hang around here for a while, you'll change your mind. And while you're at it, take a good look at this place." Her eyes scanned the table, sink, and counter, all of which were piled high with things that obviously had a home elsewhere. "That'll tell you how much help I get around here."

"Liar!" came an angry voice from the other room. "You're a big fat liar!"

"Don't you talk to your mother like that!" Tanya Ford yelled back at her oldest daughter, but there was no force behind it. Then she gave me a helpless shrug, as if to say, "See what I mean."

Nothing in my contract said that I had to handle domestic disputes, particularly between mothers and daughters. But I still had a question or two to ask.

"Tanya, did you work last night at the Corner?"

Something flickered in her eyes, a momentary flash of fear perhaps. Then she was in

66

control again. "No. I took the night off. Why?"

"Then you were here, right?"

"Right."

"Did you by chance see or hear any of what went on next door?"

"Why don't you ask old Big Nose herself, Luella Skiles," she said with venom. "She knows everything that goes on over there."

"I've already talked to her. Now I want to hear your side of it."

"My side of it. What do you mean, my side of it?" Something had sharpened her voice. "I was in bed asleep the whole time. Just ask the girls."

I waited for the voice of dissonance to come from the next room, but I waited in vain. "So you saw and heard nothing at all?" I said.

"No. Not a thing."

"Thanks, Tanya. I'll see what I can do about getting Tom out of jail."

"That's a joke, right?" If it were, she didn't see the humor.

Oakalla's jail was a low thick brick building, built in the 1950s in the same style as the City Building, that sat between the City Building on the east and the phone company to the west. It housed six cells, though they were never all full at once, and empty more often than not.

Peanut Johnstone, who also managed the telephone company, was the jailer, and his wife, Edith, did the cooking for the jail whenever it was needed, which usually averaged two or three days a week. Most of the jail's prisoners, like most of Oakalla's citizens, were basically good-hearted, God-fearing, law-abiding people, whose conscious transgressions were few, but whose weaknesses sometimes got the better of them. Hardened criminals, those who belonged behind bars and had to be kept there, were rare in Oakalla. Not so rare as to be extinct, but rare just the same.

Eugene Yuill's patrol car was parked in front of the City Building. I didn't relish the thought of talking to him, but since I needed a key to get into the jail, his would have to do.

"Morning, Eugene," I said on entering the sheriff's office, which Clarkie also shared with the town clerk. "I hear you've had a busy morning."

Eugene sat at Clarkie's desk. Up until the moment I walked in the door, he had looked very comfortable there. "Morning, Garth," he answered. "Just cleaning up some paper work, that's all." Reluctantly, it seemed, he got up from the desk and came over to the counter where I stood.

"I just wanted to borrow the key to the jail," I said.

"Why is that, Garth? You're not planning on letting Tom Ford go, are you?"

"Unless you can give me a good reason why I shouldn't."

"He killed Monroe Edmonds. That's reason enough for me."

"We don't know that, Eugene. Unless you know something I don't."

Judging by the coy look on Eugene's face, I would have bet the pot that he did know something I didn't.

"Maybe," he said slyly. "What's it worth to you?"

The question was, as I thought about dragging Eugene across the counter and tying his neck in a knot, what it would be worth to him. "Eugene, I'm only going to say this once, and once only; don't play games with me. Either you tell me what I want to know, or I'm going to get on the phone right now and call Sheriff Clark home." An idle threat since I had no idea how to reach him, but Eugene didn't know that.

"You don't have to get so sore about it," he said. "I was just joshin' you a little."

"Eugene," I spoke slowly so he didn't miss a word. "I got maybe an hour's sleep last night, after only getting a few more than that the night before. I was up at dawn and have been walking around town almost ever since, trying to get at the truth of this matter, only to find out that you've been one step ahead of me. I wouldn't mind, but you are the one who called me out of bed last night needing help, and the one who called me early this morning, wanting advice. I gave you my best advice. Go on about your regular business, and let me handle this for now."

If he were cowed by my heartfelt delivery, he didn't let on. "I'm also the one that Sheriff Clark left in charge of the town, not you," he said.

"Fine, Eugene," I said, turning toward the phone on the counter. "Have it your way."

"Hiram said Tom Ford left the Corner Bar and Grill no later than ten o'clock," he blurted out. "Call him if you don't believe me."

"Which proves what?"

"It proves that Tom Ford could have been in the house when Monroe Edmonds died. I take that back. It proves he *was* in the house when Monroe Edmonds died because he doesn't have an alibi for his whereabouts once he left the Corner Bar and Grill."

"Just give me the keys, Eugene. I'll decide that for myself."

"But I'm in *charge*," he insisted.

"Then call Sheriff Clark and ask him what you should do."

I said the magic words. Eugene unsnapped his key ring from his belt and slammed the keys down on the counter in front of me.

"Thanks, Eugene. Now, which is the key that unlocks the jail?"

"You're the one who wanted it. You can find it for yourself."

Fifteen keys later, I did find it for myself. On entering the jail, I noticed how cool it was in there. Not the airy cool of deep shade or the timeless cool of deep woods, but a dank cellar cool that got into your bones and stayed there.

Tom Ford had the jail to himself. He was in the last cell on the right, lying in the lower bunk with his eyes open and his hands clasped behind his head. On seeing me, he immediately rose and came to the door of the cell.

"It's about time somebody came to get me out of here," he said. When I didn't answer, he began to have second thoughts. "That is why you're here, isn't it, to get me out of here?"

Tom Ford hadn't shaved yet that morning, and his face was shadowed by a thick patch of black stubble that, had he been playing the movie hero, looked properly rakish. His black hair was slick with sweat and/or Vitalis, and he smelled faintly of stale beer.

Like his wife, who had kept her girlish figure, he had kept his boyish build, though he packed a lot of hard sinew on top of his six-foot frame. He had his oldest daughter's eyes, or vice versa. Alternately blue, then black, depending on the light, when lit with their own inner fire, they could see right through you. When dulled, by either booze or a bad night, as Tom Ford's were that morning, they looked as dead as two lumps of coal.

"That depends, Tom," I said, "on what kind of answers you give me to my questions."

He smiled, as if he'd just drawn to an inside straight, or thought he had anyway. "I get it," he said. "This is the old good-cop, bad-cop routine. If I tell you what you want to know, then maybe shit-for-brains will let me go."

"If you tell me what I want to know, I'm the one who'll let you go," I said. "Since I'm the one holding the keys." I held them up to show him.

"How do I know that?" he said.

"You don't for sure. But what's the alternative?"

"I could always sue for false arrest."

"Sue away. I'm not the one who arrested you. And if you're thinking about getting anything out of Eugene, you could easier get blood out of a turnip."

"I could sue the county," he said.

"You could also spend the rest of your life in prison, if things don't turn out your way."

"But I'm innocent!" he yelled.

I shrugged. "That's what they all say."

He thought about it for a moment, then said, "Okay ask your questions."

"Question number one, where were you between ten and twelve last night?"

He shook his head, as if trying to clear the cobwebs. "I honestly don't know, Garth. I was so drunk I was hugging every tree in sight, thinking they were old friends of mine. I must have hugged a hundred of them before I felt that first burst of rain and started running for what I thought was home."

It could have happened that way. I'd hugged a few trees myself in my day. The trouble with drunks is that they always have a built-in alibi — their brain. Who can argue just when it stopped working, and for how long.

"Which is when you went into Monroe Edmonds's house by mistake?"

"Yes."

"What time was that, do you know?"

"I have no idea."

"Were you wet or dry?"

"Wet. To the bone." He shivered at the

thought of it. "And cold."

That would have put him there sometime between one and two A.M., and off the hook as far as Monroe Edmonds's death was concerned, if he were telling the truth.

"What did you do once you got there?"

"I tried to find a light switch. I couldn't figure out why they weren't in the same places that they had always been."

"And when you found a light switch?"

"I sat down on the floor trying to figure out where I was. Nothing was familiar to me. I was lost in my own home."

So far so good, if we stopped right there. But no drunk that I had ever known was so considerate as to turn the lights off behind him as he went, which was what Tom Ford had done from then on. Had he really been trying to find his way out, the house would have been lit up like a Christmas tree by the time he left.

"You must have sobered up in a hurry," I said.

"Why do you say that?"

"You went to an awfully lot of trouble not to let anyone know you were there. And you didn't knock over a thing that I could see."

He gave me a sheepish grin. I almost bought it. "Just lucky I guess. There's a first time for everything."

I thought over all he'd said and decided that I didn't want to pursue it any further. In his drunkenness, he had a rock-solid alibi and enough reasonable doubt on his side to convince a jury that he was innocent of any wrongdoing. We really didn't have the grounds to hold him, but I wasn't yet ready to let him go.

"Question number two," I said. "What was it that you delivered to Monroe Edmonds's back door yesterday morning?"

"What are you talking about?"

I jiggled the keys. "Answers, Tom. Answers."

"I still don't know what you're talking about."

I started to leave. "Suit yourself."

He came right at me through the bars. Had they been an inch wider, or I a step slower, he might have had me. "God damn you!" he yelled. "Let me out of here!"

"Answers, Tom," I said, keeping my distance. "That's the only thing that will get you out of here."

He sighed in resignation. I recognized that sigh. Life wasn't fair, or at least as fair as you once expected it to be, so you cut whatever corners, made whatever bargains, with the Devil, if necessary, that you needed to survive it. And you assumed, or perhaps hoped, that everyone else did the same.

"What I carried there was a painting that I'd bought at the M and M Boys' yard sale."

"What kind of painting?" Luella Skiles hadn't described it as a painting to me, but perhaps it was.

"I don't know. It had birds and flowers on it. That's all I remember."

"Why don't you show it to me, then."

The three of us, Tom Ford, Eugene Yuill, and I, rode to Monroe Edmonds's house in Eugene's patrol car. Eugene insisted, before we even let Tom Ford out of his cell, that Tom wear handcuffs. I didn't argue. Not with me at hand and Eugene packing a gun. I didn't want any of us to get hurt, because, in a moment of desperation, Tom Ford decided that he would bolt and take his chances elsewhere. At the jail I'd seen just how fast he could move. And how quickly he could get up to speed.

It was strange to see Monroe Edmonds's house in the daylight after seeing it at night just a few hours ago. The night seemed to cast it in a harsher light, make its shadows longer, its cracks deeper. The sun, on the other hand, hid its scars, softened its rough edges, like a smile on the face of a clown.

It was also strange to share the same small space with Tom Ford and Eugene Yuill, two of the most unlikely companions I could have chosen, and not among the first ten that I would have picked to share a deserted island with me. Life did that to you, though, from time to time as a litmus test, to see if you really did have a sense of humor.

"Okay, Tom," I said at last, after we'd twice toured the entire house, including the attic, which was hot enough to roast a buffalo, and were now back down in the parlor again. "Which painting is it?"

Tom couldn't decide between a painting that hung in the parlor and one that hung in the hall upstairs. Both had flowers and birds in them, along with cows, sheep, and angels blowing horns. Both were signed and, though I didn't recognize either of the artists, that meant absolutely nothing, since I knew about as much about painters as I did about hockey players — which was to say that outside of the heavyweights like Vermeer, Van Gogh, and da Vinci, Picasso, Pollack, and O'Keefe, I knew very little. The paintings also had about an inch of dust on them and each looked as if it had been hanging there in that same spot for years.

"This one, I believe," Tom said, choosing the one in the parlor.

"Thank God!" Eugene said in relief, taking off his hat and pulling a big white handkerchief from his back pocket to wipe his brow. "Now we can get out of here." He looked at me. Something in his eyes didn't look right to me. "Can't we?"

"In a minute," I said, puzzled by Eugene's behavior. An hour ago he was ready to throw the book at Tom. Now, he seemed almost eager to buy anything that Tom told us. I wondered what had gotten to Eugene besides the heat. "I'm just curious, Tom," I continued, "as to why, if this painting struck you enough for you to buy it, only a day later you don't recognize it?"

"I bought it for the frame, that's why," he said, easily fielding my question. "I thought the old man might pay me something for it."

"Did he?"

His look grew cunning. "That's between him and me."

"Satisfied?" Eugene asked, putting his handkerchief back in his pocket and his hat back on. With emphasis.

I ignored him. "Or why on a Friday, which is a workday for most of us, you went all the way out to the M and M Boys' house in the first place?"

The M and M Boys were Mose and Martin Weidner, who lived three miles northwest of town, the last mile of it gravel.

"I can answer that for him." Eugene jumped

right in without even being asked. "Times are tough on us workingmen, ain't that right, Tom? Not every day is a working day anymore. Why do you think I took this job at age fifty-eight? Security, that's why. A man can't count on the future anymore, not the way he used to."

"Are you through?" Tom said. He stared at Eugene as he might a centipede swimming in his toilet. "The reason that I went out there is that the sale started early, at seven. I had plenty of time to go there and get back again before work."

"Why go at all?" I said. "Why make the effort?"

"Because . . ." He grasped for a straw and came up with one. "Because it's like Barney Fife here said. Times are tough on us workingmen. You have to cut yourself whatever advantage you can."

"By going to garage sales?"

"Don't knock it. Monroe Edmonds made a good living at it. So do the M and M Boys."

"Monroe knew his business. So do the M and M Boys," I said.

"It's never too late to learn, is it, Tom?" Eugene said.

"No," Tom Ford said, as his blue-black eyes burned a hole in Eugene's smile, leaving an O in its place. "It's never too late to learn."

"Of course, the M and M Boys can vouch that you were there," I said.

"Martin can. I didn't see Mose. So can Dutchman Yoder. He was just pulling up as I was leaving. And Lawrence Hess, who was just leaving as I was pulling up."

"What were you driving?"

"My pickup. The black Ford Ranger that has Ford Electric painted on each side of it." In large block letters, if I remembered right.

I looked at Eugene, who looked ill at ease, as if he no longer remembered just why we were there. Something *had* happened to Eugene from the time that we left the jail to now. He had gone from junkyard dog to Odie right before my eyes. If I hadn't known better, I would have sworn he'd had a stroke.

"I'm ready to go, if you are," I said to Eugene.

"What about Tom?"

"Why don't you ask him yourself."

"What I mean is, what do we do about Tom?"

"That's up to you," I said, not making it easy on him, which is what he wanted me to do. "You're the one who arrested him."

"Come on, Ryland," Tom pleaded. "I told you what you wanted to know."

"I don't know that yet."

"So in the meantime you're going to let me rot in that stinking jail." His voice rose in anger.

"That's up to Eugene," I said. "Frankly, my dear," I said, looking at each of them in turn, "I don't give a damn."

CHAPTER 6

I left by the back door, making sure that it was locked, while they went out the front. Luella Skiles was outside by now, for which I was grateful. I walked over to her garden where she was pulling weeds, then knocking the dirt off their roots before she slung them over the fence into the alley.

"Therapy," I said.

"Something like that," she said without looking up.

Though her aim was for the most part true, she had still managed to hang some of her weeds on her fence. They reminded me, too vividly, of the time-tattered string of hawks and owls that I had once seen hanging on a farmer's fence back in Indiana.

"The thing that Tom Ford carried to Monroe's back door, could it have been a painting?" I asked.

"I don't hardly think so. Not unless it was rolled up in something."

"I suppose that's a possibility."

"Is that what he says it is?"

"Yes," I said.

"Do you believe him?"

"Unless you can tell me otherwise."

She didn't offer to, so I assumed that she couldn't.

"There is one thing you could do for me," I said. "Walk over to Monroe's house and identify a painting."

She was tugging at a wild carrot that seemed to have a root a mile deep. "I told you that I'm not ready to go in there yet."

When the wild carrot finally gave, she didn't bother to knock the dirt off its root, but gave it a sling that carried it over the fence and the alley and landed it in the neighbor's yard next door. "Damn," she muttered under her breath.

"Nice shot," I said.

She didn't say anything.

"Tell me this, then. That painting in Monroe's study, the one in the silver frame with the sheep and angels in it, how long has it been there?"

"Years, Garth. It came with the house, I think."

"Is it worth anything?"

"I'm not sure. I don't think Monroe ever had it appraised."

"But it couldn't have been the painting that Tom Ford carried into the house?"

"Is that what he told you?" she laughed. "I thought Tom Ford was a better liar than that."

"Didn't we all."

At home I discovered that Ruth had gone somewhere, leaving me to fend for myself. I ate a bologna sandwich and a slice of cantaloupe and washed them down with a glass of milk. Not a great lunch but enough to hold me until supper. Then I walked out to the garage, got in Jessie, and hoped for the best.

Jessie was the brown Chevy sedan that I had inherited from Grandmother Ryland along with her eighty-acre farm and the money to buy the *Oakalla Reporter*. Half tortoise and half mule, Jessie ran at her own convenience, which was about twice a week, and over the years had developed a series of quirks that even Danny Palmer, the best mechanic that I knew, was hard pressed to explain.

I would take her into him to be fixed. He would straighten her out. A week later, she'd be her old contrary self again. So while neither of us would come right out and say it, we both believed that Jessie had a soul. No heart, though, unless one of steel.

I drove north on Fair Haven Road to Fair Haven Church, turned left, passed Grand-

84

mother's house and barn a half mile later, and continued on west for another half mile, before I turned north again.

As I approached the humped iron bridge that ran over Hog Run, I noticed that Hog Run ran nearly bank full. A dirty white froth bubbled at its surface, as sticks, leaves, and small logs bobbed amidst the boils and swirls of its muddy water. It had rained more in the night than I realized. With more rain predicted tonight, Hog Run might be out of its banks by morning.

Mose and Martin Weidner, the M and M Boys, lived on what loosely could be described as a farm. What animals they raised were mostly exotic animals, like pygmy and fainting goats, llamas, and peacocks. Several cats and a few chickens, most of them bantams, had the run of the place, which even in spring looked overgrazed, and by September, with its bleak bare deeply eroded gullies, looked like hell's half-acre. The animals, too, always had a tired gaunt weathered look, as if months, even years of tender loving care would be required to restore them to health again.

The M and M Boys were father and son. Mose, the father, was somewhere in his sixties. Martin, the son, somewhere in his forties. Both were gaunt and stooped, like the animals they raised. Each had a pinched face, a narrow chin, and small suspicious eyes. Each had Pinocchio's nose, though something had flattened it until it was nearly all bridge with a sharp point on the end of it. And each, nearly every day of his life, wore bibbed overalls, a white T-shirt, and high-top shoes.

I pulled into their gravel drive and shut Jessie's engine off. Three times on the way out there, I'd had to wipe the windshield, just to see to drive. The problem wasn't the dust on the road, but steam, coming up from somewhere inside the car. I took that as a sign of things to come.

Martin Weidner sat on the steps of the house, whittling. Deep in concentration, the tip of his tongue peeking out one side of his mouth like a small pink mouse, he was oblivious to everything but the block of wood in his hand. Slowly and meticulously, he carved the wood until he was satisfied that he could stop. Then he looked up at me.

"Afternoon, Garth," he said.

"Afternoon, Martin. What is it that you're working on?"

He got up from the steps to show me. "It's going to be a horse. Once I get it fleshed out some more."

I took it from him and examined it. It did indeed look like a horse. All it needed was a tail and a mane.

"Are these all yours?" On a long wooden folding table were several carved wooden birds and animals.

"All mine," he said proudly.

"What are you asking for them?" If the price was right, I might buy one.

"What do you think they're worth?" he said. Like every good trader, he didn't want to be the one to name the first price.

"I'll give you five bucks for choice."

He laughed at that. "Do you know what a lady in the Dells sells these for? Twenty-five bucks apiece, and that's not even painted. Painted they go for more like fifty."

"So what's your bottom dollar?"

"You can have choice for fifteen."

I thought it over. Five bucks and I'd be satisfied that I'd made a good deal. Seven-fifty I could live with. Anything over that and I'd be unhappy with myself. Martin Weidner's carvings were good but not something that I couldn't do without.

"I'll get back to you on that," which was another way of saying that I wasn't interested.

He shrugged. "It's up to you."

"Do you mind if I look at what else is here?"

"Look all you want," he said, not trying to hide his disappointment.

Martin Weidner went back to his whittling. I began to walk down the row of tables that lined the drive. As I did, a pygmy goat stuck his head through the fence to nibble on some grass. I could see why he did. About all that was left in the pasture were weeds and black-berry bushes.

Property of Fair Haven Church. That's what most of the tables read when I looked underneath them. Tables that once held pumpkin pie and linen tablecloths, Swiss steak and mother-daughter banquets were now cov-ered with well-travelled flea market items, whose price tags had started to fade, and whose worth was directly proportional to the amount of spare change that you had in your wallet. No true bargains were to be found. None that I could see anyway.

"Find anything?" Martin Weidner asked on my return. He had temporarily set the horse aside and sat with his legs crossed, leaning back against the step. His legs showed white at the calves. It was hard to tell them from his socks.

"No," I said.

"You should have been here yesterday. You'd have had a lot more to choose from."

I nodded, though more of the same was no choice at all. "Is your dad around?" It was cool there by the steps in the shade of a sugar maple. It felt good to be out of the sun.

"Nope," he said. "Pop's gone up to the

Rapids for the weekend. There's some kind of big doings going on up there, and he's got him a spot in the flea market. I'm supposed to join him up there tomorrow, except he called early this morning to say that last night's rain turned the place into one big mudhole, so he might be coming home early."

"Your dad doesn't like mud?" I said for something to say.

"Not since the war. He had his fill of it when he was overseas."

"World War II?" It had to be that, or Korea.

"Yeah," he said bitterly. "The only war we ever fought according to him."

"And you don't agree?"

"Oh, I agree all right." His eyes had shrunk to two hard dots. "I have to, don't I, since it's his house I'm living in, his food I'm eating. But I spent some time in a place called Vietnam." Vietnaam is the way he said it. "For a while there, we thought we had us a real war going on."

"Is that where you learned to whittle?"

He leaned over and spat on the steps, as if something had left a bad taste in his mouth. "Among other things." He looked up at me. Suddenly I didn't feel welcome. "What is it that you want with pop?"

"Nothing. I just wondered if he was around."

He picked up his knife and block of wood and started whittling again. But his strokes, instead of long, smooth, and sure, as they had been on my arrival, were short and jerky, and seemed to serve no purpose other than to keep his hands in motion.

"What do you want with me, then?" he said. "You didn't drive all the way out here for nothing."

"I was already at the farm," I lied. "It wasn't all that long a drive."

"Just the same," he said.

I watched him take a couple more strokes, long enough to see the head of the horse fly off. Then he stood, threw the headless horse as far as he could into the woods across the road, folded his knife and put it into his pocket, and sat back down again.

"It wasn't working out anyway," he said.

I didn't say anything.

"I repeat," he said, "what is it that you wanted to see me about?"

"Tom Ford," I said. "That's what I wanted to see you about. He claims he bought a painting off of you yesterday morning. I just wondered if he had."

Martin Weidner seemed to shrink before my eyes, as all of his muscles gathered in around him, like the coils of a spring. "Then Tom Ford is a liar."

"Are you saying that he wasn't here?"

"Oh, he was here, all right. What I'm saying is that I didn't sell him any damned painting."

"Do you remember what you did sell him?"

His face was closed. "I didn't sell him anything. Not that I remember anyway."

"Thanks, Martin," I said. "That's all I wanted to know."

"What's a painting got to do with anything?" he said as I rose to leave.

I studied him. If he already knew, he was doing a good job of hiding it. "That's what I'm trying to find out," I said.

"Is Tom Ford in some kind of trouble?"

"Tom Ford is in jail for murder," I said.

"Whose?"

"Monroe Edmonds's."

He looked genuinely puzzled. "Why would Tom Ford want to kill Monroe Edmonds?"

"I'm not sure he did."

"Then why is he in jail for Monroe's murder?"

"Details," I said. "Left to take care of themselves, they sometimes grow out of control."

I got in Jessie and drove away. My last statement to Martin Weidner had been my not-so-subtle attempt to rattle his cage a little in case he was hiding something. Little did I realize at the time how prophetic it would prove.

CHAPTER 7

Dutchman Yoder lived on the first farm past Hog Run on my way back to town. An old-order Amishman, and to my knowledge the only one in Adams County, Dutchman Yoder had lived around Oakalla for as long as I could remember and for just as long had been an enigma to me.

Full of folksy sayings, like "No hay smells as sweet as your own," and "A loud voice is no sure sign of a right mind," and my favorite, "If you like it . . ." here he would pound his chest right over his heart, ". . . and it feels good, get into your pocket," Dutchman Yoder tried to find the good in everything and everybody. And I believed, had someone served him up a plate of horse manure, he would have eaten it rather than hurt his host's feelings.

Still, something about him had always troubled me. He reminded me of a now-old warrior, banished long ago by his tribe for something he had done, some hideous breach of tribal mores, and was now forced to live out his life in exile among strangers. I wondered what his crime had been and why he could not go home again. Because if you really listened to his voice, to its rise and then its fall, you would hear the underlying and deepening sadness there.

As I turned into Dutchman Yoder's lane, I noticed how green and lush his alfalfa field and pasture were, how fat and contented his Jerseys looked. At the end of the lane, his small white frame house with its peaked gable and red roof sat nestled in a thick stand of Norway pines. A greying white silo stood beside his barn, and in the barn lot between the barn and the corncrib was a windmill that pumped the water for his cattle and his milk house. In the front yard was the pitcher pump that supplied Dutchman Yoder with his drinking water. Behind the house, now hidden by the pines, was his privy. Behind the privy, even deeper in the pines, his icehouse. As an old-order Amishman, he had neither electricity nor inside plumbing, so he had to carry his own water, cut his own ice, and bury his own waste when the privy hole filled up.

Dutchman Yoder wasn't home. I determined that after knocking on his door without an answer, then walking to his barn and finding his horses gone. But I didn't leave immediately. I hung briefly on the gate, looking out over the barn lot. A farm smell from my childhood had ambushed me, and I had to take a moment to savor it.

I met Dutchman Yoder pulling into his lane as I was heading out. He drove a team of matched Belgians, Bill and Bud, geldings with chestnut coats and a white blaze on their foreheads, and he sat ramrod straight on the wagon seat in his straw hat, dark blue shirt, black-button pants, and suspenders.

"Garth!" he said, recognizing me. "So seldom you are a visitor."

Tall, with blue eyes, a round face, and a full grey-white beard that looked as if it had been dusted with soot, particularly the patch nearest the center of his chin where it was darkest, he had a high whinny of a laugh, and the habit of showing all of his front teeth whenever he smiled.

I leaned my head out the window to talk to him. "Afternoon, Dutchman. How are things going?"

He looked solemn, unusual for him. "I don't know, Garth. It seems the hurrier I go, the behinder I get." Then he found his smile again. "But is that not the shape of the world, yah."

That said, we each lapsed into silence. He

was the first to break it. "So would you like to come up to the house and talk?"

"Thanks, Dutchman, but I'm on my way home. I just stopped by to see if you remembered seeing Tom Ford at Martin Weidner's yard sale yesterday morning."

"Yah. He was there. Just leaving as I was coming in."

"Do you remember if he was carrying anything?"

He shook his head. "No. I surely don't. In a hurry, he was, when I got there."

A flying grasshopper came whizzing out of the pasture and landed on one of the Belgians. The horse took one look at it and decided that he was under attack. It took all of Dutchman's strength and his harness mate's rock-solid stand to keep him from bolting.

"Whoa, Billy! Whoa!" Dutchman yelled, as he fought the huge horse to a standstill. Bud meanwhile gave Bill a curious look, as if wondering what all the fuss was about.

"Crazy horse," he said to me with a smile once Bill was under control again. "He once got stung by a hornet and has never forgotten it."

"Smart horse, I'd say."

"Perhaps. Perhaps," he said, not wanting to openly disagree with me. "But in this life, we should know the difference between hornets and grasshoppers, yah?"

"Yes," I said. "Perhaps we should." Then I realized what today was and where Dutchman Yoder had been. "You have a good day in town?" I said.

Saturday morning, June to October, we had a farmers' market in the park where anyone with produce could come to sell his goods. With his truck patch and garden, apple orchard and strawberry patch, blackberry, raspberry, and blueberry bushes, cream, butter, and Jersey milk, Dutchman Yoder kept a lot of us in Oakalla well supplied with the good things in life.

"Yah," he said, showing me his empty wagon. "A very good day indeed."

I was glad that at least one of us could say that. "Well," I said, "I guess I better head 'em out."

Dutchman gave me a puzzled look.

"It's an old cowboy expression," I said. "I used to be big on cowboys." Still was for that matter.

"No," he said, not caring if I was big on cowboys or not. "I was thinking of that young man, Tom Ford. He is headed for trouble, I think."

"With his drinking, you mean?"

"Yah. That too."

Dutchman saw and understood a lot more

than he let on. But he usually didn't share that knowledge with anyone.

"Did you see Tom Ford doing something that he shouldn't have been?" I said.

He looked away, out across his alfalfa field, which would soon be ready for its third cutting. "I think I have said too much already. A man's business should be his own, yah?"

"Give me a hint at least. Was he breaking the law?"

He turned back to me. As he did, I was struck by the purity of his eyes. No doubt in those eyes, no meanderings or misgivings. They were the eyes of a saint or an assassin.

"Yah," he said. "God's law." He gave the reins a shake. "Yah, Billy. Yah, Bud." They started on a slow trot down the lane.

Back in Oakalla, I stopped at the Marathon, Oakalla's only service station, which was at the corner of Jackson Street and Fair Haven Road. I had two reasons for stopping there. One, I wanted to talk to Sniffy Smith, who spent most of his time loafing at the Marathon. Two, I had smelled antifreeze all the way back into town.

Sniffy Smith sat on his favorite loafing stool like a king on his throne, as he traded banter with Dub Bennett who, like Sniffy, was a regular at the Marathon. A small soft man, who had barbered in Oakalla since I was a kid, and who cut hair only on Fridays now that he was retired, Sniffy had gotten his name because he had the habit of sniffing loudly whenever he was excited — which was more than a once-a-day occurrence, since Sniffy was easily excitable. I was one of the four in town who still had Sniffy cut our hair, but we were a dying breed. When Dub Bennett and Dave Troxell went, as they surely would one of these days, Danny Palmer and I would be the only ones left.

"Hello, Sniffy," I said. "Is Danny around?"

"You just missed him. He had to make a wrecker run to the south end to tow in that new schoolteacher's car, but he should be back any minute."

"New schoolteacher?" I said, not remembering any new hires.

"Came last year. Teaches sixth grade." Sniffy's eyes were on the drive. When Danny was gone, it was Sniffy's responsibility to pump gas for whoever needed it.

"I remember her now," I said. "Blonde, blue eyes, well put together. Nice smile." How well I remembered her. Her name was Amber Utley.

"And single," Dub Bennett chimed in. "Don't forget that."

A big man, nearly six-feet, six-inches tall, and about two-hundred-fifty pounds, none of it fat, Dub Bennett was one of those slow-moving and soft-spoken, when-he-talks-you-listen men, found in most small towns across America. Years ago, when a young man, he had pitched minor league baseball with enough success to earn him a shot at the Chicago White Sox. Then World War II came along, and he spent the next four years overseas. On his return, he again tried out with the White Sox, but his fastball no longer had its old zip, so he came back to Oakalla, joined his father in the coal business, then became a logger when the coal business went under and at sixty-five retired. "No regrets" was his motto, and he lived life as if he meant it.

"For all the good it does," Sniffy said about Amber Utley's single status. "She won't give a one of us in Oakalla the time of day."

"And what would you do if she did?" Dub Bennett kidded.

Sniffy gave a loud sniff, rocking back and forth on his stool. "Wouldn't you like to know."

Wouldn't we all, I thought.

"What is it you wanted, Garth?" Sniffy said, relaxing now that there were no cars in sight. Though Sniffy always volunteered to watch the drive while Danny was gone, watching was as far as it went. He hated to climb down off his stool and actually pump gas for some-body.

"Jessie's acting up again. I just wanted to get Danny's opinion on it."

"Acting up how?"

Though like me, a mechanical dropout, Sniffy considered himself a guru when it came to cars. "I'm getting a lot of moisture inside the car. I have to keep my window rolled down just to see out the windshield."

"Sounds like a heater core to me," Sniffy said. "What do you think, Dub?"

"Heater core," Dub said.

"Is that expensive?" I asked.

"You'll have to ask Danny on that one," Sniffy said. "What do you think, Dub?"

"Ask Danny."

We were all in agreement. I would ask Danny at the first opportunity, whenever that was.

"Was there anything else, Garth?" Sniffy leaned back out of sight as a car slowed, then forward again as it turned onto Fair Haven Road.

"Tom Ford," I said. "What's the word on him?"

"I hear he's in jail. What else do you want to know?"

"Has he been up to anything that I should know about?" Dutchman Yoder had seen Tom

Ford doing something that he shouldn't. It might help my cause to know what.

Sniffy scratched his head. It made me want to scratch mine, too. "Nope. I can't think of anything besides his drinking," Sniffy said. "What about you, Dub? Can you think of anything?"

Dub Bennett had risen to stand in the open doorway with his back to us. His huge frame took up nearly every square inch of it. "No. Tom Ford's always done right by me. Who says he hasn't?"

I thought about telling him and decided against it. Dutchman Yoder wouldn't appreciate the controversy it might bring. "It's just the word I got," I said. "I thought I'd better check it out."

"Speaking of Tom Ford," Sniffy said, "is it true that he murdered Monroe Edmonds?"

"That's what he's in jail for," I said, not wanting to start a controversy of my own.

"What about that painting Eugene was telling me about? What does it have to do with it? You know, the one that Tom was supposed to have bought from the M and M Boys yesterday morning."

Dub Bennett turned around in the doorway to face us. His normally ruddy face was as white as his hair. "What painting is that, Sniffy?"

Sniffy puffed up like a tree frog about to sing. He liked being in the know. Even more, he liked it when being in the know made him the center of attention.

"It had angels and flowers on it, the way Eugene described it to me. Tom Ford bought it from the M and M Boys for a song and then sold it to Monroe Edmonds. Eugene said he made a fortune on it."

Color started to return to Dub Bennett's face. He looked relieved, like a man whose biopsy had just come back negative. "I was just curious," he said.

So was I about his behavior, but I didn't know how to go about asking him.

"What about it, Garth?" Sniffy said to me. "Did Tom Ford buy that painting, like Eugene says he did?"

"Martin Weidner says not."

"Well, he ought to know if anybody does. Right, Dub?"

But Dub Bennett wasn't listening. "What was that, Sniffy?"

Sniffy gave one loud sniff of indignation. "I said Martin Weidner ought to know whether he sold Tom Ford that painting or not."

"Maybe not," Dub said, then left.

"I wonder what got into him?" Sniffy mused, as we watched Dub Bennett cross

Jackson Street then head south on Perrin Street toward home.

"Hard to say, Sniffy," I said, wondering myself. "But does it make sense to you that Tom Ford would go out to the M and M Boys' house in the first place? What I mean is, was he in the habit of going to garage sales?"

"Not that I know of, Garth. The only habit that Tom Ford has is booze."

On my way out the door, I saw Danny Palmer's wrecker pull onto the drive with Amber Utley's cherry-red Mazda RX-7 in tow. I waited for Danny to unhitch the Mazda and park the wrecker before approaching him. If possible, I wanted to be out of Sniffy's earshot.

"Afternoon, Garth," Danny said. "Jessie acting up on you again?"

Danny Palmer was somewhere in his mid-thirties with a medium build, a broad back and shoulders, quiet brown eyes, and a smile that would keep him perpetually young. All things considered, he was probably the most important person in Oakalla, or at least the one who would be the hardest to replace.

I told him what the problem was, and he agreed that Jessie probably needed a new heater core.

"Is that expensive?"

"Not in and of itself," he said, "but the labor will probably set you back some."

"Aren't you the labor?"

Danny smiled at me. As Oakalla's best mechanic, he knew his worth. "That's what I mean. It's not a five-minute job."

A car pulled up to the pumps. Already Danny was on the move. I followed him over there and was thankful when the driver stayed inside the car.

"Danny," I said, "what's the word on Tom Ford?"

"Besides the fact that he's in jail?"

"Yes. Is he involved in any scams that you know of?"

Danny washed the windshield and the rear window, then raised the hood and checked the oil, antifreeze, brake fluid, and battery water. Oakalla was one of the few places left in the country where you could still get full service for self-service prices.

"Not that I know of," Danny said. "At least I haven't had anyone in here complaining about him."

Maybe it was just my imagination, but I thought that I had seen Danny's demeanor change at the mention of Tom Ford's name. His eyes seemed to harden and his jaw had seemed to set.

He topped off the tank, took Helen Sedlack's money, and she drove away.

"You're sure about that?" I said. "Tom Ford, I mean."

"I'm sure, Garth," he said.

"Thanks anyway." It was time to move on. Pumping Danny for information that he didn't want to give would be every bit as productive as drilling for oil in Manhattan.

"As long as you're here, do you want me to check out Jessie for you?"

"No. The next time that I have time, I'll bring her in." My gaze strayed to the RX-7. Cherry red wasn't my color, and Mazda wasn't my car, but it sure would be fun to drive something like that. "What's wrong with the teacher's car?" I said.

"Timing gear, I think. She broke down and cried when I told her that, because of the holiday and all, I couldn't get parts before Tuesday."

"Did you give her aid and comfort?" Though happily married, Danny had a weak spot in his heart for Amber Utley. My weak spot was a little lower in my anatomy.

"Don't I wish," he said, his whole face turning red. "How come you've never gone after that, Garth?"

"She's too young for me."

"She's twenty-five."

"That's still too young for me." So was thirty-five, which was Abby Pence-Airhart's age, but I'd ignore that for now.

"It probably wouldn't do you any good anyway," Danny said with regret. "She's just not interested in what Oakalla has to offer."

"That's what Sniffy said." I waved at Sniffy, who was doing his best to hear what we were saying through the window. "Maybe that's why she was so upset about her car. She might have had a heavy date out of town."

Danny sighed. "Lucky him, whoever he is." Then he gave me a strange look, one that I didn't recognize at all. "Why is that you can always have what you don't want?"

That statement shocked me. I had always thought that Danny was the happiest, most contented man in the universe. "You're not serious, are you?"

We were interrupted, as someone wheeled onto the drive, revving his engine just to keep it running. The car slid past us, under the overhead door, and halfway through the bay before its driver got it stopped. Sniffy meanwhile had bailed off his chair and taken refuge against the far wall.

"Whoever her boyfriend is," Danny said, ignoring my question, "he must be into the bucks. Today she was wearing a new diamond pendant. I think it's the one I thought about buying for Sharon last Christmas up at Bill Nicewander's." Sharon was Danny's wife.

"Expensive?" I asked.

"I knew I couldn't afford it."

With that thought in mind, I left for home.

CHAPTER 8

The first thing that I intended to do when I got home was to fill Jessie's radiator with water. There was no sense in adding antifreeze, only to have it run out again. But my mind was on other things, and I forgot.

Ruth was inside, fixing supper. I looked at my Timex. Five P.M. Supper this early could only mean that Ruth was going bowling later.

"Tough day?" she said, as I sat down at the kitchen table with a groan.

She was frying ham, and I thought I smelled sauerkraut, so that meant ham, ham gravy, and sauerkraut for supper. "I thought league didn't start until next weekend," I said.

"It doesn't. But we're having a practice round tonight. God knows we need it."

Ruth's bowling team was like Avis. They tried hard, but always ended up in second place.

"Is Liddy Bennett going to be there?"

"Isn't she always. Why?" Ruth, Liddy Bennett, Wanda Collum, and Alice Culbertson made up Ruth's bowling team. At sixty-five, Wanda Collum was the youngest on the team.

I told her essentially how my day had gone and then what had happened at the Marathon. "I'm not saying that Dub Bennett's involved, but he sure acted funny when the subject of the painting came up," I said.

"So what do you want me to do?" Ruth took out the ham, then put flour into the skillet and stirred it around with her fork to soak up the grease before adding the milk.

"Find out what you can about Dub. While you're at it, see what you can learn about Tom Ford. He's up to something. I just don't know what."

She added salt and pepper and began to stir the gravy. "What will you be doing in the meantime?"

"I've got a couple stops to make, then who knows? I'm forgetting something. That feeling came over me on the way home from Dutchman Yoder's, but for the life of me, I can't figure out what it is."

"Well, it'll come to you," she said. "It always does." She set a plate of ham, a dish of raw carrots, a bowl of sauerkraut, and a bowl of gravy on the table. "While you were at it, did you ask Dutchman Yoder what he was doing at the yard sale?"

I speared a piece of ham and passed the plate to Ruth. "He's at every garage sale," I said. "He's waiting there at the post office every Friday morning for them to open the bags of *Reporter*s just so he can get his early. I know because I sometimes see him there on my way to work." Or on my way home, if the night was particularly long.

"True," she said, taking some sauerkraut and handing the bowl to me, "but does he ever buy anything?"

"I don't know. I never asked him."

"You might. The next time you see him."

"Why the sudden interest in Dutchman Yoder?" I said.

"It's not sudden, Garth. Haven't you ever wondered where that man came from and why he's still here?"

I ladled some gravy out of the bowl onto my sauerkraut. "I thought he'd always been here. He has ever since I can remember."

"Not always, Garth. He came here sometime after the war." For Ruth, *the war* was World War II.

"Has he always had the name Dutchman?" I said.

"No. His name's Henry, or some such thing. But when he came here, he could hardly make himself understood. He was Pennsylvania Dutch, he said. Old order Amish. Someone said he was more Dutch than Pennsylvania, so the name stuck."

"Dutch? It's funny, he's always sounded German to me."

"And where," Ruth said, "do you think the Pennsylvania Dutch come from originally?"

I hadn't thought about it before. After I had digested this new piece of knowledge, I said, "So what do you think he is? A fugitive of some kind?"

"Karl always thought so, but I have my doubts."

"Why is that?"

She stopped eating momentarily to give it some thought. "He doesn't act like a fugitive. He keeps to himself more often than not, but he doesn't appear to have anything to hide. It's just strange, that's all, that he would settle here when there aren't any more of his kind around. He would get lonely, I think, for someone to talk to."

"I think he is lonely," I said.

"Then why does he stay?"

"Why do any of us stay where we are? There are worse things in life than loneliness."

"Name one," she said.

I was still chewing on that thought when Ruth left in her Volkswagen a few minutes later. I washed the dishes and left them on the drain board to dry. Then I walked to the phone and dialed. Doc Airhart answered.

"Hello, Doc, this is Garth. Is Abby around?" Deep-breathing exercises would have helped at this point. And some duct tape to keep my voice from cracking. But when you stop putting your heart on the line, you stop needing one.

"She's right here. Whom did you say was calling?" I could almost see the smile on his face.

"Come on, Doc. This is hard enough as it is."

"Garth Ryland, you say? Could you speak a little louder?"

I was about to tell him where he could put his receiver when Abby came on the line. "Don't mind him," she said. "He's getting senile in his old age."

I could hear Doc laughing in the background. How long had it been since I had heard that? "What I was wondering is," I said, losing some of my confidence, "is if you wanted to make some rounds with me tonight. Concerning the Edmonds case," I felt it necessary to add.

"I'd love to, but I have some rounds of my own at the hospital to make."

"Maybe another time, then?"

"Let's not give up on tonight yet," she said. "I should be through at the hospital about

112

eight-thirty, if nothing goes wrong. What say we meet at the Corner Bar and Grill at nine. It'll be my treat."

"I'll be there," I said.

"Garth?"

I loved the way she said my name. I wished I had a recording of it to keep under my pillow.

"Yes, Abby?" I said.

"Thanks for calling."

"It was my pleasure."

My feet barely hit the ground the first couple blocks on my way to Lawrence Hess's house. Had an enemy picked that time to do me in, he would have had no trouble at all. In fact, I never would have seen him coming.

Lawrence Hess was the curator of the Pembleton Museum in La Crosse, a historical museum known statewide for its archives and collection of local artifacts that dated from the last ice age to the present. Lawrence Hess lived on east Jackson Street in the Waggoner house, which was nearly as famous as his museum. Like Luella Skiles's house, it had a wraparound porch that fronted two sides of it, and two bay windows, one that looked out on Berry Street and the other on Jackson. A carriage house with a cupola stood behind the house, along with a sprinkling of stately pines that sighed softly in the wind and always gave me the hope that all was well, even when it was not. An attached turret, the only one in Oakalla, stood at the west end of the house and gave it a brooding look, like that of a gothic castle, one that conjured up images of dusty corridors and secret panels, and skeletons in leg-irons dragging their bare bones across the floor.

Someone tooted at me as I walked along Jackson Street. I looked up to see Ruth and her cronies on their way to Portage. The Dells were closer, but as Ruth had said, with all of the tourists likely to be there this Labor Day weekend, they would be lucky to get an alley by midnight.

I found Lawrence Hess outside, furiously raking his yard as if he were trying to get it all done before dark. As I waited for him to acknowledge me, I took that opportunity to reacquaint myself with him.

A bachelor, who to my knowledge had never married, he was somewhere around forty, about five-feet, ten-inches tall, with a slender build, small delicate hands, a soft voice that bordered on feminine, hazel eyes that, hot or cold, could stare a hole in you, thinning ash-brown hair, and a love of fine wines that, to his dismay, he could never find in Oakalla. His path and mine had crossed a few times over the years, once when I did a story on him and the Pembleton Museum, and another when I did a story on the Waggoner House, which he had inherited from his aunt, and which was supposedly once a part of the Underground Railroad, though neither Lawrence nor his aunt had ever found the "safe room" where the slaves would hide. On each occasion, Lawrence Hess and I had found some common ground, so we were comfortable in each other's presence. But we would never become fast friends. I was too pedestrian for him. He was too erudite for me.

"Savages," he muttered to himself. "The world is run by savages."

"Problems, Lawrence?" I said.

"Garth!" he said, dropping the rake and putting both hands to his chest. "In the future, would you *please* announce yourself sooner. You scared the living crap out of me."

"I hated to break your concentration."

He picked up the rake and went back to work. "There is no danger of that, I can assure you." He stopped raking long enough to scan the yard. He didn't like what he saw. "Look at this yard. Just look at it, would you? If I had wanted windrows, I would have planted it in clover."

Like his person, Lawrence kept his yard immaculate. If there was a weed growing there, I couldn't find it.

"I take it someone else mowed it," I said.

"The Morrison boy. My third mower of the year, I might add. I told him specifically that I wanted it raked and bagged. I didn't care how long it took or what it cost, within reason of course." He was talking to himself, a habit with him. "I just wanted it done." He gestured with the rake in his hand. "You can see how well he listened."

"Maybe he planned to come back later," I said.

"Yes. He and the Messiah. Second comings are for birdbrains. You ought to get things right the first time."

I didn't say anything, since we had covered this ground before. Lawrence insisted that religion, all religion as he saw it, was a hoax perpetrated by the weak and ignorant upon the rest of us to keep us in line. "I don't have to prove a negative," he would say. "I don't have to prove that God doesn't exist. You do, however, have to prove a positive, that God does in fact exist, and so far no one has done that."

"To your satisfaction," I had said.

"And to yours?"

I shrugged and said, "There is a lot in a lot of religions that I disagree with. And none that I agree with completely. But I believe in God. And as corny as it sounds, I believe He believes in me."

"How can you believe in a God that you've never even seen?" he fumed. So it went until we gave up on each other.

What I couldn't explain to him, what I had a hard time explaining to myself, since above all I fancied myself as a man of reason, was that you had to take some things on faith, since, to my knowledge, the final book of knowledge had yet to be written.

"Well, what is it, Garth?" he said, impatient to get on with his raking now that dusk was closing in. "I know this isn't a social call. Though, and don't take this wrong, I would welcome one every now and again. You are one of the few in Oakalla with a brain worth picking."

"I was just wondering," I said, "what the curator of the Pembleton Museum would find of interest at the M and M Boys' yard sale?"

"Who told you I was there?"

"Tom Ford."

"And what business is that of his, if I may be so bold to ask?"

"He needed a reference. Yours is one of the first two names that came to mind."

Lawrence wore an ironic smile. Apparently his and Tom Ford's paths had crossed before. "Reference, indeed. What sort of trouble has Tom gotten himself into?"

"He's been arrested for the murder of Monroe Edmonds." I didn't tell him anything more to see what he might offer on the subject. Not much, as it turned out.

"Lovers' quarrel?" Lawrence said.

"Not exactly."

"*What* exactly, then?"

"We found Tom Ford inside Monroe's house. We found Monroe dead of a heart attack upstairs, but it's more complicated than that. We put two and two together and came up with murder." Even as I related it, I realized how nebulous it all sounded.

"Who is we?" Lawrence said. "It is my understanding that Sheriff Clark is out of town for the time being."

"Eugene Yuill."

He didn't laugh in my face as I thought he might. Instead he looked thoughtful, almost sympathetic. "The last time I heard, Eugene Yuill was driving a grain truck. My, my, we *are* coming up in the world. Rupert Roberts to Eugene Yuill, in the span of a single decade."

"What do you want me to say?" I said. "That I like it?"

Lawrence patted me on the shoulder and went back to raking his yard.

"You still didn't tell me what you were doing there at the yard sale," I said.

"Artifacts, Garth. Can you think of two better representatives of Neanderthal man than the M and M Boys?" He stopped raking long enough to give me a smile. "Was that all?"

"For now."

He resumed raking. "Do come again when you can stay longer."

CHAPTER 9

More rain was coming. The forecasters were calling for it. I could smell it in the air.

I arrived at the Corner Bar and Grill at eight forty-five and took the only corner booth in the barroom. A few regulars sat around the bar itself, and I could hear a euchre game going on in the back room. One of the three other booths was occupied by some people that I didn't know — a not-so-pleasingly-plump woman in a green pantsuit and polka-dot blouse and an equally fat man in a tank top, Bermuda shorts, black socks, and sneakers, who had probably gotten lost on their way to the Dells.

Tanya Ford came to take my order. She looked a lot better than she had that morning, more alert and alive, a blush on her cheeks and a smile in her eyes. More confident, too, as if being in demand gave her a stature that she didn't have at home.

"What will it be, Garth?"

"Bourbon and ginger ale."

"This is a first, isn't it?" What she meant was that at night I always sat at the bar where Hiram waited on me.

"I'm meeting someone here in a few minutes."

"Oh," she said. "Do I know her?" Apparently my smile gave me away and told her it was a woman.

"Abby Airhart is her name. She's Doc Airhart's niece."

"Don't know her. Is she new around here?"

"Yes. She's new around here."

When I didn't volunteer any more information, Tanya left and returned with my drink a couple minutes later. I sat nursing it, while waiting for my chance to talk to Hiram alone. I got it when he came to my end of the room, as Tanya carried a tray full of catfish and french fries from the kitchen into the dining room.

"Hiram," I said, moving over to the bar. "You got a minute?"

"About that," he said, wiping off the bar. "What's on your mind, Garth?"

"Tom Ford is on my mind. You've heard about the trouble he's in?"

"Don't know anyone who hasn't. It's about all anyone wants to talk about." He glanced up to make sure of where Tanya was. "Whenever Tanya isn't around."

"You were here last week, weren't you, when Tom and Tanya got into it?" Hiram was such a fixture at the Corner Bar and Grill that it was hard to imagine his being anywhere else.

"Here?" he said, raising his voice a little, which was as excited as he ever got. "I was right in the middle of it."

"What I was wondering was, do you remember what Tom's exact words to Tanya were before he shoved her against the bar?"

Again he looked around the barroom to make sure of where Tanya was. "I can't be exactly sure, Garth. I've slept since then. What I remember was, he said, 'Tell that fat old man to stay away from Elizabeth.' Or something to that effect." Hiram found a splotch of liquid he'd missed and used the towel to wipe it up. "Elizabeth is their oldest girl, if you didn't know."

I didn't know and was glad for the information. "Is that all you remember him saying?" I said.

Hiram nodded toward the swinging doors that separated the barroom from the dining room. Her back to the door, Tanya Ford was about to reenter the barroom. "That's the gist of it. More came before and after, but it escapes me now."

I returned to my booth, as Tanya Ford backed through the swinging door, carrying a tray full of dirty dishes. Then for the next few minutes I watched her make her rounds. She seemed to be enjoying herself, and she was very good at what she did. Nobody's empty glass, nobody's empty plate, nobody's raised hand went unnoticed for long with Tanya around. And she did it all without a hitch, with what seemed to be a minimum of effort and intrusion. That was my definition of an expert — someone who could make a hard job seem easy enough for me to want to try it. It was also my definition of a hustler.

"About ready for a refill?" Tanya asked on her return to my booth.

I looked at the Hamms clock above the bar, where my favorite log-rolling bear was about to take another tumble. Already it was nine fifteen and Abby still hadn't showed.

I handed Tanya my glass, and she took off for the bar. Moments later she returned with a refill, but when I started to pay for it, she said, "That's okay. It's already been taken care of."

I looked around the barroom. There were several people in there that I knew, but saw no one who might buy me a drink. "Who do I have to thank for this?" I said.

"Dub Bennett." She then read the question

in my eyes. "He's in the back room playing euchre."

"Since when did Dub start buying me drinks?"

"You'll have to ask him."

"Tanya," I said before she moved on, "when you get a minute, I need to talk to you."

She gave me a questioning look. "When I get a minute," she said.

While I waited for her to return, I searched for a reason that Dub Bennett might want to buy me a drink, but none came to mind. And when he left the Corner Bar and Grill a few minutes later without so much as a nod in my direction, I was even more puzzled.

"Make it fast, Garth," Tanya said. "It's a busy night."

I heard the slap of cards against the table and someone holler, "Deal." Evidently someone had filled in for Dub.

"Just one question, and I'll let you go," I said. "A couple days ago in here, when you and Tom got into it, what exactly was at the heart of it?"

"A lot of things, Garth. None of which I want to go into here or anywhere else. So, can I go now?" She had assumed a posture that said: don't tread on me. But a posture was all that it was.

"Just answer me this, then," I said. "Was one of the things Monroe Edmonds's relationship with your daughter, Elizabeth?"

As quick as Jack-Be-Nimble, she pulled a pack of Kools from her jeans' pocket and lighted one. I noticed that Hiram took note but said nothing. Good bartender that he was, he knew when someone needed either a drink or a smoke.

"Yes. But it's not the kind of relationship you think," she said. "Monroe wanted to give Elizabeth piano lessons for free. He said she had real talent. But Tom wouldn't hear of it. He said . . ." Tears came into her eyes. It took her a moment to regain control. "He said, 'What could that fat old man ever teach our daughter about anything?' " She leaned across my table and put out her cigarette in my ashtray. "I swear, Garth. Those were his exact words."

"Thanks, Tanya. That's all I wanted to know."

I took a drink of my bourbon and ginger ale and thought back to a summer night so hot and still that even the crickets couldn't find much to chirp about. Grandmother Ryland and I were sitting in the high school gymnasium along with two hundred other sweating, grumbling, disinterested spectators watching what used to be called Amateur

125

Night — before they built the park, moved it outside, and called it Talent Watch. What Amateur Night consisted of was just that, a group of local amateur performers parading their talents, or lack thereof, which was usually the case, before the Oakalla community. It was sponsored by the Community Club and was, without fail, held on what proved to be the hottest night in July.

Despite my protests, Grandmother and I always attended, because every effort (her words), no matter how miserable (my words), deserved applause. I thought then, and still think, that the real reason we went was to punish me for all of the things that I had done that she could only guess about.

On that particular night, the performers were even worse than usual, and I had threatened (with the full intention of doing so) to walk out and walk home if the next performance wasn't better than the last. Then I heard footsteps behind me. Heavy, straight-line footsteps that knew no hesitation as they made their way under the basketball goal and down the center aisle toward the stage.

Luella Skiles, who, as always, was mistress of ceremony, since it was largely her star pupils who performed, stood speechless at the microphone until she found the presence of mind to say, "And now a surprise performance by one of Oakalla's leading artists, Monroe Edmonds."

Of course, she had to say "surprise performance" because all of us who had been counting each performer with drops of his own blood knew that Monroe Edmonds wasn't on the program. But leading artist? I had to laugh at that. Oakalla didn't have any.

I laughed up until the time that Monroe Edmonds sat down at the piano and began to play. He didn't warm up. He didn't even crack his knuckles that I remember. He just sat there and pounded the keys to the tune of "Alexander's Ragtime Band" until the whole gymnasium reverberated with the sound of clapping hands and stomping feet. And when he finished, he didn't even wait for our applause, which would have been thunderous, but, just for spite it seemed, began to play a classical piece that was every bit as showy and moving as "Alexander's Ragtime Band" had been. Though, as "Alexander" had commanded our participation, this song demanded our silence, that we look inward and then upward at those personal heights that we had yet to scale, but up until that moment had seemed beyond our reach.

When he finished, Monroe Edmonds (who seemed six inches taller then and was about two hundred pounds lighter than at his death) left along the same straight path that he had entered by. The whole time Grandmother stared at me with that "See, smarty" look in her eyes that she reserved for such occasions. I didn't dare protest for fear of breaking the silence that held until Luella Skiles finally found her composure again and announced the next participant.

But no one came forward. Neither did the next person that she called, nor the next, to my everlasting relief. It was the only time that I had ever seen Luella Skiles show any emotion, as she pleaded for someone, anyone, to come forward. Her pleas fell on deaf ears, however, as first one row and then another filed out until the whole place, save for Luella Skiles, emptied.

What could that fat old man teach anybody about anything? He had taught a lot of us in Oakalla, especially me, humility.

I glanced up at the Hamms beer clock. Nine forty-five. I was about to wave at Tanya Ford and order another drink when Abby came into the barroom. I felt the tension as several pairs of eyes besides my own appraised her. But she disarmed us all with a smile.

"Am I fashionably late?" she said, as she sat down in the booth across from me.

"You might call it that."

She wore black jeans, sandals over bare feet,

and a long-sleeve blue work shirt tucked in her jeans. She also wore small silver earrings and a hint of makeup, and looked peachy keen to me.

"I'm sorry, Garth," she said. "I had a problem with one of my patients, and it took me longer than I thought it would."

"Nothing serious, I hope," I said, not able to judge by her face just how serious it was.

"He died," she said matter-of-factly. "That's pretty serious, I guess."

I felt like a fool. I started to tell her so. "Abby. . . ."

"It's okay, Garth." She took both my hands in hers. "It happens." Then she let go.

"If you'd rather make it another night," I said, "I'll understand." Big of me, now that I thought about it.

"That was my intention when I came in here," she said. "To make my apology and leave. But now that I'm here, why don't I have one drink at least."

I waved at Tanya Ford, who had been waiting patiently in the wings for us to get settled. She was a good waitress. An uncommonly good waitress.

"What will it be?" Tanya said.

"I think I'll have a draft of that Point Bock beer that I've heard so much about," Abby said. Short for Stevens Point Bock, a local favorite with a national following.

"Make that two," I said. Whiskey on beer, never fear. Beer on whiskey might be risky. But what the hell.

"By the way," I said. "Tanya Ford, this is Abby Airhart. Abby Airhart, this is Tanya Ford."

Abby rose and shook Tanya's hand. If I were to judge by the smile on Tanya's face, it was the right thing to do.

"It's good to meet you," Abby said.

"Likewise."

The barroom suddenly grew quiet. Even the euchre game in the back room hit a lull. I looked up to see Amber Utley standing just inside the swinging door, as if unsure as to where to go from there. Amber Utley was the blonde-haired, blue-eyed twenty-five-year-old elementary teacher, whose cherry-red Mazda RX-7 was at that very moment at the Marathon for repairs. I had never seen her in the Corner Bar and Grill before. Maybe she had wandered in there by mistake.

"May I help you, miss?" Hiram said, noting her distress.

Amber Utley had a head full of curls to go with her blonde hair and the kind of body that even a priest would sneak a second look at. She wore a white T-shirt with hot pink lettering that said "Let's Party" on the front of it, hot pink L. A. Gear tennis shoes, and a pair of jeans that left little to my imagination.

"I'd like a twelve-pack of Old Milwaukee, please," she said in a small breathy voice that reminded me of Marilyn Monroe.

"Coming right up." Hiram almost tripped over himself in his hurry to serve her.

Tanya Ford, however, seemed less impressed with Amber Utley. Tanya headed straight for her with our two drafts of Point Bock beer, and Amber Utley had to step out of the way or risk getting run over.

Hiram then returned from the cooler with a twelve-pack of Old Milwaukee. Amber Utley paid him and left the way she'd come.

I was watching Tanya Ford watching Amber Utley when Abby said, "Friend of yours?" Though she was still smiling, I noticed the chill in her voice.

"No," I said, realizing that I had paid more attention to Amber Utley than I should have.

"Then would you like for her to be a friend of yours?"

I felt my ears turning red. Guilty as charged. "Drink your beer, please, before it gets warm."

"You didn't answer my question."

Neither was I going to.

We sat drinking our beer, as the euchre

131

game continued in the back room, and one and two at a time, the regulars continued to wander in and out of the Corner Bar and Grill. Abby seemed fascinated by the place, like a kid at her first real movie theater, as her eyes greedily took in everything, including me.

"Do you mind if I smoke?" she said.

The question took me by surprise, even though it wasn't entirely unexpected. "Be my guest," I said as I slid the ashtray her way.

But she wouldn't let me off that easily. "No," she said. "Do you *mind* if I smoke?"

She had me on the horns of a dilemma. As a nonsmoker who up until then had assumed a laissez-faire attitude toward the whole issue, would it have been hypocritical of me to say that it's okay for everyone else in the world but not for you?

"Yes," I said. "I mind. But I don't expect you to not smoke on my account."

"Good," she said, taking a pack of Winstons from her purse and lighting one. "I was hoping you'd say that."

When we stepped outside an hour or so later, the smell of rain was near and bold, and no stars shone in the sky. We walked the two blocks along Colburn Road to Doc Airhart's house then stopped at the front door. "Well, here we are," Abby said.

"I enjoyed it," I said.

"So did I. More even than I hoped I would."

"Maybe we can do it again some time."

"I'd like that."

I touched my hand to her cheek. She laid her hand on mine and held it there a moment. Then we said our goodbyes, and she went inside.

On the way to Monroe Edmonds's house, I played back our final conversation before I had walked her home. We had been talking about Monroe Edmonds and what I had learned so far about his death.

"Do you think he'll try again?" she had said.

"Who?"

"Whoever was in the house last night before Tom Ford got there."

"We don't know that anyone was in the house before Tom Ford got there. Or do we?"

She shook her head no. "It just seems likely, that's all. If Tom Ford didn't stop that elevator between floors, someone else had to."

Which was why I was now on my way to Monroe Edmonds's house. If someone else besides Tom Ford had been in the house and had indeed been looking for something as Tom Ford probably had been, then he might return under the cover of darkness and resume his search.

I cut through the alley that ran beside the United Methodist Church and turned south once I reached School Street. Approaching the school, I realized that I was also approaching Amber Utley's apartment, which was the upstairs apartment in the first house north of the school. I had passed it several times within the last year on my way elsewhere, and nearly every time, despite my avowed lack of interest in Amber Utley, I gave it a longing look. As with Babbitt, who also knew better, Amber Utley was my fairy child. I couldn't imagine a lifetime with her, but I could imagine one long delicious night.

Tonight, I stopped and stared up at her window. Though the curtains were pulled, a light was on behind it, and I could see someone moving about inside and hear muffled voices. A man's voice and a woman's voice by the sound of them. So someone had Amber Utley, a twelve-pack of Old Milwaukee, and a three-day weekend all to himself. Life didn't get any better than that.

I came to Monroe Edmonds's house, stepped into the shadow of Luella Skiles's giant pine, and waited to see what might happen. The rain, which so far had held off, seemed right at the edge of town. As I listened, I thought I could hear it in the cornfields and the bean fields beyond, a gentle patter that soon built into a roar. Not all storms required thunder and lightning, or wind that spun the leaves inside out and sent your lawn chairs skidding across your patio. Some storms were silent except for the rain. They came on "little cat feet" and made no show of force, save for that opaque silver curtain, dropped straight down. But when they left, yards had been turned into ponds, and rivers ran in the streets.

I thought that I heard the house shudder — someone's misstep perhaps that had turned into a fall. Edging closer to the house, as far as the pine's shadow would allow me, I felt the first drops of rain. It was either now or never. Soon I would be too wet to care what happened.

As I tried the front door, I was surprised to find it unlocked. Stepping inside, I thought I heard the back door quietly close. A chilling sound, one that made the damp night seem even cooler than it was, it told me that yes, someone else was in the house, and perhaps had been in here last night as well.

Not trusting myself to make my way through the house in the dark, I went out the front door and around the south side of the house to the back. There I stopped only long enough to scan the backyard before I was driven inside by the rain. Then the hair on my nape began to tingle. What I smelled was that old, oddly medicinal smell from my childhood that I couldn't quite place — the same smell that I had noted less than twenty-four hours earlier, as Monroe Edmonds lay dead in his elevator.

CHAPTER 10

Had I not heard Ruth rummaging about the kitchen, I would have slept longer than I did.

First, while waiting out the storm in Monroe Edmonds's house, I had called Luella Skiles to tell her where I was and not to be alarmed if she saw some lights come on. Then I had made a methodical search of the house to see what, if anything, was missing. Nothing was that I could see, but since it wasn't my house, I couldn't be sure.

"How did your bowling go?" I asked Ruth, as I poured myself a cup of coffee and sat down at the kitchen table.

"It went," she said. She appeared to be making caramel cinnamon rolls, something that she did from time to time when the weather began to cool.

"What about Liddy Bennett? Did you learn anything from her?"

Ruth was chopping pecans. With a vengeance, it seemed. "I learned where both gutters were. She's the only person I know who can throw a hook and a fade on the same ball."

"I mean about Dub Bennett."

"No. She was pretty closed mouth all night, which is unusual for her."

"Maybe Dub warned her off."

"That's what I'm thinking."

After she finished chopping the pecans, Ruth got out the mixing bowl, measured out some flour, sugar, and cinnamon, added an egg and some milk, and began to mix the batter by hand. She usually used the mixer, but I could tell that she needed to work off some frustrations. Bowling did that to her, as golf used to do that to me — before I gave it up.

"What about Tom Ford? Did anyone have any bright ideas about him?"

"Not a one. If he's up to something, he's doing a good job of keeping it a secret."

"Maybe Dutchman Yoder is mistaken about him."

"I doubt it, Garth. There's not much in this town that goes on that Dutchman Yoder doesn't see. But because of who he is and the way he's dressed, people just don't pay that much attention to him."

"In other words, he doesn't count."

"Yes. When you get right down to it."

She got out her tin baking pan and put the dough in it, set the oven, and put the pan

138

inside. Then she started on the pecan-caramel icing, which was my favorite part of the whole operation.

"How did your night go?" she asked.

How had my night gone? Part of it had been terrific, the rest less so. "It went," I said, using her tactic.

"You ask Abby out?"

Damn, I thought. How did she know?

"We met for a drink at the Corner Bar and Grill."

"How did that go?" Intent on the icing, she wasn't even looking my way. But I knew she had her radar on.

"Very well."

I thought I saw her brows rise ever so slightly. Antennae, I called them. When they were up, I was usually in trouble.

"It's not what you're thinking," I said.

"I didn't say anything."

"You didn't have to. But, to ease your mind, we said our goodbyes at her front door."

"You're a grown man, Garth. She's a grown woman. What you two do in private is your own business."

I heard her but didn't believe her. Ruth was liberal in a lot of ways but not when it came to casual sex. Or bed hopping, as she called it. She believed in commitment for commitment's sake and felt that anything less, which included sex outside of marriage, or the promise thereof, was wrong.

"What I meant was, when I said things went very well is that I like her a lot. As a person, I mean. Not just as a woman."

"I'm listening."

"And today, tomorrow, next week, or next month, whenever I see her again, I think she'll be the same person that she was last night."

"What you mean is, she's normal."

"Yes. But in an exceptional sort of way."

"So when do I get to meet her?"

"I don't know yet. Maybe as early as this afternoon."

Satisfied that everything was under control, Ruth brought her cup of coffee to the table and sat down. "So what else happened last night that I should know about?"

I told her about my visit to Lawrence Hess and then my trip to Monroe Edmonds's house. In the retelling of it, when I came to the part about the old familiar smell, I again felt the hair on my nape rise.

"You don't recognize the smell?" she said.

"I recognize it. I just don't know what it is."

"Same difference. Do you think he found what he was looking for?"

"No."

"Why not?"

"I just don't think he did, that's all."

"Then do you think he'll be back?"

I had to give that some thought. Meanwhile I could smell the rolls baking in the oven. I wished they'd hurry up.

"No," I said. "There was no reason for him to leave when he did, not with it starting to rain. I think he came to the same conclusion I did, that whatever he's looking for, isn't there."

"You keep saying *he*. Could it be a she?"

"I hadn't thought of that, but it's a possibility."

She got up to check on the rolls and sat back down again. "What does Lawrence Hess have to do with all of this?"

"I'm not sure that he has anything to do with it. But he was out at the M and M Boys' yard sale just ahead of Tom Ford . . ." I stopped. Something clicked in my brain, but I couldn't make the connection. "Maybe he saw something there that could shed some light on the matter."

"Like the painting that Tom Ford says he bought?"

"That's right," I said, feeling stupid. "I forgot to ask him that."

"Your mind was probably on other things."

"Probably." I wouldn't give her the satisfaction of denying it.

"There's something else you might consider, Garth. How did Tom Ford, or Lawrence Hess for that matter, know to be out at that yard sale when the *Reporter* wasn't even out yet?"

"I'll ask Lawrence that when I see him later today."

"And Tom Ford? When are you going to ask him?"

"About Monday, I figure. Twenty-four more hours in jail should soften him to where he might talk."

"It doesn't bother you that he's in all probability innocent of Monroe Edmonds's murder?"

I kept smelling the rolls and hoping they'd hurry up. "A little. But not enough to keep me up nights."

"Rupert Roberts would never allow it," she said, bringing out the heavy artillery.

"I know. That's the difference between Rupert and me, why he was a real lawman and why I'm not."

Ruth got up to take another look at the rolls, then stood by the oven, warming herself. "One other thing I wonder about is how everybody keeps getting into Monroe Edmonds's house so easily?" she said. "Didn't Monroe keep it locked? Aren't you keeping it locked now?"

"You'll have to ask Eugene Yuill about that. He was the last one in there yesterday. He and Tom Ford, if I remember right."

"Speaking of Eugene Yuill, what's he up to lately? I haven't seen hide nor hair of him."

Now that she mentioned it, I hadn't either.

When the rolls were finally done and out of the oven, Ruth iced them. As soon as they cooled enough not to burn our mouths, we began to eat them. We both made pigs of ourselves, but that was the whole idea.

"You going to church?" Ruth asked, using a napkin to wipe her mouth.

"No. Are you?"

"I thought I might. I haven't been all summer."

Neither had I, but that was beside the point. "Then I'll walk you part of the way there."

"Let me guess," she said.

"You'd be wrong."

While Ruth went upstairs to get ready for church, I cleaned off the table and put what dishes there were on the counter beside the sink. There weren't enough to wash, and Ruth always knew when I just rinsed them off, so I'd let her worry about them.

The phone rang. I answered it. "Garth, what's this I hear about Ruth pumping Liddy for information about me last night." It was Dub Bennett, and he didn't sound happy with me. "It seems like you've got enough to do without sticking your nose in everybody's business."

"Just covering all the bases," I said. "A man gets murdered in his own home, I'd sort of like to know why."

"Who said anything about murder? The way I hear it, Monroe Edmonds had a heart attack, plain and simple."

"Who told you that?"

"Eugene Yuill. Last evening at the Corner Bar and Grill. Before he left he said that if you came in, I was to buy you a drink for him, and he'd settle with me later."

That explained the drink at least. "Was Eugene in uniform?" I said.

"No. As a matter of fact, he wasn't. He said he was taking the night off. He said he was sick of the job already, the way it always pits neighbor against neighbor. In fact, he was even talking about resigning."

"So he bought me a beer?"

Apparently Dub didn't know how to respond, so he didn't even try.

"I'm sorry to hear about Eugene," I said. "But he told you wrong about Monroe Edmonds. He did die of a heart attack, but it isn't as simple as that."

"That's your opinion."

"That's also the acting coroner's opinion."

"A young heifer just out of medical school is what I hear."

"And Doc Airhart's opinion."

"An old quack who's over the hill."

I glanced outside where the sun was up and hard at work, mopping up after last night's rain.

"Dub, I'm going to hang up now before I say something that I might regret."

"Sure. You can dish it out, but you can't take it."

Click. I hung up, then waited there by the phone to see if he would call back. When he didn't call back, I walked to the back door to take a look outside. Such a beautiful morning. I wished I were out in it. Alone, in a canoe. Miles and miles from here.

"Who was that on the phone?" Ruth asked on her way down the stairs. She wore red high-heel shoes, a lightweight blue suit and belt, and on the lapel of the suit, the diamond brooch that Karl had given her on their twenty-fifth wedding anniversary. Sometimes I forgot how truly beautiful Ruth was and had been. It was always a shock to be reminded again.

"Dub Bennett," I said.

"What did he want?"

"For us to stay out of his business."

Ruth shrugged it off. "We must be on to something then."

"He also said that Eugene Yuill was out of uniform at the Corner Bar and Grill last night and that he's thinking about resigning."

Her answer was "I wouldn't get my hopes up."

"But what happened to him, Ruth, between yesterday morning and last night. When I first talked to him yesterday, it would have taken the Second Cavalry to get that uniform off of him."

"Maybe nothing happened, Garth. Maybe the job got too big for him, that's all. It wouldn't be the first time."

"Maybe. But I don't think so."

Ruth and I walked together as far as Doc Airhart's house, where I sat down on the bottom step of the porch while Ruth went on to church. I didn't have long to wait. A couple minutes later, Elizabeth Ford and her two younger sisters came bounding down the church steps and took off for home. I had to run to catch up to them.

"Elizabeth," I said, as I pulled alongside her. "Could I talk to you a minute?"

Elizabeth and her two sisters all wore white dresses that they'd outgrown by several inches. Each had a blue ribbon tied in her hair, and each looked neat and freshly scrubbed.

Elizabeth Ford gave me the once over, then sent her sisters on ahead. "Don't run," she said. "And make sure you look both ways when you cross the street."

"Do your sisters have names?" I said.

"Joanna is the middle one. She's nine. Wendy is the little one. She's six."

"And you are how old?"

"Twelve. In April."

Twelve. Had he lived, that would have been close to my son's age.

"Why does that make you sad?" she asked.

We were walking along the alley south of the church, the same alley that I had walked a few short hours ago after leaving Abby at her doorstep.

"I was just thinking about someone," I said.

"Who's that?"

"My son."

"Why does that make you sad? Did you have a fight or something?"

We came to School Street and turned south. "No. He's dead. Sometimes, like today, I realize how much I still miss him."

"Sometimes I wish I were dead. Then I wouldn't have to listen to my folks fight all the time."

"Do you think that would solve anything?"

She shrugged. "It would for me."

"They'd still go on fighting, with or without you around to hear it. So what's to gain by it?"

"Maybe a little peace for once in my life."

I knew exactly how she felt, but I couldn't let her know that. "That's an awfully big price to pay for a little peace."

She smiled at me. I was relieved to see that she still could. "I've thought of that, too. I'm already twelve. If I've stood it this long, I can stand it a few years longer."

We walked the next half block in silence, until we came to Amber Utley's apartment. "My old teacher lives here," Elizabeth said, stopping to show me. "Upstairs."

I followed her eyes to the upstairs window but saw only a square pane of glass. "What was your teacher like?" I asked when we were moving again.

"She's nice," Elizabeth said. "And she tried really hard to get us kids to like her. But she's not really my type, if you know what I mean."

I nodded, trying to look wise.

"Elizabeth," I said, realizing that we'd soon be at her house. "I have to ask you some hard questions, and I need some straight answers. Are you up to that?"

"Is this about Mr. Edmonds?"

"Yes."

Her face was the picture of resolve. "Then I'm up to it."

I slowed my pace, so that we would have more time to talk. "The first thing I need to know is, did Mr. Edmonds offer to give you piano lessons?"

"He did. But my dad wouldn't let him. At least that's what my mom said." She seemed to have her doubts.

"I think your mom's shooting straight with you on this one," I said.

She didn't say anything.

"Were you and Mr. Edmonds friends?" I said.

"*Good* friends," she emphasized. "It seems I was always over there doing something for him, like washing his dishes or cleaning his house. He wanted to pay me, but I wouldn't let him. Except for mowing his yard. I charged him five dollars a week for that." She wore a scowl that darkened with each step toward home. "I know it needs mowing now. But the mower's broke, and Dad hasn't gotten it fixed."

"You mow your own lawn, too?"

"I mow the yard, do the laundry, wash the dishes, clean the house." She listed these like a litany of grievances. "I know Mom says I don't do anything around there, and I don't whenever she's there. I figure that's her job.

149

But the rest of the time, I do. And the house is a lot cleaner, too, than when she's there."

I kept my mouth closed and my eyes on the sidewalk.

"But to hear Mom tell it, I'm the laziest, most ungrateful kid who ever lived." Elizabeth Ford's eyes burned with anger. "At least she can't call me stupid. I've got the grades to prove it."

"Back to Mr. Edmonds," I said, looking up and seeing that we had less than a block to go. "Did he ever . . . ?" I stopped. I didn't know how to put it.

"Did he ever molest me? No. He patted me on the shoulder sometimes. You know, when I was messing around on the piano and I'd do something good, but that was the only time he ever touched me."

"Sorry. But I had to ask."

"That's okay. Mom asked me the same thing a couple weeks ago. Only she was asking about Dad."

"And you told her?"

"I told her that he never touched me where he shouldn't. If he ever did, I'd kill him in his sleep."

I looked at her to see if she was serious. She was. "Does your father ever beat you and your sisters?"

"No. He knows better."

"But he does beat your mother?"

"Sometimes. When he's been drinking." She frowned, as if she were unsure of herself. "I'm not taking his side of it, but Mom usually starts it. She hasn't learned when to leave well enough alone."

"In what way?"

"Dad. He can get mean when he's drunk and say all kinds of hateful and hurtful things. But if you leave him alone and let him sleep it off, he's usually okay by morning." She smiled. It looked a little forced but was otherwise intact. "Dad's not a bad guy when you get to know him. Just a little messed up. He was doing okay in college, too, until I came along. Then he had to quit and go to work for Grandpa. Things might have worked out for him if he could have stayed in school."

"Do you blame yourself for that?"

She shook her head, as her long brown hair swirled around her face. "It's not my fault Mom got pregnant. Her fault either, though Dad blames her for it. It was an accident, that's all. Nobody's to blame for it."

I stopped, took her by the shoulders, and made her look at me. There was a tear at the corner of each eye. "Are you sure about that?"

She used her fist to wipe her eyes. "Well, okay, it hurts sometimes, knowing that I might have messed things up for them. But the way I figure it, that was a long time ago. If they haven't gotten things straightened out by now, that's their fault."

We crossed School Street and stopped in front of Monroe Edmonds's house. "He was a great guy. I'm going to miss him a lot," she said.

"Do you have any idea who might have killed him?"

She shook her head no.

"Do you remember seeing or hearing anyone in his house the night he died?"

"No," she said, fighting back the tears. "Not the night he died. But other nights, after I was already in bed, I'd hear his piano playing. And sometimes people laughing." The thought of it seemed to anger her.

"Are you sure it wasn't at Miss Skiles's house next door?"

"I'm sure. Besides, Miss Skiles never plays the piano anymore. Mr. Edmonds told me that."

I walked her to her back door. Part of me hated to leave her there because of all the burdens waiting inside. The other part said not to worry. Elizabeth Ford could take care of herself.

"Elizabeth," I said, struck by a sudden thought, "by any chance did Mr. Edmonds ever give you a key to his house?"

"Sure," she said, brightening. "He gave me one just in case he was out of town and needed me to check up on his place. I keep it on a nail, just inside the door."

"May I see it?"

She went into the house after the key but returned empty-handed. "That's funny," she said. "I was sure it was there. It always is."

"When was the last time you remember seeing it?"

She squinted as she tried to remember, as if narrowing her vision would help her narrow her thoughts. "I can't say. Since it's *always* there, I never pay any attention to it."

"Has it ever disappeared before?"

"No. Not that I know of."

"Thanks, Elizabeth. You've been a big help. Elizabeth?" She was reaching for the door when I stopped her. "Did you by any chance see the painting that your dad said he sold to Mr. Edmonds?"

She looked puzzled. "What painting is that?"

"Never mind. I forgot that you would have been in school."

I crossed the alley into Monroe Edmonds's yard, then glanced back at Elizabeth Ford. She hadn't moved from the spot but still stood with her right hand resting on the back door. She appeared to be deep in thought.

CHAPTER 11

Luella Skiles didn't seem glad to see me, but that was nothing new. In Sunday school I had been her chief antagonist whenever I was there. Not only could I not carry a tune, I usually drowned out all of those around me who could. That was when we sang a song I liked. The rest of the time, which was most of the time, I stood there mouthing the words and feeling foolish.

"What is it now, Garth?" She didn't invite me inside.

"A couple questions, that's all. Then I'll leave you in peace."

"That certainly would be a welcome change."

She stepped outside onto the porch. She wore baggy grey slacks and a short-sleeve white blouse that had a small tear in the shoulder and brown paint spots all down the front of it. "You're not going to church today?" I said.

"Does it look like it?"

I couldn't imagine the United Methodist Church without Luella Skiles in it. Even after she had stopped playing the organ, every Sunday, she was there front and center in the third row — a dusty icon that I no longer feared but still paid homage to.

"Nice day," I said, noticing how deep blue the sky had become.

"Get on with it, Garth, please. Some of us have lives of our own."

"Okay, I'll get on with it. To your knowledge, was Monroe in the habit of locking his doors at night?"

"He didn't used to be. But after his persistent late-night visitor, I persuaded him that it might be a good idea to lock them from then on."

"By his persistent late-night visitor, you mean the intruder that you called Sheriff Roberts and then Sheriff Clark about."

"Yes," she said sharply. "What else would I mean?"

"Elizabeth Ford told me that she heard Monroe's piano playing long after she was in bed. And voices and laughter. That's what else you might mean."

She seemed less startled by that information than the fact that I knew it. "Well, the child is not wrong about that. I, too, have heard the same thing."

"You told me yesterday that Monroe Edmonds was always in bed by ten. Or were you mistaken?"

She found something in the far reaches of her yard to look at. "I wasn't mistaken. Monroe usually turned the lights out at ten. But not always."

"Do you happen to know who it was there in the house with him?"

"No." With her head turned, it was hard to tell whether she was lying or not.

"Is it true that Monroe wanted to give Elizabeth Ford piano lessons?"

"Yes. Against my better judgment."

"Why against your better judgment?"

She turned to face me. She had a familiar look in her eyes, her dour Sunday-school look from years past. "Monroe was a talent, but he was no *teacher*. That girl deserves better."

"Then she has talent?"

"Unlimited talent. I've tried to tell her parents that, but it's like talking to two stumps. They are like you in that they cannot conceive of anything beyond the obvious."

"What is the obvious?"

"They are flawed. Therefore, their daughter must be."

"How is that like me?"

"I'll leave that up to you to decide."

"How is it that you know about Elizabeth's talent? I thought you had nothing to do with the piano anymore."

"I don't. But that doesn't make me deaf. Now if you will excuse me." She went back inside and closed the door.

Eugene Yuill lived in a small rental house that sat behind Doc Cook's old house along Gas Line Road. Doc Cook was Oakalla's longtime veterinarian, who developed a blood clot and died after a cow had kicked him in the leg. The rental house was what used to be his office.

Squeezed into three tiny rooms, bedroom, parlor, and kitchen, with a broom closet and a half bath, and sided with patchwork squares of brown linoleum, the house seemed to suit Eugene Yuill just fine. He had lived there for most of his adult life.

Though Eugene's patrol car was parked in the drive, he didn't answer when I knocked on his side door, which was also his front and only door. I knocked again, harder this time, shaking loose a shower of rust from the screen that gave my arm an instant tan. Then I went to each window, all four of them, and tried to look inside, but a shade was drawn on each. Either Eugene wasn't in there, or he didn't want to be disturbed.

I continued east along Gas Line Road until

I came to Berry Street where I turned north. With a twinge of guilt, I had passed the long low cement building that housed the *Oakalla Reporter* and in which I spent most of my waking hours. For two days running, I had not darkened its door. There wouldn't be a third.

Lawrence Hess had managed to rake all of his grass down to its roots and was now in the process of bagging the grass. He wore faded navy-blue dress pants, a long-sleeve white dress shirt with the sleeves rolled up to his elbows, loafers without socks, and brown cotton gloves. Watching him, his look of distaste as he wrestled with the grass, I decided that even on this first Sunday of the new NFL season, probably no one in Oakalla would invite him over for pretzels and beer.

"Are you allergic to grass or something?" he said to me, as he straightened and used his shirt sleeve to wipe his brow.

"Sorry. I didn't know you needed help."

"Then you haven't been paying attention."

I held the bags open and tied them after Lawrence had filled them with grass. We then carried them to the alley that ran behind his carriage house. One of the few true alleys left in Oakalla, it ran half the length of town, from Perrin to Park Street, and was, for me who loved alleys, a beautiful sight to behold.

"It's bad enough that I have to rake the

damn stuff," Lawrence said. "Now I'll have to pay someone to haul it away."

"You could always just let it grow."

"As you could just stick with running a newspaper." He stopped to wipe his brow again. "But we both know that's not going to happen."

"Is there something in the air today?" I said. "It seems that everybody is on my case."

"Here. Make yourself useful."

He handed me a coffee can full of rainwater that I used to prime his pitcher pump while he worked the handle. Once the water began to spill out, he wetted his sleeve and meticulously dabbed it here and there on his face, like someone applying makeup.

"Be my guest," he said, handing me the tin cup that hung on the pump.

He again worked the handle while I filled the cup. The water was ice cold but had a slight artesian taste to it that I didn't care for.

"What do you think?" he said, after I'd drunk half a cup and thrown the rest away.

"I've had better."

"So have I. That's why I never drink the stuff."

"Thanks for nothing," I said.

"You're quite welcome."

Before we moved on, Lawrence set the empty coffee can back on top of the well. "As long as we're here, it would be just as easy to fill it," I said.

"No," he said, with a hint of a smile. "Let God do it."

We entered the shade of a nearby pine, where it smelled refreshingly, and deceivingly, like the North Woods. "Two visits in two days," Lawrence said, taking off his gloves and showing me his blisters. "To what do I owe the honor?"

"Senility," I said. "Yesterday when I was here, I forgot to ask you if you remembered seeing a painting at the M and M Boys' yard sale?"

"What kind of painting?"

"I was hoping you could tell me."

He didn't spend much time thinking it over. "No. There was no painting there that I remember."

"Are you sure? It's important."

"I'm sure, Garth. It's my business to be sure."

What he meant was that as curator of the Pembleton Museum, which on a shoestring budget had built its collection of rare artifacts one find at a time, he couldn't afford a false step or to overlook anything of possible value.

"We all have our bad days," I said.

"True. But this wasn't one of them."

"Did you see anything else there that . . ."

"That someone would have murdered Monroe Edmonds for? No. I would have bought it if I had."

"Whatever the cost?"

His smile said that he knew what I was up to and was one step ahead of me. "Within reason."

"Were you the first one at the yard sale, or did someone beat you there?"

"I believe I was the first one."

"May I ask how you got there so early?"

"That's easy. I read about it in the *Reporter*."

Again something teased my mind, then eluded me. "But the *Reporter* wasn't out yet."

"I know. But Dutchman Yoder isn't the only early bird around here. Two can play that game as well as one."

"You were there when they opened the sacks?"

He shook his head, looking disappointed in me. "Garth, you know me better than that. Unlike Dutchman Yoder, I have no scruples when it comes to opening sacks. I do it myself. Besides, my paper's usually near the top anyway."

"I'll remember to put it at the bottom from now on."

"A wasted effort," he said with certainty.

"I'll find a way around it."

"Any other ideas on the subject as to why someone might want to murder Monroe Edmonds?" I said.

"You're sure he was murdered?"

"Yes. I'm sure." At least Abby was, and that was good enough for me.

"No," Lawrence said. "I have no idea why someone might want to murder him. I've seen all of his stuff. Together it makes a nice collection, but no single piece is worth killing someone over."

"What about your collection, is it worth killing someone over?"

Through the grapevine, I had heard that Lawrence Hess had his own personal collection of artifacts here at the Waggoner House, one that he kept under lock and key and didn't allow anyone to see.

His face was frightening to behold. I had never seen such a fierce look on him before. "I would kill anyone — man, woman, or child, who stole one piece of my collection. Now, does that answer your question?"

"In spades," I said. "Thanks for your time."

Lawrence didn't answer. His mind was somewhere else, on his collection perhaps. Wherever it was, whatever it had fastened itself on, had cast his face in shadow.

"Lawrence, are you all right?"

"I'm fine, Garth." I'd brought him back to the present, but he looked weary, as from a long journey. "It's an occupational hazard."

"What is?"

"Nostalgia."

"You didn't look nostalgic to me."

He smiled. He had said exactly what he meant. "That's because you don't know where I've been."

CHAPTER 12

As usual, Ruth and I ate Sunday dinner on her good china in the dining room. As soon as the last dish was dried and put away, I called Abby. Doc Airhart answered.

"You again," he said.

"Me again. Is Abby there?"

"I don't know. I'll have to ask her. It's Garth," I heard him say. "Are you here?"

"I'm here," she said into the receiver. "We're just finishing up dinner."

"Same here."

"What did you have?"

"Pot roast. How about you?"

"Pot roast."

"It must be the water," I said.

She laughed. "Probably."

"What I was wondering was, if you would like to take a drive later?"

"I'd love to. Your car or mine?"

I thought about Jessie and rejected that idea. She would strand us somewhere just for spite.

"How about yours?"

"Fine. I'll meet you there within the hour."

"She's coming here," I said to Ruth after I'd hung up.

"I heard." She didn't look pleased. "You might have given me fair warning."

"The house looks fine. It always does."

"That's what you say."

Forty-five minutes later — just after I had sat down from burning the trash, stacking the magazines, dusting the living room, and brushing my teeth — a car pulled up out front. I didn't recognize the car, but I did the driver, who was Dr. Abby Pence-Airhart.

"Abby's here," I said, jumping up from my chair. I felt like a schoolboy about to introduce his prom date to his mother. If either didn't like the other, no matter what, it was going to be a long afternoon.

"Then show her in," Ruth said.

I held the door open for Abby, who was wearing khaki shorts, a marigold tube top, sandals, and a great big smile. "I didn't know where we were going on our drive," she said. "I hope this is all right."

"You're fine," I said. "Just fine." The way I said it brought added color to her cheeks. And mine.

"Abby, this is Ruth Krammes," I said, holding my breath. "Ruth, this is Abby Airhart."

What I feared was one of those long awkward pauses where no one would know quite what to say, and therefore, say nothing, leaving me to break the silence. Abby, however, was already on the move. Before Ruth could even give her a second glance, Abby put her arms around her and gave her a big hug. Damn! I thought. That was the worst possible thing to do.

Followed by "Garth's told me so much about you."

"I'll bet he has," Ruth said, halfheartedly returning Abby's hug, which was more than I expected her to do.

"No. I'm serious. He said he couldn't have gotten along these past few years without you."

Had I said all that, or was she making it up as she went along? Whatever the case, she couldn't flatter Ruth into anything. I knew because I'd tried.

Undeterred, Abby continued. "I hope you don't mind my stealing him for the afternoon. I promise to have him back by dark."

"Why should I mind?" Ruth said.

"Oh, I don't know," Abby replied, losing none of her good humor. "I thought you guys might be planning to watch a football game or something."

As a matter of fact, we had been planning

to watch the Packers, which I had forgotten about. I started to say that, but Ruth cut me short.

"We were. But I decided I wanted the house to myself. So why don't you two run along and let me do that."

Fine with me. I was already out the door, when Abby, who seemed to be enjoying her stay in the lion cage, said, "You're welcome to go with us. I can sit in the backseat."

"No," Ruth said, though she seemed pleased with the invitation. "We'll all have a better time if I stay right here."

"Thanks," Abby said.

"You're welcome."

Outside, I opened the driver's side door of Abby's dark red Honda Prelude as she got in. Then I got in on the other side.

"Where to?" she said.

"Groundhog Falls. I'll point you the way."

"Why don't you just drive us there? That might be easier."

"Why don't you drive there and I'll drive us back," I said. "That way you can learn the roads."

"Good idea."

"I thought so."

We soon put Oakalla behind us, as we drove south on Madison Road. The Prelude's sun-roof was open, both windows were all the way down, and even though she didn't know the road, Abby was speeding merrily along. I laid my head back on the seat and smiled. I hadn't had this much fun in a long time.

"Well, what do you think?" she said anxiously.

"About what?"

"Ruth. Do you think she likes me or not?"

"It's hard to tell with Ruth. I won't know until I get home and maybe not even then."

"As soon as you do know, call me."

I looked over at her — her straw-colored hair fluffed by the wind, her eyes on the road, her hands light and steady on the wheel. Concentration. She had it in abundance. And just the right touch.

"I don't care what Ruth thinks," I said. "I like you."

She momentarily glanced at me, then back to the road again. She was grinning from ear to ear. "I know."

Groundhog Falls was a small falls on the west fork of Stony Creek that dropped about fifteen feet into a deep pool. A cavelike opening had been hollowed out beneath it, and a lot of people liked to stand in there under the falls, while they fished the hole below. Thirty-pound catfish had been caught in there, as well as several trophy walleye and smallmouth bass.

168

The main attraction, however, was the falls itself. In spring, when its waters ran free, pink and white with dogwood blooms; or in the first light of a barefoot summer day; or the last light of knife-edged winter's eve; or in repose, when it gathered itself in pools, and autumn leaves fell upon its flat bare stones. It was a place to collect your thoughts and go refreshed to meet a new day.

I told Abby where to turn, and we began to wind our way back a narrow paved road. The weeds alongside it had been flattened by the runoff from the recent rains, and there were gravel trails across the road itself, where coming off a slope, water had jumped the ditch and laid its own path. No rain in sight today, though. Nothing but blue sky as far as I could see.

"This is fun," I said.

Abby just smiled and kept on driving.

When we reached the turnaround at the end of the road, I was surprised to see that we had Groundhog Falls to ourselves. Normally a couple other cars at least would be out here, sometimes as many as a half dozen. Why, I wondered? I didn't have to wait long to find out.

Something very dead was nearby. Its stench enveloped us before we had taken more than a few steps in the direction of the falls. Then it worsened as we went along, until I wasn't sure that we should go any farther.

"This is a test, right?" Abby said, while holding her hand over her nose and mouth. "To see if I'm really cut out to be a pathologist?"

"Right. It's a test."

"What do I get if I pass?"

"To keep your dinner down."

She began to look a little green in the gills. "I wish you hadn't said that."

I wished I hadn't either.

Long before we ever reached the falls, I could hear it roar. Not a happy, spring, flex-your-muscles roar, but a swollen angry roar from absorbing too much water in too short of time. After all, it should be at rest now, preparing for its long winter's nap. And like a boxer forced to slug it out late in his career when he should have been sitting ringside aging gracefully in the afterglow of triumph, Stony Creek seemed to want to hurl its load downstream all at once and get it over with.

"This is it," I said, as we came out of the woods at the edge of the creek. "Groundhog Falls."

"Impressive," she said, as we watched a brown wall of water tumble over the falls into the boiling soup below. "And scary."

We made our way up the rain-slickened

path beside the falls until we could see our way upstream. About fifty yards ahead, where a newly fallen cottonwood had created a logjam, someone's cow, a Holstein by the looks of it, lay wedged in the branches of the cottonwood. Having spent a large portion of my boyhood in and around streams, I knew that when the waters receded, the cow still would be hanging there — for months to come, long after the vultures and maggots had eaten their fill, until it was literally skin and bones.

"I'm ready to go back now," Abby said.

It was my turn to drive, and I didn't waste any time getting out of there. I was surprised at how well the Prelude hugged the curves and what a pure pleasure it was to put my foot into it and have something happen. I had been driving Jessie too long, I decided. I had almost forgotten what driving could be.

"You look like you're having fun," Abby observed.

"I am. A high old time. So where to from here?"

"Why don't we just drive? It's a good day for it."

"Why don't we."

So we drove and talked and laughed and watched the afternoon pass all too quickly. The best part of it was that it didn't really matter what we talked about. Sharing came easy with her.

"Do you ever see your former wife?" Abby asked as we were on our way back to Oakalla. The sun was low in the sky. The air had started to cool.

"No. There's no reason to. The last I heard she was married to a lawyer in Milwaukee and was doing okay."

"How long ago was that?" She was smiling, but I thought I could see a hard edge to it.

"Four or five years ago. She sent me a Christmas card. I haven't heard from her since."

"Let me know if you do."

"You'll be the first."

"You say you have a son?"

"*Had* a son. He died in infancy."

Jason Arthur Ryland. September 1, 1979– September 1, 1980. We'd buried him close to a red pine, where he would have sun in the morning, shade in the afternoon, and the pine's lullaby at night. His stone was grey, like his eyes, and small, like he was in life.

"I'm sorry," she said.

"So am I," I said, wondering why it still hurt so after so many years had passed. "He was such a happy little guy, so full of chortles and snuggles that despite what the doctors said, I thought . . . I thought that because

I loved him so much, God wouldn't let him die. When he did die, I lost my faith for a long time. I'm just now getting it back."

"What did he die from?"

"Congenital heart failure. There was nothing we could do."

She reached over and took my hand in hers. We didn't say anything more the rest of the way home.

"You're welcome to come in," I said as we sat parked in front of my house.

It was sunset. The house, the car, the street itself was bathed in an orange light.

"No," she said. "I need to make my rounds. I'm surprised that someone hasn't beeped me before this."

"So that's what that is on your belt. I thought it was a garage door opener."

"Very funny," she said. She leaned over and kissed me lightly on the lips. Then she got out of her side of the car, I got out of mine, she slid in under the wheel, closed the door, and drove away.

"Put your seat belt on!" I yelled after her. But I don't think she heard.

Inside the house, I went straight to the kitchen, where I popped two bowls of popcorn, took a couple mugs out of the freezer and filled each with a Leinenkugel's from the refrigerator, then carried it all into the living room where Ruth sat watching "Sixty Minutes."

"Thank you," she said, as I handed the popcorn and then the Leinenkugel's to her.

I watched the last segment of "Sixty Minutes" with her, then several commercials in a row until Andy Rooney came on. Ruth liked Andy Rooney more than I did, but we both agreed that the show wouldn't be the same without him.

"Who won the game?" I said.

"It wasn't the Packers."

"Did we have a bet on that one?"

"No. On the Bears and the Lions. You won." Meaning so did the Bears.

"So what do you owe me? The usual?" The usual was a Friday night supper at the Corner Bar and Grill.

"Either that or a used bowling ball."

"I'll take the usual."

"I thought you might."

"So," I said, finally getting up the nerve to ask her, "how did you like Abby?"

"I like her," she said. Her eyes were still on the television where "Sixty Minutes" was about to go off the air. "She comes on a little strong, but there's nothing wrong with that. A faint heart never won a fair hand."

"Meaning mine?"

"Who else would I mean?" She got up,

turned off the television, and returned to the couch where she would read until bedtime. "Garth, all I care about the girl is that she treat you right. And from what I've seen of her, she'll do just that."

"Thanks, Ruth," I said from the heart. "You know that your opinion means a lot to me."

"Maybe more than it should," she said. But I could tell that she was pleased.

I got up and walked to the front door. Twilight outside — bronze at the far edge of the earth, black trees against a lavender sky. A perfect end to a perfect day.

CHAPTER 13

The phone rang. In my dream, it was my alarm clock, and I was a twelve-year-old paper boy back in Indiana. It was raining, and I didn't want to go out into the rain, especially not in the dark.

A figure appeared in my doorway. Not my mother, I finally decided as things began to take shape around me. She was too tall for my mother, too broad in the shoulders. It had to be Ruth.

"It's for you," she said.

"What is?"

"The phone call."

"What do they want?"

"I don't know. You'll have to ask her."

"Her?" I said, rolling out of bed. "It's not Abby, is it?"

"No. It sounds like Luella Skiles to me.

Wearing yesterday's boxer shorts, I made my way past Ruth and started down the stairs. "What time is it, anyway?"

"Going on two A.M."

"Same time as her call to Eugene Yuill."

"I thought of that."

"Yes, Luella?" I said when I reached the phone.

"I don't recall identifying myself."

"Ruth guessed who it was."

"That doesn't surprise me. Not in the least."

I glanced outside where the stars shone brightly in a blue-black sky. At least it wasn't raining, as it had been in my dream.

"The reason I called," Luella Skiles said, "is that I believe there is someone in Monroe's house again. Not believe," she corrected herself, "I'm sure of it."

"Did you call Deputy Yuill?"

"I did and he came, but that was a half hour ago, and I haven't seen or heard a thing from him since then."

"I'll be there as soon as I can."

"I would appreciate it."

"Damn," I said as I hung up the phone.

"What's wrong?" Ruth asked.

I told her.

"I thought you said he wouldn't be back," she said. "That he had given up on finding what he was looking for."

"It appears I was wrong."

In the time that it normally took me to tie

my shoes, I put on jeans, a sweatshirt, and tennis shoes. Then I took off walking for Monroe Edmonds's house. I would have taken Jessie, but I was in a hurry.

No lights were on in the house when I got there. Neither did I hear anyone in the house, despite Luella Skiles's assertion to the contrary. While waiting in the side yard for a large dose of courage to carry me inside the house, I thought I heard someone groan. It seemed to come from around back.

"Don't hit me again," Eugene Yuill said, throwing up an arm to protect himself, as I shined my flashlight at him. He sat slumped over the back stoop. I was thankful that he'd thrown up his arm at me, instead of reaching for his .38 Police Special.

"It's Garth Ryland," I said, as I approached him. "And I have no intention of hitting you."

"Garth, is that really you?" He wasn't sure he believed me.

"Yes, Eugene, it is."

He bent over and groaned again, then began to sob in relief. It took a while for all of the terror to wash out of him.

"I'm sorry," he said, using his arm to wipe his eyes. "Sitting here bawling like a baby."

I stood beside him on the stoop. Not knowing what to do, I had yet to do anything. An arm around his shoulder might have helped him, but then again it might have broken him.

"I'm going inside, Eugene. Are you going to be all right?" For all I knew, at that very moment, someone could be carrying the entire contents of Monroe Edmonds's house out the front door.

Eugene started crying again — silently this time. I had a decision to make. Either I could stand there and watch over Eugene or I could go on inside. The house could wait, I decided. Eugene needed my help more than it did.

"I'm sorry, Garth. I'll get it together in a minute."

"That's okay. He's probably gone by now anyhow."

"Damn," he said, smacking his fist against the rotten pillar, causing the whole stoop to shake. "I forgot about that."

I remained standing. He remained sitting on the stoop. A band of fleecy white clouds, so thin they barely dimmed the moon, drifted overhead, then moved on.

"Do you want to tell me what's going on?" I said.

He swiped angrily at his eyes with the back of his hand. "Me. That's what's going on. Mr. Eugene Yuill, who up until now had never done anything in his small shitty life but drive a grain truck. And this job, which is proving a whole lot harder than I thought it would be."

I couldn't argue with that, so I kept quiet.

"Oh, I can do the routine stuff, like checking the pressure in the pump house and adding that salt to the water every couple of days. And I can smile at the kids and tip my hat to the ladies and fill out the accident report for any fender benders we have. You know, all the easy stuff. But once the sun goes down, that's a different story. Every time I get a call at night . . . I swear to God, Garth, my heart starts racing a hundred miles an hour by the time I even pick up the phone. That's why I called you the other night when I got the call from Luella Skiles. I just couldn't make myself come down here alone. And that's why I stayed in my house all day today with the shades down and the phone off the hook."

Another band of clouds, a little longer and a little thicker than the one before, passed by overhead. Another storm, perhaps still far to the west, was headed our way.

"Then, just when I was thinking I was safe and put the phone back on, I got a call from Luella Skiles to come here. I knew it was a do-or-die situation. If I couldn't handle it on my own, then I wasn't fit to be deputy sheriff, and I might as well turn in my badge. So I came. My knees were knocking, and I was having trouble breathing, but I came. Nothing at first. Not a soul in sight and not even a whisper coming from the house. I tried the front door, and it was locked, so I came around back to see what might be going on here. That's when I discovered that the door had been jimmied." He got up to show me, then had to grab the pillar for support while he regained his balance. "Anyway, you can see for yourself."

I walked over to examine the door and jamb. The jamb was splintered at the lock, the door forced open. They looked as if someone had taken a pry bar to them.

Eugene said, "So I thought to myself, are they in there or not? As quiet as it was, I couldn't be sure. And why go in if I wasn't sure, because I could watch the house just as well from here." He sat back down on the stoop. "So I started to walk away, give myself a little distance where I could see the whole house, when crash! All hell breaks loose inside. I couldn't ignore that, so I started running for the door. That's when someone hit me in the back of the head. That's the last thing I remember until you came along."

"The person who hit you wasn't the person in the house?"

"No way, Garth. It couldn't have been."

"And you haven't been in the house at all?"

"No. I never got that far."

"Then maybe it's time you did."

A look of panic came over him. Only my presence there kept him from bolting. "I can't, Garth. Not now. I just can't."

"Then I'll go and you can watch the front door for me."

"What if something happens to you in the meantime?"

"Call 911."

I went in through the back door, turned on the kitchen light, and made my way to the parlor, turning on lights as I went. There, I discovered the first of several disturbing things. Someone had cut out the oil paintings, leaving three empty frames.

As I started up the stairs, I did a gut check. All along I had thought that only one person was involved. Now, if I were to believe Eugene's account of what had happened to him, I knew there were at least two people involved, maybe more. One I might be able to handle if he were unarmed. Two or more would put me at a definite disadvantage. Not wanting to be stupid about this, I went back for the fireplace poker.

At the top of the stairs, I discovered what all the noise had been about. Someone, deliberately it seemed, had toppled Monroe's china cabinet, breaking the glass and most of the R. S. Prussia dishes inside. Then he had begun bouncing Monroe's tinware off the walls. One piece had gone through the window on the landing. I could see the night air lapping at the curtain.

I stepped around the china closet, went on down the hall, and stopped at each room in turn. Someone, a couple people by the looks of it, had spent a lot of time and effort moving furniture. What puzzled me was that, unlike before, they had made no effort to hide their trail.

The elevator was my last stop. I opened the door and almost plunged into the abyss before I realized that the cage wasn't there. I hit the top button and waited as the cage, creaking and groaning, slowly made its way up to me. The elevator had been on the second floor the last time I was in it. After the volunteer firemen had taken Monroe's body off on the first floor, I had ridden the elevator back up to see if anything was wrong with it.

Now it arrived empty. That's the way I preferred it, no bodies, no prowlers.

"Eugene, I'm coming out," I said before leaving by the front door.

"Got you."

As I stepped outside, I saw him strap his gun back in its holster and was thankful that I'd said something. "No one home," I said. "But there has been. The place is a wreck."

"That doesn't figure," he said, speaking my own thoughts. "Why come here and trash the place?"

"I don't know, Eugene. But in the lines that Alice made famous, 'this gets curiouser and curiouser.' "

"Alice?"

"Of Wonderland."

He still didn't get it.

"Never mind. It's been a long day."

He touched the knot on the back of his head and winced as he did. "You're not telling me a thing."

"Eugene," I said. "The other day when you, Tom Ford, and I were here, do you remember locking the front door on your way out?"

He gave me a sheepish look. "No, Garth. I don't remember. But I must have because it was locked tonight."

"Not necessarily. I've been in there since then."

He looked down at the ground. "No. Then I don't remember."

"Do you remember what Tom Ford had in his pockets when you booked him at the jail?"

184

"His billfold and some loose change. That's all."

"No keys?"

"No. No keys of any kind."

"Was he still wearing the same clothes that he was in when we saw him earlier that night?"

"I think so. It looked like he'd never been to bed."

I felt someone watching me and turned around to see Luella Skiles standing at her bay window.

"Why don't we go ask Tom what he was wearing," I said.

Eugene hung his head. He couldn't look me in the eye. "That might be hard, Garth. Tom Ford's not in jail."

"Then where is he for God's sake?"

"I don't know where he is. He escaped from my custody early yesterday afternoon when I was bringing him back to the jail. As soon as I came to a stop, he jumped right out of the back of the car and took off running. I had a shot at him, but I didn't want to risk it for fear of hitting somebody else."

"Why didn't you say something to somebody?"

Eugene raised his head to look at me. I wished he hadn't. The look on his face almost broke my heart. "Because when I arrested

Tom Ford that morning, I forgot to read him his rights."

"That's why you were so scarce around town?" I said when I finally got over the shock of it. "You were afraid you would meet up with Tom Ford and then what would you do?"

He nodded. "At first I thought Tom Ford was the perfect solution to all of my problems. Arrest him for murder, and maybe the word would get out that I was one tough hombre, not to be messed with. That way, maybe I could cut me some slack until Sheriff Clark got back, and nobody would be the wiser."

It made sense to me. It also explained why Eugene had been such a basket case in Monroe Edmonds's house when we were there looking for the painting with Tom Ford. Why then hadn't Eugene's plan worked out the way he wanted? Probably because life never did.

"So what are you going to do now?" I asked.

"I don't know, Garth. What do you think I should do?" His sadness seemed to have deepened — all the way to the bottom of his being.

"Stay on at least until Sheriff Clark gets back. We'll need someone to patrol the streets and generally keep his eye on things until then."

"What about those calls that come in the night?"

"If nothing else, refer them to me."

"I don't know, Garth. I'll think about it. That's all I can say."

He started toward his patrol car. I'd seen two-hundred-year-old turtles move faster.

"Eugene," I said. "In what direction was Tom Ford going when you last saw him?"

"South. Toward the school."

South was also the direction of Tom Ford's house and beyond that the railroad. But I couldn't see Tom Ford hopping a freight and heading for parts unknown. Not unless there was a six-pack on board.

"Was he still in handcuffs?" I asked, remembering that he was the last time I saw him.

"Yes."

"Then he couldn't have gone far."

"That's what I figured," Eugene said. "That's why when Luella Skiles called me tonight, I figured it had to be Tom. I also figured that if I could catch him in the act and arrest him proper, then I could set things right."

"It wouldn't have mattered anyway, Eugene. The most we could have gotten Tom Ford for the second time around would be breaking and entering." Or entering and breaking, as things had turned out.

"Even if it turns out he killed Monroe Edmonds?"

"Even if it turned out he killed the president."

"You're kidding me, aren't you, Garth?"

Was I kidding him? I didn't believe so. Justice was neither as swift nor as sure as it once was in this country. But then neither was injustice.

"I wish I were, Eugene."

He took off his deputy's hat and gazed at it — tenderly it seemed. Then he creased the crown of the hat and put it back on. I liked the effect. It made him look more cowboy than cop.

"See you around," he said.

I followed his gaze to Monroe Edmonds's house, which, swathed in shadows, was wearing its mean face again. Thinking that he was talking to it rather than to me, I didn't say anything. Then he got in his patrol car and drove away.

CHAPTER 14

Three hours later, I rolled out of bed and had the juice poured and the coffee on before Ruth ever made her way down the stairs.

"It's a holiday," she grumbled on her way into the kitchen, "or have you forgotten that?"

I had forgotten that, but it wouldn't have made any difference. Once the alarm clock inside my head went off, I either had to get up or spend the next hour thinking about it before I got up.

"You want me to cook breakfast?" she asked, stopping at the stove to pour herself a cup of coffee.

"No. Juice and cereal will be fine. But I would like to pick your brain before I leave."

"Where are you headed?"

"The farm. I've got some heavy thinking to do."

Ruth sat down across from me at the table and after she had added sugar and half-and-half to her coffee, and then taken her first sip, I told her how last night had gone.

"You say there were at least two people inside and at least one outside?" she said.

"That's what I believe anyway."

"Working together?"

"I don't know that. But I assume so. Otherwise, why would they all be there together?"

"Maybe whoever was inside beat whoever was outside there."

"That's possible," I said. "But then why take the chance of coldcocking Eugene if you weren't involved?"

While she thought about that, I glanced outside. Just up, the sun seemed to be having a hard time getting going today.

"Maybe he didn't want whoever was inside to get caught," she said.

"Why? If they were after the same thing, that would be two fewer people to worry about."

"Unless they knew what he knew and might spill the beans."

"Which is what?"

She thought some more, then said, "Let's put that on the back burner for a while. What else is bothering you?"

"Whoever was in there last night had to jimmy the back door to get in. Friday night, when this all started, Tom Ford and whoever else might have been in there that night didn't break in. I'm sure of that. Tom might have used a key, but I can't prove it." I told her about the key that Monroe Edmonds had given Elizabeth Ford and that was now missing.

"It would have been easy enough for Tom Ford to have used the key and then hidden it somewhere," she said.

"If he were the first one in Monroe Edmonds's house that night."

"You don't think he was?"

"I'm not sure, Ruth. I haven't sorted it all out yet. But for argument's sake, let's say that Tom Ford wasn't the first one in the house, but that someone else beat him there. Assuming that Monroe Edmonds locked his doors that night, which Luella Skiles said that he had been doing of late, then that means that whoever was first in there either had to have a key or was already in the house when Monroe locked the doors."

"Which is it?" she said.

I glanced outside where the sun was still struggling to make itself known, as the shadows gave grudgingly, if at all.

"I think he was already in the house, probably in the basement. When Monroe got in the elevator and started upstairs to bed, it would have been easy for him to open the basement door and pull the master switch.

With Monroe trapped in the elevator, he could search the house at his leisure."

"Then how did the elevator get to the second floor?"

"I don't know, Ruth. Unless he ran it up there before he left."

She took a drink of her coffee. I took a drink of mine. Already mine had started to grow cold.

"Why would he do that if he wasn't through searching the place yet? He couldn't know that Monroe Edmonds had died in that elevator. And you said yourself that you thought he returned again Saturday night, so that means he hadn't found what he was looking for."

"Now think, Ruth. I'm sure he returned Saturday night. I smelled him, remember?"

"So why run Monroe Edmonds up to the second floor when there was still business at hand?"

"Maybe somebody interrupted his search. Tom Ford, for instance."

Ruth was skeptical. "Think about it, Garth. You're in someone else's home. You've got him trapped in the elevator, and you're in the process of searching the place. Someone else comes in unannounced. Now, what would you do?"

"I'd get the hell out of there as fast as I could."

"You wouldn't take the time to run Monroe Edmonds up to the second floor?"

"No."

She gave me her cat-that-ate-the-canary smile. "My point exactly."

An hour later, I sat in a rowboat in the middle of Grandmother Ryland's pond. The sun was bright but not as warm as I hoped it might be. My resident muskrat was taking a lap around the pond, as was my perennial coot. Otherwise, I had the place to myself.

A century ago, it now seemed, Grandmother and I had come to the pond with our cane poles and can of worms to fish for bluegill and sunfish. They didn't run large. Eight inches was tops, and there weren't many of those. But the fun was not in how large a fish we caught, or how many, but in the excitement that each fish brought, particularly at the end of Grandmother's pole.

Normally a stoic, who could tranquilly face down a snorting and pawing Guernsey bull or a sharp-billed old Leghorn setting hen intent on keeping her only egg, Grandmother rarely got excited about anything. Except bluegill and sunfish. The instant the bobber went completely under and stayed there, she would give a hard yank on her pole, and with a whoop they could hear in Oakalla, throw the hapless fish over her shoulder and halfway to the barn. Caught up in her excitement, her absolute joy at catching something, I'd forget what I was doing and watch her, instead of watching my own line. Consequently she always caught more fish than I did, and, it went without saying, had a better time of it.

Yet, if there was a memory to put in my pocket and keep for all time, it was of Grandmother and me, as we walked up the lane toward the house. The stringer slung over my shoulder, dust puffing up between my bare toes, a smile on my face as wide as the sky, I couldn't have been happier.

I watched the coot dive and then surface a few feet away. I watched the muskrat glide into his hole among the cattails at the far end of the pond. I felt the sun on my bare back, as it untangled the knots that the past few days had put there. I let my mind wander and the boat drift. Then I knew what my mind knew and had forgotten.

Late Thursday evening, as I was about to finish the final draft of my weekly column, I had received a phone call from someone that I took to be Martin Weidner, though he had never identified himself.

"On that yard sale three miles northwest of town," he had said, "the one advertising antiques and collectibles, I want you to add, 'Friday only, World War II stuff.' "

"I'm not sure I can do that at this late hour," I said.

"Well, do what you can."

So I had done what I could and somehow squeezed it in. Only out of respect for those who had fought in World War II, I had eliminated *stuff* and put *mementoes* in its place. So the addition had read: Friday only, World War II mementoes.

Mose and Martin Weidner were both home that Labor Day morning. Evidently Mose had gotten rained out on Saturday night and come home from Wisconsin Rapids. I was still surprised to see him there. Ordinarily if there was a buck to be made, Mose Weidner was somewhere making it. It was equally surprising to see that he had no flea-market tables set up to snare whoever might be out his way. For once in his life, Mose Weidner was spending his holiday idle, like everyone else.

"Morning, Mose," I said as he approached Jessie. "I thought you might still be up at the Rapids."

Both Martin and Mose Weidner had been standing on the front steps in their bib overalls and white T-shirts. But they hadn't appeared to be sunning themselves.

"Got rained out," Mose said. "Mudded out is more like it."

"That's right. Martin said you'd had your

fill of it in your day."

Mose gave Martin a look that I usually reserved for poodles and pay toilets. "Oh, he did, did he? Martin's just full of information these days."

The two of them had apparently been feuding, so what to me had seemed an argument on the front porch was probably just that. Martin's silence seemed to confirm my observation. He was in no mood to talk to anyone.

Glancing from one to the other, I saw something else besides anger on their faces, something that made their flattened Pinocchio noses, their small close-set beady eyes almost cartoonlike in their apprehension. Both were afraid of something, though Mose Weidner's fear seemed more primitive, closer to the core. If I were to guess, I'd have guessed that Martin was more afraid of Mose than he was of whatever it was that Mose feared. Thinking back to the last time I was here, I recalled seeing no such fear on Martin's face then, which meant that Mose must have brought it home with him.

"What's on your mind, Garth?" Mose said. "Martin and I were just about to drive into town to see what's doing there."

I glanced ahead and saw their new GMC pickup and attached camper shell parked alongside the house near the back door. A long pair of skid marks led up to its back tires.

"What I was wondering was who bought all the World War II stuff at your yard sale Friday?"

"What World War II *stuff* are you talking about?" Mose Weidner seemed surprised at my question.

"What you had advertised in this week's *Reporter*."

"I didn't have no World War II stuff advertised." He turned to Martin, who was trying his best to be invisible. "Martin, what the hell is going on?"

"Nothing, Pop. I don't know what he's talking about."

"Find a copy of Friday's *Oakalla Reporter*," I said to Mose. "Then you'll see what I'm talking about."

"Boy," Mose said, as if he were talking to a child instead of a forty-year-old man, "go get me last Friday's *Reporter*."

"I can't, Pop," Martin said, looking to me for help. "I burned it."

"I might have been mistaken," I said, trying to give Martin some slack. "I might have the wrong yard sale."

"No. You ain't mistaken," Mose said. "That boy has been selling things out from under me my whole life. Tell him what happened,

Martin, after your mother died."

"No. That's nobody's business but ours."

"Tell him or I will."

"Then you go right ahead. I don't have to listen."

Martin turned his back to us, as if that would keep the truth away. It was sad to see the transformation in him between Saturday and now. Saturday he had been his own man, confidently wheeling and dealing as he whittled his horse. Today he was back to being his father's son.

"That's okay," I said to Mose. "We can save it for another day."

"No. You'll hear it now," Mose insisted. "Then Martin can tell us what he did with all that World War II *stuff* that he don't know nothing about."

With his back still to us, Martin hugged himself. Like Martin, I had to look away.

Mose Weidner said, "The deal was, after the boy's mother died a few years back, I had this whole house full of stuff that I didn't need no more, so I invited a man in to look at it to see what he might give me for it. What we couldn't strike a deal on, I'd then sell at auction, which I did. What I didn't realize. . . ." His eyes fell heavily on Martin, who continued to ignore us. "What I didn't realize was that my only son here was gathering up a pile of my things on the sly, and as soon as my back was turned, he tried to sell them to the man for next to nothing. Now what do you think about that? Is that loyalty, or what?"

"You had no right," Martin mumbled.

"What's that, son? I didn't hear you."

Martin turned to face us. He might have feared his father, but at that moment he hated him more. "I said you had no right! Not to sell Mama's things. Not her personal things, all her little keepsakes that she had on her dresser and along the windowsills." Tears began to stream down Martin Weidner's cheeks. "Hell, Pop, she wasn't even cold yet."

"Mama's boy," Mose Weidner said to me. "Always was. Always will be."

"Eat shit and die, old man," Martin said, as he started down the steps.

But Mose reached out and grabbed him by the strap of his bib overalls and jerked him down to the ground. "The stuff, Martin. The World War II stuff. *My* World War II stuff. What happened to it?"

Martin Weidner looked up at him with hate in his eyes. He reminded me of a dog who had been kicked once too many times and would bite the next time, no matter what the consequences.

"That fag that runs the museum in La Crosse bought most of it. I gave the rest of it away."

"You *gave* it away?" Mose Weidner was beside himself. "Do you know what that *stuff* as you call it went through with me? Three years of hell, that's what."

"So what?" Martin said, as he rolled away from Mose and got to his feet. "Mama went through a lifetime of hell with you, so I figure we're even."

Mose Weidner began to lose some of his anger. Sadness took its place. "Do you hate me that much, Son?"

"I don't hate you at all, Pop. Not when I'm thinking straight. But I don't love you either. I don't know which is worse."

Martin Weidner started in the direction of the barn. Mose Weidner watched him go. I got in Jessie and left.

CHAPTER 15

Approaching Dutchman Yoder's lane, I saw a car pull out of it. The car was a two-tone green Chevy Bellaire that looked even older than Jessie. Luella Skiles was driving it.

I found Dutchman Yoder in his garden where he stood in the midst of squash, eggplant, peppers, and cucumbers, picking tomatoes. After each one was picked, he would carefully wipe it with a cloth and put it into the wooden basket he carried. He reminded me of Grandmother Ryland and the care she used to take with her eggs, as if each were a prize find, as if there weren't a dozen more in her basket just like it.

"How do you keep your garden so clean?" I asked. No weeds were in sight. Every row was as bare as my savings account.

"A little of this and a little of that." He made hoeing motions. "What is it called, elbow grease?" He straightened and looked beyond his garden at his cornfield, where goldenrod, jimsonweed, and Queen Anne's lace had overtaken the fence row. "But weeds, too, have their beauty, don't you think?"

Yellow, violet, and white, the weeds did brighten up the fence row, if I looked only at their pretty heads and ignored the rest of them. "Maybe," I said without enthusiasm. "At this time of year at least."

"Yah," Dutchman Yoder said. "But is this not the time of year in which we are living." Then he smiled, showing me most of his teeth.

"You might have a point, Dutchman."

"Yah. I sometimes do." He clasped me on the shoulder, and we began to walk toward his house. "So what is it that brings you here so early in the day?"

"Wasn't that Luella Skiles I just saw pulling out of here?"

He nodded, looking solemn. Right behind his ready smile was the ever-deepening sadness that I had noticed of late.

"She came here to buy some butter for her table," he said.

"Is she a regular customer?"

We had stopped in the shade of a sugar maple that grew at the edge of the garden. In his long sleeves, long pants, and hat, Dutchman didn't seem to notice the cool breeze sifting down from the north. But I, in my shorts and T-shirt, felt its chill.

"No, she is a sometimes customer," he said.

"That often?"

"Well, perhaps a hardly ever."

I wondered why Luella Skiles would suddenly take it upon herself to drive all the way out here to buy some butter from Dutchman Yoder when she could have stopped at Heavin's Market there in town and saved herself the trip. Dutchman Yoder seemed to be wondering the same thing.

"Maybe she has company coming," I said. "Wanted to do a little something special."

We started walking. I was relieved to be out in the sunshine again. Already I had goose bumps on my arms and legs.

"Yah. That must be it," he said.

"There was another reason why I stopped by," I said. We came to Dutchman's back stoop, which was shaded by the thick stand of pines that continued on into the woods as far as I could see. "The last time I was here, you hinted to me that Tom Ford was headed for trouble. I need to know what that trouble is."

"For your own reasons?" he asked.

"For a lot of reasons."

He sat down on the stoop with his basket of tomatoes beside him. I folded my arms across my chest and tried not to think about being cold.

"It is important that I tell you?"

"Very important."

He thought about it some more, while I rubbed my bare legs together, trying to start a fire.

"I would like to tell you, Garth, but a man's business is his own, if it is not a hurt upon the rest of us."

"Are you saying that Tom Ford has committed no crime?"

"No crime? Yah. That would be one way of saying it."

"What would be another way?"

His eyes met mine. Their purity was blinding, even in the shade. "Perhaps that is the only way of saying it," he said.

"So you won't help me?"

"No, my good friend, I won't help you."

"Thanks for your time." I needed to get into the sun before my teeth started chattering. But Dutchman Yoder had a question for me.

"Luella Skiles," he said. "If she were not after butter, what would she be doing here?"

"I don't know, Dutchman. You'll have to ask her."

"She and Monroe Edmonds were good friends, yah." It wasn't a question.

"In their early days, yes. I'm not so sure about lately."

"Friends stay friends," he said sadly. "They do not pass with age. Only with death."

I could have argued that with him but didn't. My friend Ron Richards hadn't passed from my life through age or death. Just neglect.

"Do you ever miss your friends, Dutchman? Your family?"

He looked up at me with those keen eyes of his. He knew exactly what I was asking, but he didn't try to sidestep it.

"Every day, my friend. Each and every day."

"Then why don't you go home?"

His smile was radiant. And no teeth at all showed. "I will. Perhaps soon, I will."

I got in Jessie, rolled up my window, turned on the heat, and started home. A mile later I began to thaw out just as the windshield fogged completely over. Either I turned off the heat and rolled the window back down or I spent the rest of the way home wiping the windshield with the handy-dandy rag that I now kept in the front seat for just that purpose. I decided to wipe the windshield. I didn't want to be cold ever again.

At home I told Ruth about my morning, as for lunch we ate Campbells chicken noodle soup and grilled cheese sandwiches. I had intended to fill Jessie's radiator with water as soon as I got home, but as my father was fond of saying, the road to hell was paved with good intentions.

"I wish Rupert were here," I said, wondering how many times in the past couple of years I had said that — ever since Rupert Roberts had resigned as sheriff of Adams County and started living the gypsy life of a retiree. "I'd even settle for Fillmore Cavanaugh, but he's with Rupert."

Captain Fillmore Cavanaugh of the Wisconsin State Police had retired just a few months ago. He was my last link with the old guard of lawmen, who had taught me the ropes and kept my head above water when I first came to town. Without Rupert or him at the helm, I often felt like the first mate on the sinking ship, Oakalla.

"Where are they now?" Ruth asked.

"I don't know. They and their wives are off on another one of their jaunts. Rupert said not to expect them back before next week sometime."

"And you think this whole business has something to do with the war?"

"I did this morning on Grandmother's pond. Now, I'm not so sure."

"What changed your mind?"

"Mose Weidner. He didn't know about his missing World War II items until I got there.

206

He was already upset about something else. He and Martin both. And the only thing I can figure, since Mose was out of town, is that Martin made it a point to tell him about what happened to Monroe Edmonds."

Ruth took a saltine out of the package, broke it, and dropped it in her soup. She liked to eat her saltines one at a time. I preferred to break a handful into my soup and let the whole sorry mess get good and soggy before I ate it.

"Why do you suppose Martin did that?" Ruth said.

"My guess is because they are somehow involved."

"Then maybe Tom Ford told you the truth after all," she said. "Maybe there really was a painting, and that's what Mose is so upset about."

"Lawrence Hess says not."

"Maybe Lawrence Hess is lying."

"I've considered that possibility."

"And?"

"And I'll know more after I've talked to him this afternoon."

Ruth waved her hand at me, which meant either she'd burned her mouth on the soup or wanted silence for the next few moments. So I ate my soup and tried not to slurp too loudly.

"You realize, don't you," she said, "that another party has just been added to the mix."

"If you're talking about Luella Skiles, I was wondering myself what she was doing out at Dutchman Yoder's place. I think so was he."

"I'm not talking about Luella Skiles. Dutchman Yoder, either. I'm talking about the man, whoever he is, who bought the things from the M and M Boys after Clarissa Weidner died. She couldn't have died more than two or three years ago. Maybe whoever was in her house nosing around saw something that he wanted but knew better than to try to buy on the spot with Mose around. So he bided his time and then sent Tom Ford to buy it for him a couple years later."

"And who might this mystery man be?" I said. I had a guess, but that would spoil it for her.

"Monroe Edmonds would be my first choice."

Monroe Edmonds was likewise my first choice.

"It makes sense," I said. "And it would explain why Tom Ford got out there so early, since he wouldn't necessarily have been going to the garage sale but on a special mission. But if it were something truly valuable, then why didn't Mose Weidner sell it long ago?"

"Maybe he didn't know its value."

"Not likely, Ruth. He's been in the business too long."

"Nobody knows everything about everything," she said. "That includes Mose Weidner, who once sold me a silver inlaid copper teapot for a dollar."

"How many years ago was that?"

"Several," she admitted. "He was just starting out."

"Try to buy the same teapot now and see how far you get. Not that I'm saying that Mose Weidner can't make a mistake," I said before she could counter, "but if he has anything that even smells like money, you can bet that he will find the right person to put a price on it."

"Then maybe Mose stole it," she said. "That's why he wouldn't sell it."

"Stole it for what purpose?"

"Just to have it."

I couldn't buy that and told her so. "Mose Weidner doesn't seem like a sentimental man to me. If he stole something, it would be with the idea of selling it later."

She went back to eating her soup.

"Unless he stole something really big or thought he had. Then he might be afraid to sell it," I said.

"Or couldn't sell it," she said. "Because everyone was afraid to buy it."

"You think that's it, don't you?"

"I think that's a possibility."

A few minutes later, I left for the east end of town. Though big and bright, the sun still didn't seem to be putting out much heat. Volcanic ash perhaps, or more likely ice crystals too fine for my eyes to see were blocking its rays. It reminded me of a winter sun, and of some people I knew. With the faces of cherubs, they could throw two-hundred-watt smiles at you that could light up an airport, yet not warm up a matchbox. Sometimes it happened that way. Cold hearts and gentle people sometimes slept in the same bed.

"Garth!" Lawrence Hess said on answering his door. "Three visits in three days. I must say you flatter me."

"Cut the crap, Lawrence," I said. "If you'd have levelled with me the first time, one visit would have been enough."

Lawrence wore a short-sleeve, Army-green jumpsuit that made him look cool and efficient and strikingly military. With some brass on his shoulders, he easily could have passed for an Army officer.

"Is something wrong, Garth?"

"No, Lawrence. I just stopped by to admire your outfit."

He twirled around to show me all of it. "Do

you think it's really me?"

"I don't know. I'll reserve judgment for later."

"Do come in, Garth," he said. "It appears you have a lot on your mind."

Inside didn't feel any warmer than outside, but Lawrence Hess didn't invite many people into his home, so I took him up on it. Immediately I was glad I did. The Waggoner House was worth seeing all over again.

Two wide oak staircases, both with curved walnut banisters and walnut newel posts, led up to a white-posted four-cornered balcony that overlooked what only could be described as a great-room. A teal-and-ivory Persian rug at least twenty feet square covered only the heart of the hardwood floor. A crystal chandelier, big enough to light a circus tent, hung from the high domed ceiling directly over the rug. A gallery of original oil paintings ringed the room. But otherwise, the room was bare of furnishings. Not even curtains on the windows.

"Is this your first time in here?" Lawrence asked.

"No. I was in here once before when I did the article on it. But you were in the process of remodeling then."

"So what do you think?"

I was walking around the room, glancing

211

at each painting in turn. All were what I took to be modern art. Some I liked. Some I didn't like. The more abstract a painting was, the harder it was for me to identify with it.

"Impressive," I said. "It's almost like a cathedral in here."

"Or a museum? Which is the way some of my so-called friends have described it."

"I like either one, Lawrence. Both give me a sense of wonder, and of peace."

"Peace, yes," he said. "Peace is nice."

I looked at him. I never knew for sure when Lawrence was sharpening his claws on me. "It is nice," I said, "for those of us who know so precious little of it."

"My sentiments exactly, Garth. I wasn't being catty."

We stood in the middle of the room right under the twelve-ton chandelier. I wondered, if I shouted, would I get an echo?

"I'll come right to the point, Lawrence. What was it that you bought from Martin Weidner and what else of value did you see there?"

He walked over to one of his paintings, took a handkerchief from his pocket, and dusted the frame. "I must be getting old. One of us anyway. I thought I had answered those very same questions recently."

"Not about what you bought from Martin.

You're avoiding that question entirely."

Walking over to another painting, he began to dust its frame. "If I may be so bold to ask, why is that any business of yours?"

"Monroe Edmonds is dead. I think what you bought might have something to do with it. Or didn't buy, which is more likely."

"What I didn't buy were a pair of boots, a uniform, canteen, mess kit, and ammunition boxes — stuff that you once could buy for a dime a dozen in any Army surplus store. If somebody killed Monroe Edmonds over any of that, then you're dealing with a nut case and not somebody that I can help you with."

"What about the things that you did buy?" I said.

"You won't take my word for it that they're of no great value to anyone but me?"

"Not this time, Lawrence."

"Very well, then. Follow me."

He started up the west staircase. I did as he asked and followed him. He stopped in front of a large white door with a brass knob and waited for me to catch up to him. The door led into the turret.

"Before I let you in here, I have to have your word that what you see in here stops at this door," he said. "There are some people in Oakalla who might not understand."

"Is any of it stolen?" I said.

213

"Not by me. I can't speak for everyone I've ever dealt with."

"Then you have my word."

I expected at least one lock on the door. Instead we walked right in.

"Don't you keep it locked?"

"There's no need. The ghosts keep everyone else out."

I studied him to see if he were kidding. He didn't appear to be.

Then he turned on the light, and I saw what he meant. If ever a room was haunted, this one was.

"Chilling, isn't it?" he said. "But in its own way, magnificent."

Had the room been stacked with mummies, or had a circle of stuffed carnivores bared their teeth at me, I would have been less awed than by what I saw. I felt my hands grow cold and my head start to spin as I tried to grasp the enormity of it. Lawrence said nothing. He saw the effect that the room was having on me. It was having the same effect on him, though he already knew what awaited him there.

On either side of the curved room with only a narrow walkway in between, like a diagonal bisecting a circle, were gathered the relics of World War II. German weapons, uniforms, and accessories on one side. British and American weapons, uniforms, and accessories on the other side. Except for old war movies, I had never seen such vintage weapons, such vintage uniforms, or so many swastikas gathered together in one place in my life. Lawrence was right. It was magnificent. But chilling had been his first word. And chilling, it was. I could almost reach out and touch the horror packed within that room.

"Go ahead," Lawrence said. "You can look at them. They won't bite."

"I'd rather you'd tell me what I'm looking at."

So like a general reviewing his troops, Lawrence led me among his treasures, stopping every couple feet or so to point something out. "Browning Colt .45 and holster," he said, reaching to his left. "Nine millimeter Walther P38, standard German issue after 1938," he said, reaching to his right. "Lee-Enfield .303 and .3 Garand, otherwise known as the M-1. Manser Kar 98, 7.92 millimeter. German officer's uniform. Notice the bullet hole in the left front pocket. British major's cap, sans bullet hole. Silver Star and Distinguished Flying Cross. Iron Cross and Croix de Guerre . . ."

He continued to drone on, but I had stopped hearing him. Part of me wanted to turn and run. The other part, the part closest to my heart, wanted to take each memento aside and hear its story. To whom do you belong? Did he die or is he still alive? Was it stripped from his still-warm body, or years later, did his children sell it when he went to the veterans' home? Or did it become an emblem of shame, and thus, he gave it away. Or did he sell it for a package of cigarettes and a bottle of Thunderbird wine? So many mysteries. So many unanswered questions. No wonder ghosts walked here. Where else were they to go?

"These are what I bought from Martin Weidner." Lawrence's voice brought me back among the living. "I haven't decided yet where they should go."

Three badly tarnished medals lay in a small cardboard box. Lawrence took them out one at a time to show me.

"This is a Victory Medal," he said, handing me a small bronze medal with what looked like a bald buxom woman embossed on it. "The Purple Heart." A heart-shaped medal with a cameo of what appeared to be George Washington. "And, of course, the Bronze Star." Which, except for its blue-and-white ribbon, looked exactly like a bronze star.

As I held all three in my hand at once and felt their combined weight, I had a new respect for Mose Weidner. "It appears Mose was somewhat of a hero," I said.

"So it appears." He seemed less impressed than I.

"And this is all you bought there?"

"That's it."

"May I ask what you paid for them?"

"A dollar each. He wanted two, but I said I wouldn't pay that."

"What are they worth?" I said.

"What I paid for them. That's all anything's worth. What you pay for it."

I handed the medals back to him. He put them back in their cardboard box.

"Sad, isn't it?" he said. He had stopped on his way out to survey the room one last time before leaving it. "The last great war. Where the powers of darkness and light were so clearly defined. When we knew what we were fighting for, and that if we lost, civilization as we knew it would end. Over here," he said, nodding to the American-British side, "the white hats — valiant warriors one and all, but with superior resources and far superior numbers. And over here . . ." He paused, out of respect, it seemed. "One small country, no bigger than Minnesota and Wisconsin combined. And it came within an eyelash, an *eyelash*, Garth, of conquering the world." He turned off the light but had yet to open the door. I could feel the room closing in around us. "Now it's united again. Doesn't that scare you just a little bit, Garth?"

"Frankly, Lawrence," I paused for a long deep breath as the walls moved ever closer, "it scares the hell out of me. Particularly with all that's going on over there now."

He opened the door. It was all that I could do not to trample him on my way out.

"Yes. It does have a familiar smell to it, doesn't it?" he said.

We walked back down the stairs. Again I made a circle of the room, looking at each painting in turn, but saw none that looked out of place.

"What is it that you're looking for, Garth?" As if he didn't know.

"Lawrence, did Mose Weidner ever show you a painting that he might have for sale?"

When he failed to answer right away, I knew that Mose had.

"Lawrence?"

"I'm thinking, Garth. It seems to me that at one time several years ago he did mention something about a painting. He drove all the way over to the museum to see me, which seemed strange in itself, since we can't live more than five miles from one another. He asked if I was interested in coming to his house to look at something. What might that be? I said. A painting, I think he said. Couldn't he bring it here to show me? He'd rather not.

Then could he describe it for me, please? Not offhand. Then could he tell me where he got it? He didn't remember." Lawrence was eyeing a cobweb that hung just out of reach. "At that point I began to lose interest. Even if he did have something of archival value, which I doubted, the chances were nine in ten that it was stolen." He wadded up his handkerchief and threw it at the cobweb, knocked the cobweb down, then caught the handkerchief on its way down. "Not that I'm totally above that sort of thing, but not in my own backyard, and certainly not if it would put Pembleton at risk."

"So you never went to look at the painting?"

"No. I never did."

"Why didn't you tell me this earlier when I asked about Tom Ford?"

"Because I didn't think of it earlier. I didn't think about it until you were long gone from here." He wore a look of disgust. "While doing yard work, one has more than ample time to think."

"Would you have told me if I hadn't brought it up?"

"A moot point, since you did bring it up."

I was almost ready to leave. "About the ghosts upstairs, are they real or just your imaginary watchdogs?"

Lawrence put both hands in the pockets of

his jumpsuit and peered up the stairs. I thought I saw fear in his eyes.

"They're quite real, I assure you. Not only have I heard them on a number of occasions, but I have gone in there the next morning to find some of my things moved."

"But never anything stolen?"

"Never." Lawrence's eyes had begun to water. He believed what he was saying and was making a believer out of me. "Oddly, they seem to prefer Greek crosses."

"You mean anything with a swastika on it."

"Yes. That's what I mean."

"How long has this been going on?"

"A long time, Garth. Ever since I've lived here."

"Which is what?"

"At least fifteen years."

"Then it appears they're here to stay."

He glanced fearfully over his shoulder, as if afraid the ghosts had broken down the door and were at that very moment on their way down the stairs. "One might think so."

I left by the east door. As I walked down Berry Street toward my office, I didn't notice that it had gotten any warmer out.

CHAPTER 16

I spent from then until supper working on the next edition of the *Oakalla Reporter*. After supper I went back to my office and worked a few hours more. Most of what I did was to make phone calls and answer the phone. I had a good network of sources, who not only did not mind telling me what was going on around town, but became fractious when I didn't touch base with them every other day or so. They saved me a lot of legwork, and I really should have paid people, like Sadie Jenkins, who called every day and were a lot more faithful and diligent than employees I had known. But that would have upped the ante too high — for me who couldn't afford it and for them who were not now bound by schedules and deadlines, but were free to call whenever they pleased. Or so they told me whenever I brought up the matter of money, and I was just cheap enough to believe them.

Late that evening I had tried to call Abby,

but Doc said that she was at the hospital and would likely be there for a while. He then asked me what I wanted to do with Monroe Edmonds's body, which was still in his basement. I said that I didn't know, since no relatives had turned up to claim it. He said he wasn't running a boardinghouse for corpses. I said he'd better get used to it, since Abby was taking up his old trade. Over his dead body, he said. I took that as a joke and hung up.

On my way home that night, I noticed that the sky had a whitish cast to it that stretched from horizon to horizon. Some stars were out, but they were fuzzy, more like splatters of paint than points of light, more like an artist's rendering of them than real stars in a real night sky. The trees, too, were blurred and still. No flutter of wings, as some bird found himself a better perch. No wind rustling the leaves. No creaks and moans from the trees themselves. A night muted by the long tendrils of a slow-approaching storm, and apprehension.

Where was Tom Ford? That was the question that I had asked Ruth at supper and nearly everybody else that I had talked to that day — the question that I had pondered on and off all afternoon and far into the night until I finally fell asleep with it on my mind.

I awakened late that next morning. I blamed

it on the sky, which looked like grey cheese-cloth and threatened rain at any moment. Ruth was already up and had the coffee on and a load of clothes in the washer. She didn't care what the weather outside was. She had planned to wash clothes today and by damn, she would. If she couldn't hang them outside, which she infinitely preferred, she'd use the drier. That's what I liked about Ruth. Full speed ahead and damn the torpedoes. She got things done. Most of us usually just thought about it.

"You're up early," I said, pouring myself a cup of coffee.

"No. You're up late." Then she noticed that I still stood at the stove with my coffee in hand. "Is something the matter?" she asked.

"No . . ." I started to lie my way around it but decided that there was no reason to. "I woke up with Luella Skiles on my mind. For some reason, I'm worried about her."

"Then why don't you call to make sure she's all right?"

"What if she is all right? I'd feel stupid for getting her out of bed."

"You won't get her out of bed. If I know Luella Skiles, she beat both of us up."

"Then why do I tell her I called?"

"Make up some lie. You're good at that."

"Thanks for the vote of confidence."

Ruth didn't answer. The washer had just stopped spinning. She was already on her way to take the clothes out of it.

I called Luella Skiles, who answered on the second ring. "Luella, this is Garth Ryland."

"I guessed who it was. What do you want, Garth?"

"I saw you out at Dutchman Yoder's yesterday . . ."

"As I saw you," she said before I could finish. "If you're wondering what I was doing there, I went to buy some butter for a friend of mine from Chicago who is visiting this week."

"No butter in Chicago?"

"Not Jersey butter, Garth." She paused, then said, "And what was it that you were doing there?"

"I was looking for Tom Ford. You haven't by chance seen him around the neighborhood lately, have you?"

"I thought Tom Ford was in jail." She seemed disturbed by the news that he wasn't.

"So did I. Until late Sunday night."

"You might have told me." She sounded out of breath. From fear? I wondered.

"Is something wrong, Luella?"

"No. Nothing's wrong. I had a late-night visitor, that's all."

224

When she didn't elaborate, I asked, "How late?"

"Sometime after midnight, which is when I went to bed. I thought I heard him on the stairs, but when I finally screwed up my courage enough to come out of my bedroom and confront him, he was gone."

"Did he take anything?"

"No. Not that I know of."

"How did he get in?"

"A key, I would imagine, since the doors were locked. I keep mine hidden under the mat at the back door. When I went looking for it, I didn't find it where I'd left it."

"You mean it's gone altogether?"

"No. Just moved from one side of the mat to the other."

"Then perhaps you'd better find a new hiding place for it."

"Don't be . . ." She had started to say, "Don't be silly, Garth," then changed her mind. "Perhaps I will."

"The sooner the better, Luella."

"I'm aware of that."

"Is there anything else that you need to tell me?" I said.

While I was waiting for her answer, I thought I saw a drop of rain streak the kitchen window. When I heard Ruth start the drier, I knew that I hadn't been seeing things.

"No. I guess not," she said.

"Remember Luella, Monroe Edmonds had a late-night visitor the night he died."

"I haven't forgotten, Garth." Her voice had gone dead.

"And Tom Ford, you're sure that you haven't seen him?"

"Absolutely sure. Is that all, Garth?"

While I was deciding, she hung up on me.

"Well?" Ruth said, as I picked up my cup of coffee and sat down at the table.

"She's okay, but she says that someone else besides her was in her house late last night."

"Do you believe her?"

"I don't know what to believe anymore, Ruth. It would make things a lot easier if Tom Ford would show up."

"If he doesn't?"

"I don't know. I'm at a standstill until then."

We listened as a burst of rain raked the window. Then silence. Just a warm-up for the main event.

"Well, I'd better get going," I said, "if I'm going to beat the rain."

"You're not going to eat breakfast?"

"I've got some peanut butter crackers in my desk at work. I'll eat those if I get hungry."

"What about lunch? I promised Aunt Emma that I'd take her up to the Rapids today."

226

Ruth's Aunt Emma, now pushing ninety, was a former Army nurse, who, when she was sober, which was about half the time, had a razor-keen mind and a tongue to match. Though Ruth denied it, Aunt Emma was about the only person in Oakalla that she paid deference to, and about the only person in Oakalla who knew more about its people and its history than Ruth did.

"What's Aunt Emma doing in the Rapids?" I said. "I thought Crazy Days was over for this year."

"She's going to her eye doctor for her annual checkup. He keeps telling her that if she keeps on drinking, she'll develop glaucoma, and she keeps on disappointing him."

"Well, say hello to her for me."

It started to rain in earnest just as I left for my office. Not a brutally hard rain that stung as it hit, but a steady in-your-face rain out of the east that given enough time, would soak even your imagination. Someone once said (probably Euell Gibbons who also liked to eat tree bark) that he liked to walk in the rain, that it was no more to him than taking a cold shower. What I had always wondered was who among us delighted in a cold shower? Nobody that I wanted to share my knickers with, I didn't think.

Once at my office, I hung my raincoat up

to dry, then used some paper towels to wipe my face and hands. The next order of business was to put a pot of water on the hot plate for instant coffee, then to scrounge up all the peanut butter crackers that I could find. Three packages of crackers were all that I came up with, and two of them were stale. But I ate every crumb and even licked the cellophane.

I loved my office in the rain. It gave me a sense of solitude and well-being that I could find nowhere else. I loved the big oak desk and the swivel chair that used to sit in the boiler room of my father's dairy back in Godfrey, Indiana. I loved the feeling that they had brought with them — one of security and intense belonging. I loved the smell of newsprint and printer's ink, of the musty walls and dusty corners that surrounded me. No other place on earth belonged to me as much as my office did. No other place reflected me in quite the same light. That was why I tried to keep it pure and simple, and out of time's reach.

But I found no peace in my office that day. The rain darkened my corners, steamed my windows, seeped into my toes, and generally threw a wet blanket over the place. Where was Tom Ford? I had the overriding feeling that was fast becoming a certainty that if I didn't find him soon, something bad was going to happen.

I walked to the Corner Bar and Grill for lunch. At my back now, the rain dived at my legs and dribbled down my neck, driving me along at a pace that was a half step faster than I wanted to go. But perhaps it knew that.

The Corner Bar and Grill was crowded for a Tuesday. The rain had brought people out and into town. You couldn't cut grass or work in your garden. You couldn't wash your car, rake your lawn, or burn your leaves. It was too wet to plow and too windy to stack BBs. So you might as well come into the Corner Bar and Grill, fill up the place, take Garth's seat at the counter, and eat the last piece of pecan pie.

"What will it be, Garth?" Bernice, the owner and noon waitress asked. "It will have to be short order because we're out of everything else."

I had squeezed myself onto the end stool beside the jukebox. I would be all right until somebody decided to play the damn thing.

"I'll have a cheeseburger with fried onions, macaroni salad, and a glass of milk," I said.

"Sorry, we're out of macaroni salad. It was on special today."

"Pea salad then."

She didn't look hopeful. "We might have a spoonful left. I'll see."

"Bernice, I hate to ask," I said as she was

writing down my order, "but when you make your rounds, will you ask if anybody's seen Tom Ford lately?"

"I'll do what I can, Garth. But you can see what a zoo this place is."

"I'd appreciate it."

While I was waiting for my order, a skinny gum-chewing brunette in jeans and boots approached the jukebox with what looked like a gunnysack full of change. I thought about falling to the floor on the pretense of picking up my napkin and pulling the plug, but someone would just put it back in again. So I listened to ten different versions of how someone's heart had been broken by love. The songs themselves weren't bad if you liked country music, which I did, but they surely didn't do much for my morale.

Not nearly as much as my cheeseburger with fried onions, and pea salad, which was more than respectable for the bottom of the barrel. Feeling that I'd live now at least, I waited for Bernice to finish her rounds, so that she could tell me what she'd learned about Tom Ford.

"Sorry, Garth," she said as she wiped the counter in front of me. "Nobody's seen hide nor hair of him."

"How can that be?" I muttered. "Surely the man has to eat."

"What's that, Garth?" Bernice was busy collecting the dirty dishes two stools down from me. By the looks of all of them, Baby Huey had eaten there.

"Nothing, Bernice. Is Hiram around?"

"He was a couple of minutes ago. We got so busy, I had to call him in." She loaded the dishes onto her tray and started for the kitchen. "I'll give him a holler for you. I'm going that way anyway."

"Thanks, Bernice."

"Just remember me in your tip."

"Don't I always?"

I picked up my check, laid down my usual dollar tip, and awaited her return. "Sorry Garth," Bernice said. "He must have slipped out the back."

That proved to be too bad. Had I talked to him then, I might have saved a couple lives and me one of the worst nights of my life. But as they say, timing is everything.

"That's okay, Bernice. I'll try to catch him later."

"He comes in at six tonight, if you're wondering, and will be here until two or closing, whichever comes first."

I paid my bill and went back out into the rain.

At five that evening, it was still raining and showed no signs of stopping. A small pond

231

had formed there in my yard outside my office, but so far no ducks or kids had showed up to play in it. A lone robin, though, who had braved the rain all day, was having a heyday with all of the earthworms and night crawlers that the rain had brought to the surface. Hog heaven. If there was such a place, that robin had found it.

I beat Ruth home by the time it took me to hang up my raincoat in the front closet and walk into the kitchen. She wasn't nearly as glad to see me as I was to see her. But a day with Aunt Emma could do that to you.

"Supper will be ready within the hour," she said curtly, after hanging up her raincoat and plastic hat in the utility room. "If that's what you're wondering."

"I just got home," I said. "I haven't had time to wonder." A bourbon and ginger ale was on my mind when I walked in the door, but with supper an hour away, I decided to hold off for a while. "So how was your day?" I said.

"About like every day with Aunt Emma. A survival test. Except today was worse because of the rain."

"Was she drinking again?"

"Again?" Ruth gave me a harsh look. "When did she ever stop? But that wasn't the problem. For her, she was practically sober."

"What was the problem, then?"

I listened to the rain as it beat against the house. It sounded as if it was swinging to the north. A cold rain was about to get colder.

"Monroe Edmonds was the problem. She couldn't let up on him, not for one minute. She's like a badger with a bone when she gets that way."

"Did she offer any insight into his death?"

"Later, Garth. I'm not in the mood to talk about it now. Not if you want any supper tonight."

"I'll be in the living room," I said. "As soon as I fix me a drink."

"You might want to hold off on that. Unless you want to drink and drive."

She had my attention. "Where might I be going?"

"Dutchman Yoder's. He should be home by now."

"Where has he been?"

"The Rapids. We saw his horses and wagon parked along the street when we went into the doctor's office. They were gone when we came out again."

"Where along the street?"

She had to think about it. "Across from the bank, I think it was."

"You're absolutely sure about that?"

"Call Aunt Emma and ask her if you don't

233

believe me. She's the one who pointed them out to me."

She was absolutely sure. She wouldn't involve Aunt Emma otherwise.

"That doesn't sound like Dutchman Yoder at all," I said. "Why drive a wagon all the way to the Rapids in the rain?"

"That's what we said. In fact, those were our exact thoughts."

"Did you see him again on your way home?"

"No. That was another thing that bothered us. With cows to milk, he should have been on his way home."

I thought about giving him a call, then realized that he didn't have a telephone. "I guess I'd better go check on him," I said without enthusiasm.

"It's up to you. If you stay here in the warm and dry, no one will be the wiser."

Somehow she always knew the right button to push.

Putting on my wet raincoat was the hardest part of going out into the rain again. It felt cold and wet against my skin, even though I knew it was perfectly dry on the inside. Well, almost perfectly dry — if I didn't count sweat.

Jessie's windows began to steam before we were even out of the garage, and I had to wipe them constantly just to see the road. It was fortunate for me that no one else was driving

Fair Haven Road then because I needed all of the road just to stay between the ditches. It was also lonely with no one else out and about. I wondered where all of those people who had crowded into the Corner Bar and Grill had gone. Not anywhere north of town, I decided.

Before I ever reached the end of his lane, I knew that Dutchman Yoder wasn't home. His cows were bawling in that pained pitiful way that cows do when they need to be milked. They had all gathered around the barn, waiting for someone to let them inside. I wasn't the one they were waiting for, but I let them in anyway, then climbed up into the darkened mow to throw them down some bales of hay. Maybe that would take their minds off their udders for a while.

From there I went to the room built around the silo, where the smell of green silage almost overpowered me. Holding my breath, while looking into the silo itself, I could hear pigeons fluttering and cooing somewhere above me and see what looked like the body of a dead pigeon lying on top of the silage. Dutchman Yoder wasn't in there, though I halfway expected him to be.

A barn swallow darted past me on its way outside as I entered the stable where Dutchman kept his horses. One glance told me that the horses weren't there. A second glance told me that one, their feed bin was nearly empty and two, Dutchman Yoder wasn't inside it either.

Outside, I made a quick search of the milk house, machinery shed, and corncrib before ending up at the house. With nightfall nearly upon me, I was relieved to find both doors to the house locked. I really didn't want to go in there in the dark looking for Dutchman Yoder.

Happy feet. That's what they call the feet of a chicken quarterback who won't stand in the pocket. Happy feet because they won't stay still and are always on the move, looking for someplace to run.

I had a bad case of happy feet that evening. Standing there on Dutchman Yoder's back stoop, with the rain pelting down and the night closing in around me, with the cows bawling for their master and the black pines moaning a primordial prayer, I wanted to cut and run so badly that my shoes started to smoke. But I had one place left to go.

The path to the privy was carpeted with a layer of pine needles softer and deeper than my living-room carpet at home. Tunnellike, it led through an opening that began to squeeze down as I approached the privy until I was encased in a stillness as thick as the pines themselves.

It had rained all day. I had seen, heard, and felt it. But there a step from the privy, the needles were dry enough to crunch underfoot and give me pause for thought. What awaited me in there? The cynic in me said nothing. The coward said that either I would find Dutchman Yoder's lifeless body, or that he, pitchfork in hand, would jump out at me like a grinning jack-in-the-box. I opened the door. The cynic turned out to be right.

The trip back to Oakalla proved uneventful. It continued to rain. Jessie continued to steam. I continued to wipe the windshield every few seconds. It wasn't until I was a block from home that I realized that I had forgotten to search the icehouse.

At home Ruth waited for me in the kitchen. As soon as I was inside the back door, she began to set supper on the table.

"What took you so long?" she said. "I was about to call out the militia."

For some reason, that struck me as funny. "I *am* the militia, Ruth. Eugene Yuill and I."

"Somebody, then."

I took off my raincoat and hung it in the kitchen doorway where it would dry faster. "The reason that it took me so long was that I couldn't rouse anybody, so I went looking to see what I might find."

I watched as peas, pork chops, and fried potatoes went on the table. That night, she could have served liver and onions, and I would have eaten it and thought it was good. I was just thankful to be home and out of the wet and cold. Something that Dutchman Yoder couldn't say.

"What did you find?" Ruth said.

"Nothing. The cows are bawling like they need to be milked. The horses aren't in the barn. There's no sign of him anywhere."

"Well, sit down and eat before it gets cold. We'll talk about it later."

"You want a gut feeling, Ruth?"

"If you keep it short."

"Dutchman Yoder is dead."

"Why can't he just be gone?"

"One or the other, then. I don't think he's coming back."

She shrugged and didn't say anything more. Soon I was too busy eating to think about it.

"You want coffee?" Ruth asked when we'd finished.

"Coffee sounds good to me."

She poured us each a cup, then sat back down at the table. Since I was still chilled from the rain, the coffee hit the spot. The only way it could have been any better was with a slug of Irish whiskey in it.

"Aunt Emma," I said. "You said that she

had some thoughts on Monroe Edmonds."

"*Some,* Garth? She had a whole day's worth of thoughts on the matter. But it was like being back on the threshing ring, you could hardly see the wheat for the chaff."

"Give me the wheat, then." I had settled back in my chair with my coffee cup in hand. If I'd have had my druthers, I wouldn't have had to go out again.

"Follow the booze. That was one of her comments. If we want to find Tom Ford, we need to follow the booze."

"That was it?"

Ruth nodded. "I told you, Garth. It was a long day."

"What else did she have to say?"

"Something of interest, though I don't know what we'll do with it. She said that Mose Weidner and Dub Bennett served in the same outfit during the war. The Seventh Army, Third Infantry Division, I believe. Then after the war, they stayed in Germany for a while until they were mustered out together."

"The Seventh Army wasn't like your friendly neighborhood Cub Scouts, Ruth. It took in a lot of men. So did the Third Infantry Division."

"All I know is what she told me."

Listening to the rain, I thought it seemed to have let up a little. Maybe it would quit before I had to go out into it again.

"Any other gems of knowledge and/or wisdom?" I said.

"She did say that years ago Monroe Edmonds and Luella Skiles *were* sweet on each other and had even planned to be married, but at the last minute they backed out of it."

"Did Aunt Emma say why?"

"Aunt Emma thinks that Luella is the one who pulled the plug. Here she was a graduate of the Juilliard School of Music about to marry a railroader. What would they ever have in common?"

"Music, for one thing. That's what they'd have in common."

Ruth shot me a caustic glance. "I'm only repeating what she told me."

"Did she have any thoughts on the trouble that Tom Ford might be involved in?"

"She did." Ruth gave a half smile, which might mean anything.

"Well?"

"She said follow the booze."

"I think Aunt Emma's getting a little addled in her old age," I said. Later I would regret that statement.

CHAPTER 17

The rain didn't quit after all, but altered its form to smaller, harder drops that bit almost like sleet. I walked to the Corner Bar and Grill, shook off my raincoat and hung it over an empty barstool, and sat down. Unlike earlier that day, the Corner Bar and Grill was nearly deserted, and instead of in loud happy voices, those few people there, eight in all counting me, spoke in whispers. Even the haze that always hung around the booths seemed listless, unable to rise more than a couple feet above the floor. But the effect wasn't entirely unpleasant. For someone who loved quietude as much as I, it was almost narcotic.

"What will it be, Garth?" Hiram, the bartender, asked.

If I wanted Irish coffee, here was my chance. Hiram made the best around. "What I really need is some information." I looked around to see where Tanya Ford was and saw her go into the dining room with a tray full of munchies. "The night that Monroe Edmonds died, which would have been Friday, Tom Ford was here until about ten, is that right?"

"Right. He left sometime about then. Though I can't give you the exact minute."

"Did he leave with anyone?"

"Not that I recall."

"Was he drinking with anyone, who might have followed him out of here a few minutes later?"

Hiram scratched his chin, while he waited for Tanya Ford to clear the barroom on her way to the kitchen. "Not that I know of, Garth. But Friday is usually a busy night in here. It's hard to keep track of everyone."

Tanya Ford came out of the kitchen, took a long look at Hiram and me, then went into the dining room.

"I think she's on to us, Garth."

"Just one more question. What was Tom Ford's condition when he left here? Was he falling down, tree-hugging drunk, like he told me he was?"

"Not that I could tell. You know me, Garth. I won't serve anyone once they get in that condition." He smiled, and I immediately knew what he was smiling about. "Unless it's Wilmer Wiemer on his yearly binge." Who would then pay someone to drive him home.

"And you have no idea where Tom was

headed that night?"

"No idea whatsoever. One minute he was here. The next minute he was gone."

"Thanks, Hiram. You've been a big help."

Hiram went on down the bar where he stopped to pour Mickey Williamson another draft of Leinenkugel's and to fix Buddy Comer another Canadian and water. Meanwhile Tanya Ford came to the swinging doors that separated the barroom from the dining room and stood there staring at me as I watched in the barroom mirror. Wearing a long-sleeve pink blouse, tight grey jeans, dangling pink earrings that matched the blouse, and pink lipstick to match the earrings, Tanya looked about the best that I had ever seen her look. With Tom Ford away, she seemed refreshed and increasingly more confident. Then she noticed that I was watching her in the mirror and disappeared back into the dining room.

Seeing his opportunity, Hiram came back my way on the pretense of wiping the bar. "Garth, remember the other day when you asked me what it was that got Tom and Tanya to going at each other, and I said it was Monroe Edmonds?"

I said that I remembered.

"Well, I got to thinking about it. You know, trying to fit it all together as to what came first and what came after. That part I told you about their little girl and Monroe Edmonds, that came closer to the middle than I realized when I told you about it."

"What came first, Hiram?" Already I had the feeling that I wasn't going to like it.

He glanced over his shoulder to make sure that Tanya wasn't within hearing. "Tom said, *'And another thing.'* That came first."

"What came after?"

" *'Too.'* That came after. 'And another thing, you tell that fat old man to stay away from Elizabeth, too.' "

I stared straight ahead at the man in the mirror across the bar from me. He didn't look happy with himself.

"Hiram, I wish you would have told me that a few days ago."

"Hell, Garth, I wish I would have, too. But it didn't come to me until the middle of the night, and I haven't seen you since."

"Have you said anything to Tanya about this?"

Hiram took offense. "What? And ruin the mood she's in. I might not be the world's greatest thinker, but I know what's good for me and what's good for business. I'm not about to rock the boat when there's nothing to be gained by it."

"She has seemed to be happier lately," I said.

"Who has?" Tanya Ford asked.

I hadn't seen her approach us. Hiram had but too late to warn me. He immediately found something else to do at the other end of the bar.

"You have," I said. "I was just remarking to Hiram how good you looked tonight."

She shrugged it off. "Some nights I get lucky, and everything falls into place." She was smiling, but her eyes were small and hard, like two peas that had withered on the vine. "What else were you and Hiram talking about? I noticed that you were careful to talk only when I wasn't in the room."

"A couple things," I said. "Do you have any idea where Tom went when he left here Friday night?"

"None whatsoever. Furthermore, I don't care where he went or if he ever comes back. So why don't you just butt out of my life from now on." She turned her anger on Hiram, who was pretending not to listen. "And that goes for you, too. For once in my life, I'm happy. I want to stay that way."

Hiram raised his hands as if in surrender, then found some glasses that needed washing. But I stayed where I was. Unlike Hiram, I didn't have to get along with Tanya Ford.

"You're still here," she said.

"I still have questions that need answers."

"Why?" Her facade started to crack. She wasn't quite as hard as she was trying to be. "Why can't you leave it alone? I don't want him back. Can't you see that? Neither do the girls. I don't care if he's guilty or innocent. I just want him *gone*."

"That would make things easier . . ." I said.

"You're damn right it would." She started to cry in spite of herself.

"For now, it would make things easier. But it wouldn't solve anything for either one of us. You would always have to wonder if and when he's coming back. I would always have to wonder where he went and why."

"I'll take that chance," she said. "For some Goddamned precious little peace for once in my life, I'll take that chance. Remember, you're not the one who lives with him. I do. And my little girls do. It's as much for them as for me that I'm asking you to, LEAVE IT ALONE!"

It grew quiet in there. The looks that Mickey Williamson and Buddy Comer gave me weren't exactly friendly.

"Is he bothering you, Tanya?" Mickey Williamson asked.

Mickey Williamson was a construction worker, who stood about five-ten, weighed somewhere around two-twenty, and who could carry a keg of beer or a keg of nails with equal ease — up a sixteen-foot ladder if he had to, one in each hand.

"Yes, he's bothering me," she said. "But I don't need your help."

"Well, if you do . . ."

He turned back to his beer. Buddy Comer, who weighed as much as Mickey, but was a couple inches shorter, turned back to his Canadian and water. All at once, I felt several pounds lighter.

"So why don't you go," she said. "Before I sic Mickey on you."

At the sound of his name, Mickey shot me a wicked glance. I could almost hear my bones cracking.

"When I get the truth," I said.

"I told you the truth, okay. I don't know where he is."

"About you and Monroe Edmonds."

"Me and Monroe Edmonds?" She tried to laugh it off. "What about me and Monroe Edmonds?"

"That's what I'm asking you. If I were to get a search warrant for your house, would I find the key to his back door in one of your pockets?"

"That's ridiculous," she said. "I don't know where . . ."

"Elizabeth told me," I said, while she was still off guard. "About his late-night visitor.

How she always came on Friday."

"That's a lie!" she said. Which it was, since Elizabeth had told me no such thing. But like a lot of us who want the last word, Tanya Ford didn't know how to quit when she was ahead. "Friday isn't even my night off." Then she realized what she'd done. "Shit," she said. "I didn't mean that."

"Have a seat," I said, patting the stool beside me. "Let me buy you a drink."

"I can't. I'm working. You can't drink while you're working. It's house policy."

Hiram brought her a beer anyway. "Screw the house," he said. "I can cover for you."

She looked subdued as she climbed on the stool beside me and took a drink of her beer. "What do you want to know?" she said. "Were Monroe and I having an affair? Yes. If affairs are of the heart. No, otherwise."

"But you were there last Friday night and had been there on several other nights in the past?"

"Yes. To play the piano. Monroe was teaching me. He said I had a gift, though mine wasn't as great as Elizabeth's." She took another drink of her beer and stared off into space for a moment. "I guess I was flattered more than anything else. It was the first time that anyone had said that I had a gift for anything. I very much wanted to believe him."

"How did it all start, the lessons I mean?"

"By accident. One day this past summer, Tom was off who knows where, and I'd just put the girls to bed when I heard this music coming from next door. Just what I need, I thought. I finally get a minute to myself, and the old man next door cranks up his piano." She smiled as she relived that night. "But the longer I listened, the better I felt, so finally I had to go over there and tell him how much I enjoyed his playing." She paused, as if needing a cigarette, but I didn't have any to offer her. "One thing led to another, and the next thing I knew, I was sitting there beside him on the piano bench with my hands on the keys. Playing. If you can imagine that. I can't."

She excused herself, bummed a cigarette off of Mickey Williamson, and returned with it and an ashtray.

"Anyway," she said, looking more confident with a cigarette in her hand, "it was fun. More fun that I'd had at any time since I was a kid. Or since Tom and I hooked up, which was when I was practically a kid." She took a long drag on her cigarette, savoring it. "It was always fun with Monroe. And easy. Had he been a few years younger, or had I been a few years older . . ." She raised her brows. "Well, who knows? Stranger things have happened."

"Then Tom found out."

At the mention of his name, she mashed out her cigarette and gave the ashtray a ride down the bar where Hiram caught it before it slid off.

"Yes. Tom found out. He came home earlier than usual one night last week and saw me leaving by Monroe's back door. That started the argument that we finished the next night in here." She closed her eyes and shook her head. She looked about as unhappy as someone could. "If anything's ever finished with Tom. I'm not sure it is."

"So what were you doing home Friday night," I asked, "if it's not your day off?"

"That's easy enough to answer. When Tom shoved me into the bar, I bruised my back. That, plus the fact that I couldn't face everyone up here just yet, was enough to keep me home." She smiled at me. "My house isn't quite the wreck that you saw on Saturday or nearly as bad as Elizabeth probably told you it is. She and I just have different standards. We probably always will."

I didn't comment. I was still trying hard not to take sides.

"Then you didn't plan on seeing Monroe Friday night?" I said.

"Not at all. He was the last thing on my mind until he called."

"What time was that?"

"Five or six. Sometime in there. He was surprised to find me home, since I'm usually at work by five. He asked me if there was anything wrong. I lied and said no, that I'd just taken the night off, that's all. Then why not come over later, he said, after the girls are in bed? I said I'd have to see but not to count on it."

I waited while she bummed another cigarette. Hiram meanwhile set the ashtray down on the bar in front of her and then went about his business.

"Eleven. That's usually the time I got over there. At her age, it's hard to get Elizabeth to bed much before ten, and then I'd have to wait for her to get to sleep." Her eyes narrowed. Tanya Ford and her daughter, Elizabeth, it seemed to me, would always be on a collision course. "Or at least until she pretended to go to sleep, which turns out to be the case. But that night I really had no intention of going over there, until I went to turn out the kitchen light and saw what I thought was a flashlight go on, then off again." I waited for her to knock a roll of ashes into the ashtray. "I wondered what was going on, if Monroe was having trouble with his lights or something, so I went over to find out. But the back door was locked."

"Is that unusual?"

"Yes and no. Unusual in that he would never lock the door if he thought I might be coming over. Some nights I'd find him in bed reading, and the next thing I knew he'd be down there playing the piano in his robe and pajamas."

"Did he always take the elevator to bed?"

She looked away momentarily, as if she knew what was coming next. "Always. Because of his weight, he couldn't get up and down the stairs anymore."

"What happened after you couldn't get in the back door? Did you come back home after the key?"

"Yes. And you're right, it's still somewhere at home. In the pocket of whatever I was wearing that night." She wore a vague, near-panic look. "I'm sorry. I can't even remember what it was."

"It's not important," I said, seeing that she was about to flounder. "But what you saw that night is important."

"I didn't see anything. That's the trouble. The moment I came in the back door, I could have sworn I heard the front door close. My first instinct was to turn on a light, which I did."

"And it worked?"

"Yes. Why wouldn't it?"

"Never mind." She'd figure it out for herself soon enough.

"So I went on into the house," she said, "until I got to the stairway. Then I was almost afraid to go any farther."

"Had you called out to Monroe?"

"Yes. Several times. And he hadn't answered. That's why I was afraid."

"What about when you first came over and found the door locked? Did you call out to him then?"

"I might have. I don't remember."

"Go on," I said, afraid that she wouldn't.

She took a deep breath to calm herself. "Well, finally, I went on up the stairs to Monroe's bedroom. But he wasn't there. He wasn't anywhere upstairs. Okay, I thought. He was probably playing games with me, which he sometimes did. You know. Little things to tease me, like fooling with the foot pedals when I was trying to play the piano." All but forgotten, her cigarette had almost burned down to bare skin. "So I'd just take the elevator downstairs and maybe get the jump on him."

She turned my way. Her face told me just how terrible that next moment had been. "Do I have to go on?"

I reached over and took the cigarette out of her hand before she burned herself, and

253

put it out in the ashtray. "Only to tell me if the elevator was up or down when you pushed the button."

"Neither," she said. "It was somewhere in between. I remember because it got there a lot faster than it should have."

"You're sure?"

"Yes."

If everything else that she had told me was true, I had to believe that I was right about Monroe Edmonds's death. Whoever had killed Monroe Edmonds was already in the house waiting when Monroe started up to bed that night. He had then pulled the master switch and in so doing, killed Monroe. More chilling was the realization that he knew Monroe's habits well enough to know just when he would be able to pull the switch. That meant he must have stalked Monroe in the past.

"Did you smell anything out of the ordinary?" I asked.

"I smelled Monroe. It made me sick at my stomach. I threw up the second I got home."

"Besides Monroe."

"No, Garth. Working up here has about ruined any chance I have of smelling anything. That and these." She held up her cigarette butt.

"Earlier you said that when Monroe called you, he seemed surprised to find you home.

Why would that be if he was calling you in the first place?"

"He wasn't calling me. He was calling Elizabeth. He said that he wanted her to come over for a minute."

"Did she go?"

"I think so." She thought about it some more. "Yes, I'm sure she did. I was watching television at the time, so I wasn't paying much attention, but it seems she came back with something."

"Square or round?"

She sat with her elbow resting on the counter, her chin resting on her fist. "Round, I think. Long and round. And green."

What was long, round, and green that a twelve-year-old girl might want? Not any twelve-year-old girl, but a particularly bright, talented, and articulate girl named Elizabeth Ford.

I felt the barstool slide out from under me as my feet hit the floor. I grabbed for my raincoat.

"Shit."

It was my turn to say it.

CHAPTER 18

I didn't run to Elizabeth Ford's house, but it was the fastest walk that I ever took in my life. Relax! I kept telling myself. She's safe at home, either sitting on the couch watching television with her sisters or curled up in bed with a good book. Nothing to worry about, Garth. Nothing at all.

When I reached the back door, I was relieved to see lights on inside and hear the television going. I almost didn't knock for fear of scaring her and her sisters, but for my own peace of mind, I had to know that she was all right.

It took a long time for anyone to answer the door. As I stood there waiting, I felt the rain for the first time since I'd left the Corner Bar and Grill. Like the Energizer Bunny, it was still going.

Elizabeth's youngest sister was the one who finally answered the door. She carried a stuffed bear in one hand and was rubbing her eyes with the other. She didn't look as if she had been watching television. She looked as if she had been in bed asleep.

"Is Elizabeth here?" I said.

She didn't answer right away. For a moment I thought that she wasn't going to answer at all. "I'm not supposed to talk to strangers. Lizbeth says."

It was hard to refute that logic. Neither did I want to. "Then go get Elizabeth for me. Please, Joanna, it's important."

"I'm Wendy." She stuck her chin up defiantly at me.

"Wendy, then. Would you please go get Elizabeth for me?"

"Can't," she said, losing some of her courage.

"Why not?"

"She's not here."

"You're sure?"

"I'm sure. I looked." Her lower lip had started to tremble. She put both arms around her bear and laid her head against it.

"What about Joanna? Is she here?"

Again I waited for her answer. "In bed. Asleep."

I hoped asleep was all she was. "Does Joanna know Elizabeth is gone?"

She shook her head.

"May I come in, Wendy? I promise not to hurt you."

She nodded.

"Thank you."

I followed her inside, through the kitchen and into the living room where the ten o'clock news had just come on. "This is Lizbeth's room," she said, pointing to the first room on the left past the living room. "But she's not there."

The door to the room was closed. Before I opened it, I said, "Does Joanna sleep with you or Elizabeth?"

"Me." She pointed down the hall. "That's our room."

I breathed a sigh of relief. It was short-lived, however, when I opened Elizabeth's door and smelled an all-too-familiar smell. Wendy wrinkled up her nose and made a face, so I knew that I wasn't imagining it.

"Stinks, huh?" I said.

"Awful."

I went on into the bedroom and called out to her in case Elizabeth was hiding in there somewhere, but she didn't answer. Her bed was still made. He had been waiting for her, it appeared, just as he had for Monroe Edmonds.

"When did you girls go to bed?" I said to Wendy. Glancing around the room — at the bookshelves that someone had made out of old boards and concrete blocks, at the small collection of dolls arrayed in colorful homemade costumes inside a plastic pink dollhouse, at the rows of dresses hung neatly in the closet, I saw no sign of a struggle.

"Nine o'clock," Wendy said. "Lizbeth always makes us go to bed then on school nights."

"And Elizabeth, does she go to bed then?"

"Yes. Right after we do."

"Then why is the television still on?"

She looked up at me. She still wasn't sure if she trusted me or not, or how much. "I got scared."

"When you got up and found Elizabeth wasn't there?"

"Yes."

"What caused you to get up?"

"I heard someone's voice. I thought Daddy was home."

"But he wasn't home?"

She shook her head. She was close to tears. "No. No one was. Except me and Joanna."

I called Luella Skiles and asked her to come over for a while, which she did, no questions asked. Which surprised me more than a little.

The trip back to the Corner Bar and Grill took me longer than I intended. I kept stopping to weigh a thought, then dismiss it. I didn't notice how wet I was until I stepped inside the Corner Bar and Grill and saw the puddle form at my feet.

Tanya Ford was waiting for me. She had known when I left that all was not well at home.

"What's wrong, Garth?" she said.

As I told her, a look of panic came over her. Without a word, she went after her coat and started for the door. I caught her arm on the way past.

"Take Mickey with you," I said.

"Whatever for?"

"In case he comes back."

"In case *who* comes back?"

"I don't know. Just take Mickey with you. Buddy, too, if he wants to go."

"No thanks, Garth. I can't even handle one man. What would I do with two more of them?" Then she left.

My next move proved brilliant. I did nothing because I didn't know where to go or what to do. I just stood there like a drowned rat, dripping all over the floor of the Corner Bar and Grill.

Amber Utley came into the barroom, wearing a beige raincoat with a matching hood, bare legs sticking out from under the raincoat, and hot pink L. A. Gear tennis shoes on her bare feet.

"I'd like a twelve-pack of Old Milwaukee, please," she said to Hiram.

Though not as obviously nervous as on Saturday night, she didn't seem completely at ease, either. And she looked more haggard than one might have expected on the heels of a three-day vacation. But I had heard that sixth graders could do that to you.

Then Aunt Emma's much maligned words of wisdom came back to haunt me. "If you want to find Tom Ford, follow the booze."

I nearly ran over Amber Utley in my hurry to get to Hiram. But the smile that she gave me said that all was forgiven.

"Stall her," I whispered to Hiram on my way to the phone.

Hiram went to the cooler as if he hadn't heard, but once there, he began looking for Old Milwaukee in all of the wrong places. Meanwhile I made a call to Fritz Gascho, owner of the hardware store, who said that yes, a pretty blonde schoolteacher had bought a hacksaw late Saturday afternoon. I thanked him and hung up.

"Okay," I said to Hiram. "You can go ahead and serve her."

"What's up?" he asked, as he bent down to pick up the twelve-pack of Old Milwaukee.

"Old Milwaukee. Is that Tom Ford's brand

of beer?" I hoped it was, or I was going to feel awfully stupid.

His once-a-year smile appeared on his face. "As a matter of fact, it is."

Then I noticed Mickey Williamson and Buddy Comer eyeing Amber Utley. They were probably wondering what I was wondering — just what was on under her raincoat, if anything? Now all I needed was for one of them to hit on her.

"Give me the beer," I said to Hiram. "I'll pay you for it later."

"If you can pull it off, Garth," he said, sizing up the situation, "it's on the house."

"Ready?" I said to Amber Utley. I held the twelve-pack in one arm and offered her my other one.

She just stared at me, as if perhaps I'd just flashed her. This wasn't working out as I hoped, but then things rarely did.

"Pardon me?" she said, still hesitating.

The longer the pause went, the worse it got. I felt like an actor, now center stage, who knew the right lines but for the wrong play. To make matters worse, Mickey and Buddy had started to notice me.

"Tom sent me," I said, still smiling. "To see that you got home safely."

I didn't have to say anything more. She took

262

off running for the door. The twelve-pack of Old Milwaukee and I followed her; all the while I hoped that Mickey and Buddy weren't following us.

It took me a block to catch up to her. But then I had a handicap.

"You come home without this," I said, shoving the twelve-pack at her, "Tom's not going to like it."

She started to speed up. I caught ahold of her arm and slowed her down. "Let me go," she said, struggling to break my grip. "Or I'll scream."

"Will you at least hear me out?" I let go of her, then chased her through a puddle of water.

"What's to hear?" she said.

"You're harboring a fugitive. That's a felony in this state."

"Says who?"

"Me. Deputy Sheriff Garth Ryland."

"Oh, shit," she said, stopping dead in her tracks. "I thought you just ran the newspaper."

We faced each other under the streetlight at the corner of School and Poplar. "Here, hold this." I handed her the Old Milwaukee, then dug out my wallet to show her my special deputy's badge. One of these days, I'd have to shine it up.

"It looks official," she said as she held it up to the streetlight.

"It is official."

I put the wallet back in my pocket. She handed the beer back to me. We continued on toward her apartment at a more leisurely pace.

"How much trouble am I in?" she said.

"Not much. If you'll help me with Tom."

"He says he's not going back to jail, no matter what."

"He might not have to. Has he been in your apartment since Saturday?"

"As far as I know. I've been out a time or two for beer and groceries, but he's been too scared to leave." Something in her voice said that Tom Ford wasn't quite the bargain she once thought he was.

"Has he said anything to you about what's going on?"

"No. Only that if he could ever find that painting, neither one of us would ever have to worry about anything again."

"What painting is that?" I said, playing dumb.

"The one 'that fat old man,' as he calls him, paid Tom to buy for him."

She unbuttoned the top of her raincoat and pulled out a diamond pendant that probably went about half a carat in all. "See. Here's what he bought me with part of the money."

I had stopped to admire the pendant, and what was under it. No matter how I approached the subject, or whatever disclaimers I made, Amber Utley was still a whole lot of woman.

"Nice," I said.

She smiled at me. I could feel my clock start ticking. "I'm glad you think so."

When we stopped on the sidewalk below her apartment, I said, "Do you have your key with you?"

"Yes. But if I know him, Tom has the door locked from the inside."

"Is he still wearing his handcuffs?"

"Yes. But I sawed the chain in two."

"Then we'll have to play it by ear."

"Fine with me. Anything to . . ." She took a deep breath as tears welled up in her eyes. "To get this over with."

I followed her up the wooden stairs to her apartment where she knocked quietly on the door. "Tom, honey, it's me."

"Are you alone? I thought I heard two sets of footsteps." He must have been waiting by the door.

"Of course, I'm alone." She sounded irritated. "What you heard was my lugging this damn beer up the steps."

He started to undo the lock. I motioned for

her to yank on the door then get out of the way.

"You're sure you're alone?" He wasn't at all sure himself.

"Yes, goddamnit, I'm sure. Now open the frigging door."

He unlocked the door and eased it partway open, so that he could see the stairwell before he committed himself. Amber Utley yanked on the door with all her might, tearing it from his hands. At that same instant, I delivered a two-hand chest pass of Old Milwaukee to Tom Ford.

The force of it knocked the wind out of him and sent him stumbling back into the apartment. I didn't want him to catch his breath. Tackling him with my shoulder, I drove him over a coffee table and into a couch. Meanwhile someone ran past us on into the apartment. I assumed it was Amber Utley.

Tom Ford was younger, stronger, and more desperate than I, and try as I might, I couldn't hold him down. He broke away from me and started for the door. I tackled him again before he could reach it. We rolled over on the floor, smashing into the coffee table, before he struggled to his feet with me still hanging on. He was reaching for a table lamp to bash over my head when it exploded right before his eyes. He might not have heard the gunshot, but I did. I let go of him at once.

"Stop it! Both of you!" Amber Utley yelled. "Before you wreck the place."

I looked around. The only thing that I could see broken was the table lamp that she herself had shot. But I didn't think that this was the time to point that out to her.

"Give me the gun," Tom pleaded, taking a step her way. "Like a good little girl."

She kept her pistol pointed at him. She had no intention of giving it up.

"I'm not your good little girl," she said fiercely. "I'm not your good little any-thing. Now sit down on the couch and don't move."

"Come on, honey," he wheedled, still not believing her. "This is Tom, remember?"

"How could I forget?"

"Meaning what?"

"Meaning sit down on the couch and don't move."

"Bitch," he said, as a whole new counte-nance came over him. "Some friend you turned out to be."

I glanced at the couch. It was one of those slick imitation-leather oversized jobs that would probably stay in the apartment when Amber Utley moved on. But it looked as if it would hold Tom Ford.

"Tom, sit down on the couch," I said when

he didn't offer to move. "I think she means business."

"You're damn right, I do," she said. Then she eased her way around him until she stood beside me.

"So that's the way it is," he said. "You found yourself a new boyfriend."

"Sit down and shut up, Tom. You're already in enough trouble the way it is," I said.

"I didn't kill that old man. I don't care what anybody says."

"I know you didn't."

Finally I said something that he would listen to. "Say that again."

"I said that I know you didn't kill Monroe Edmonds. I don't know who did, but it wasn't you."

"Then what's this all about?"

He glanced from me to Amber Utley, who stood beside me with her pistol still pointed at his chest. Part of him wanted to believe that this was some sort of conspiracy against him. Part of him, it seemed, liked being a victim because it gave him every reason he needed not to do anything with his life.

"You're still a fugitive. As a material witness, if nothing else," I said. "So sit down before I think of something else to charge you with."

He thought it over, then sat down on the

couch. I heard Amber Utley sigh in relief as she lowered the pistol. She then went into the bathroom, taking it with her. A moment later, I thought I heard her throwing up.

Meanwhile Tom Ford sat on the couch staring at me. I sat on the floor staring at him. We neither one had much to say to the other.

"You're wondering how I got into this, aren't you?" he said.

I glanced around the apartment. Saw a large-screen color television with a built-in sound system complete with speakers, a mound of big fluffy brown-and-white pillows that matched the couch, a sprinkling of wall decorations tastefully done — all in all, a cozy little love nest. Add Amber Utley to the mix, and I didn't wonder at all.

"No, Tom. I wonder how you're going to get out of it."

Amber Utley came out of the bathroom and without a glance our way went into what I presumed was the bedroom and closed the door. She was probably sick of both Tom and me by now.

"It was Elizabeth," Tom said, as if I hadn't said anything. "She's the one who introduced me to Amber. At the school's open house last year."

"Tom, I'm more interested in the painting that you bought from Martin Weidner."

"What painting is that?"

"The one that cost Monroe Edmonds his life. The one that might cost Elizabeth hers." Tom Ford needed some shock therapy to improve his memory.

"What about Elizabeth?"

"Someone kidnapped her tonight. I'm sure it's the same person who killed Monroe Edmonds."

He gave me his how-dumb-do-you-think-I-am smile. I wanted to shove it down his throat. "You're putting me on, right?"

"Call your wife and find out. Better yet, let me call her for you."

I heard the bedroom door open as Amber Utley came into the living room. She had shed her raincoat and wore a sea-green housecoat that, while she was still standing, barely came to her knees. When she sat down on one of her big fluffy pillows and crossed her legs Indian style, it barely covered her thighs. But Tom Ford seemed not to notice. Familiarity, I guess, breeds contempt.

"Let me get this straight," Tom said. "Are you saying that someone kidnapped Elizabeth tonight?"

I looked at my trusty Timex. "Less than two hours ago."

He studied me, like a poker player who had just been raised beyond his limit. He didn't want to believe me but couldn't afford not to.

"Why, for God's sake?"

"Because Monroe Edmonds gave her the painting you bought for him."

"Gave it to her? Why?"

"For safekeeping perhaps. More likely, as an investment in her future."

He gave me a puzzled look. He didn't understand. I doubted that he ever would.

"What are you saying, Garth, that the old man and Elizabeth had something going?"

"I'm saying that Elizabeth has musical talent, real talent from what I understand. Monroe Edmonds saw it and wanted to nurture it. So he bought her a ticket to the future."

Tom still looked puzzled.

"The painting that you told me about," Amber said. She pulled out her pendant to show him. "The one that bought me this."

Tom wore a tight-lipped smile that said for her to keep quiet. He was the man here, and he would do the talking.

I said, "What was the deal, Tom, that Monroe pitched to you?"

"I don't have to answer that," he said. "That was between Monroe Edmonds and me."

"A lump sum would be my guess. Pay what

you had to for the painting, and the rest was yours. Or was it? Or was the rest supposed to go to Elizabeth?" Which was more likely the case.

"Which she never got and will never get," he said savagely. "A lousy hundred bucks. That was supposed to be my share. I bought the painting for fifty, which was fifty less than what Martin Weidner was asking for it, I get a hundred, and Elizabeth is supposed to get what, eight-fifty? For piano lessons, for Christ's sake! When I can't even afford insurance for my truck."

"You told me that money was yours," Amber said. "You didn't tell me that you stole it from Elizabeth."

"What are you crying about?" he said. "You got what you wanted out of the deal. As for Elizabeth, what's she done for me lately?"

"How much of the money is left, Tom?" I said.

He reached into his jeans as far as the handcuff on his wrist would let him and pulled out a handful of change. There were a couple crumpled Abe Lincolns among it, but that was all.

"Expensive pendant," I said.

"Some of it went for a tape deck for my truck that I've been wanting. The rest for this and that." Booze, in other words.

272

"Did you get a good look at the painting?" I said.

"Just a glimpse to make sure that it was the one that the old man wanted. Dutchman Yoder showed up about then, so we had to put it away."

"What was the painting in?"

"A green canister of some kind. Martin said it was Army issue and probably was used to hold maps at one time."

"Did Martin say where the painting came from?"

"A trunk up in their attic. Old man Edmonds saw it when he was there a couple years or so ago, looking through their stuff after Martin's mother died." Tom Ford shook his head at the folly of it. "But from what I saw of the painting, I can't see what all of the fuss was about. A house. That's what it looked like to me. Not a very good house at that."

"Do you remember anything else about it?"

"No. That's all. I told you I didn't get a very good look at it."

I wasn't sure that I believed him. "Then why did you come back that night and try to steal it?"

"Why not?" he said. "If some fool was willing to give me a thousand dollars to buy it, some other fool might be willing to give me a lot more than that to sell it to him."

"Or kill you for your trouble."

That thought seemed to sober him, that and the fact that his daughter was missing. "You don't think Elizabeth's in any real danger, do you?" he said.

"You'd do better asking Monroe Edmonds."

I left Tom Ford sitting on the couch and Amber Utley sitting on her big fluffy pillow, and went out into the night.

CHAPTER 19

At home, I stopped only long enough to tell Ruth where I was going before I climbed into Jessie and drove north on Fair Haven Road. The rain had turned to drizzle, and the temperature had dropped a few degrees, which made it perfect for condensation both inside of Jessie and outside. Had her windshield not been fogged and had I not suffered from night blindness, I still would have had trouble seeing the road.

I drove past my first turn and had to back up on Fair Haven Road. Then I drove past my second turn and had to back up again, nearly ending up in the ditch. But the worst was yet to come.

I heard Hog Run before I ever saw the humped iron bridge that passed over it. Stopping in what I hoped was the middle of the road, I got out of Jessie and walked up to the bridge to make sure that it was safe to cross. Just a few feet below me, and rising ever nearer to the bottom of the bridge, Hog Run raced and roared, as if it just couldn't wait to overrun its banks and be set free.

Back in Jessie again, I drove with my head out the window until we were safely across the bridge. That accomplished, I thanked God and drove on.

No lights burned in the M and M Boys' house. No outside security light showed me the way, as I pulled into their drive and got out of Jessie. An uneasy feeling, powered by fear, said to get the hell out of there while I still could.

Their front door stood all the way open. "Anyone home?" I yelled inside.

In the silence that followed, I thought I heard someone breathing. Panting was more like it. The pant of a cornered animal.

"I'm coming in," it seemed necessary to say.

Once inside the door, I fumbled for a light switch, found three of them in a row, and tried them all in turn. None of them worked.

I went back out to Jessie, took the flashlight out of her glove compartment, and turned it on. Nothing. I smacked it on my thigh a couple times, tried again, and was rewarded with a bright wide beam. But like everything else that had to do with Jessie, that might mean absolutely nothing a moment from now.

I didn't announce myself the second time

that I went inside. Perhaps that was a mistake. The breathing seemed louder and even more fearsome than it had before. I didn't like the sound of it. Not at all.

Not wanting to give anything away, I kept my flashlight off and walked as quietly as I could. Despite its low clouds and drizzle, the night was not completely dark, and enough light filtered into the house for me to see shapes and shadows and to feel my way past fixtures and furniture. But when I got to the kitchen, I had to turn my flashlight on. I felt as if I were walking in maple syrup.

Not maple syrup after all. Blood. A river of it led to the stairs.

The heavy breathing was coming from the top of the stairs. What it looked and sounded like was that a kill had been made in the kitchen, then the body dragged up the stairs where the beast of prey was now guarding it.

To get to the stairs, I had to cross the rest of the kitchen floor, which was lacquered with the prey's blood. To get up the stairs, I had to face the beast itself.

A word of warning might have helped. But I didn't give it.

Click! I will never forget that sound as long as I live. It was the sound of a gun being cocked. The blast that followed blew the glass out of the back door. I lay flat on the stairs in a puddle of blood — afraid to move, afraid even to take a breath for fear that it would be my last.

Click. I knew what I was facing now — the second barrel of a double-barrel shotgun. His first shot had been head high, designed to take my head off. Who knew where his second might go?

"Martin, or Mose, if that's you, this is Garth Ryland." The words would either kill me or save my life. But a fifty-fifty chance was better than none at all.

No answer from above.

I didn't dare move. Not until he acknowledged me. I tried again.

"I'm coming up the stairs now. Whatever you do, don't shoot."

I started to rise then thought better of it. Whoever was up there, be it Martin, Mose, or someone else, didn't have his full wits about him or he wouldn't be sitting at the top of the stairs, holding a double-barrel shotgun.

Boom! I felt the blast part my hair as it blew out the rest of the door. Had his second barrel been a skeet instead of a full choke, I would have been dead.

I gathered myself and scrambled up the stairs before he could reload. A wasted effort, as it turned out. Mose Weidner didn't have the wherewithal to reach for another shell.

He sat at the top of the stairs with the shotgun beside him and Martin Weidner's head in his lap. As I shined my flashlight down into Martin's face, I saw that he was dead. Long dead by the looks of him. As pale as pale can get, he had a slit on his throat that ran from ear to ear and was wide enough to stick your whole hand into it.

"Mose, what happened here?"

He didn't answer me. He sat there without speaking, rocking his dead son. I knew that he was in shock. What I didn't know was that he had been shot. Not until I saw the blood seeping out from between his fingers — blood that was too fresh to have come from Martin.

But when I tried to move Martin's head out of the way to examine Mose's wound, he bent over, wrapped both arms around Martin's head, and began to wail. And the harder I tried to wrestle Martin away from him, the harder he fought and the more he bled. Finally I gave up.

I went downstairs looking for a phone, found one in the kitchen, and discovered that the line was dead.

"Mose, I'm going for help," I yelled up at him. "Hang in there."

But I doubted that he heard me, or much cared if he had.

Back inside Jessie, I cursed her all the way to the iron bridge that ran over Hog Run, then talked her tenderly across it until we were safe on the other side, and began cursing her again. All the time I knew that it was a mistake. Jessie never let any reproach go unpunished. But I had to take my frustrations out on something, and with her leaky heater core and steamy windshield, she was a big target.

On my way past Dutchman Yoder's, I noticed that all was still dark there. No sense in trying to call from there anyway since he didn't have a phone.

At Grandmother Ryland's, I let myself in the back door and called Abby. I didn't know who else to trust with Mose Weidner's life.

"Hello?" she said, with a question in her voice, as if she were expecting bad news.

"Abby, it's Garth. I need your help."

"You've got it."

I told her where I was and where the problem was. "But tell those idiots from Operation Lifeline to take it easy," I said. "Especially crossing that iron bridge over Hog Run. You go in there, you might not come out again."

"I'll tell them. And, Garth?"

"Yes?"

"Thanks for calling *me*. It means a lot."

I got in Jessie and drove back to Mose Weidner's house. It never occurred to me to wait at the crossroads for the Operation Lifeline ambulance, so that I could lead it safely to the right place. It never occurred to me because Abby had never been riding in it before. Damn! I thought. Damn. Damn. Damn.

Mose Weidner hadn't moved from where I'd left him. Neither had he released his grip on his son's head. But something in his eyes had changed. No longer focused, they looked distant and strangely at peace. Hurry, Abby. Mose Weidner is dying.

I went back outside. Soon I saw the flashing red lights of the Operation Lifeline ambulance bounce over the iron bridge and come my way. Dumb, I thought, for me to stand here in the middle of the road waving this flashlight at them. They'll probably run over me.

But they didn't run over me. As soon as Abby jumped out of the ambulance, I led her inside.

"Watch your step," I said as we crossed the kitchen floor.

"Is that what I think it is?"

"Exactly."

"Then how can he still be alive?"

"It's not his. Most of it anyway."

"Then whose is it?"

"You'll meet him shortly."

At the top of the stairs, Mose Weidner looked up at Abby and smiled. He must have thought that she was his guardian angel.

"You can see the problem," I said.

Behind us I heard the people from Operation Lifeline starting up the stairs. It sounded as if they'd brought the whole regiment.

"Not yet!" Abby yelled down to them. "Stay where you are."

Then she knelt beside Mose Weidner and began to talk to him. Within a matter of seconds, he released his grip on his son and let me drag Martin's body off of him.

"Now!" Abby yelled back down the stairs.

"How is he?" I asked, after she had pulled down Mose's bib overalls and examined his wound.

"Not good."

"Can you save him?"

She looked up at me. Her eyes said no. "I can try."

I got out of the way while they stuck a needle into Mose's arm and began giving him blood. Then they put an oxygen mask over his face, strapped him on a stretcher, and carried him downstairs.

"Are you coming?" Abby asked.

"In a little while."

"Wish me luck."

"Luck," I said.

The house became quiet again, and dark, once the ambulance pulled away. I took a tour of it to see what I could see but found nothing that told me what had happened here, or why. Only Mose Weidner could tell me. And at the moment he wasn't talking.

My last trip up the stairs was a deliberate one. The blood had started to dry and, like paint when it starts to dry, had become tacky. Smack, smack went my shoes all the way up the stairs. Smack, smack, smack.

Martin Weidner lay on his back with his arms out and his legs spread. His eyes were open. His bib overalls and white T-shirt were soaked with blood.

I knelt and closed his eyes, then shined my flashlight up and down his body, searching for what I had glimpsed a moment earlier. There it was in his right hand. A small link chain, like that on the trinkets in gum-ball machines, stuck out from between his fingers, like the tip of a rat's tail.

Prying open his hand proved easier than I thought it would be. He seemed to want to give me its contents, now that he was through with it.

A rabbit's foot. Martin Weidner's hand held a rabbit's foot that was designed either to go on a larger key chain or to serve as a key chain itself. Turning it over, I saw a round white sticker that was almost buried in the soft fur. The sticker read: Keep me near and you'll always have good luck. In smaller letters around the edge of the sticker were the words: Fickle's Store, Oakalla, Wisconsin.

That gave me pause for thought. Fickle's Store hadn't been in business since I was a kid.

CHAPTER 20

I drove to the hospital and called Ruth from there. She must have been close to the phone because she answered on the first ring.

"Thank God," she said. "I was about to call the state police."

"Then you heard the ambulance go through?"

"Both times. When I called the hospital, all they would tell me was that somebody had been shot. Where are you, anyway?"

"The hospital. And it's Mose Weidner's who's been shot." Then I told her the rest of it.

"Where does it all end?" she asked when I finished.

"I don't know, Ruth. I'm not sure it ever does."

"Well, keep me posted."

"I'll be sure to."

I hung up and went looking for Abby. I'd forgotten how I looked until I saw a couple of nurses staring at me. The Night Stalker. There in my bloody raincoat with mud all over the rest of me.

Abby found me before I found her. She yelled at me just as I was about to take the elevator to the second floor. One look at her told me that things had not gone well.

"I'm sorry, Garth," she said. "We lost him on the operating table."

"Want a cup of coffee?"

"Yeah. I could use one."

We were a matched pair, Abby and I. I had blood all over my raincoat. She had blood all over her blue surgeon's gown. We both looked tired and defeated.

We took the elevator down to the canteen where she sat down at a table and lighted a cigarette while I got the coffee out of a machine.

"Cream or sugar?" I asked.

"No. Black."

"I should have said nondairy creamer," I said as I sat down.

She gave me a smile, though her heart wasn't really in it. "It wouldn't have made any difference."

We sat in silence as she smoked her cigarette, and I drank my coffee. Even silence with her felt good to me.

"A penny for your thoughts," she said.

"I don't have any. I'm too tired to think."

"Me, either." She reached into the pocket of her gown then laid a slug on the table. "Here's what I took from Mose Weidner's liver. It looks like a nine millimeter to me. Either that or a forty-five."

I picked up the slug and examined it. It had flattened slightly but was otherwise in almost perfect shape.

"Not many nine millimeters in Oakalla," I said. "Forty-fives either. Most of the people around here own shotguns and rifles."

"That was my thinking."

I handed the slug back to her, and she put it back in her pocket.

"Too bad Clarkie's not here. He could tell us what it is," I said.

"Clarkie?"

"Sheriff Clark. He's at a seminar right now."

She took her first drink of coffee. "I hear that's no great loss."

"Don't believe all that you hear."

Another silence, but shorter this time.

"Did Mose Weidner say anything to you at all?" I said.

"Nothing that made any sense to me. Maybe it will to you. When we were there in the back of the ambulance together, he grabbed ahold of my wrist, and said, 'Bugs Bunny.

Tell Bugs Bunny I got it back.' "

"You're sure that's what he said?"

"I'm sure that's what I heard. I'm not sure that's what he said."

"Sorry. It doesn't make any sense to me, either."

"Well, I guess it will keep for now."

"I'm not so sure about that."

I told her about Elizabeth Ford, who was still missing.

The tiredness that I saw in her only moments ago disappeared right before my eyes. "Then why are we sitting here?" she said.

"Because I don't know where to go."

She reached into her pocket and took out the slug. "This might tell us, if it would."

"I know someone whom we could ask."

"Who's that?"

"Uncle Bill!" we said in unison.

"Damn," Abby said a few minutes later. "I don't have my keys with me."

Since Abby's car was at home, we had gone in Jessie to Doc Airhart's house. I drove while she kept the windshield wiped. We made a good team.

She rang the doorbell and waited for Doc to answer it. Glancing up at the nearby streetlight, I could barely see the rain. Smokelike, it sifted down through the trees and fell upon the sidewalk without a sound.

The porch light came on, and the front door swung open. "It's a little early for trick-or-treaters, isn't it?" he said.

Doc wore grey flannel pajamas, his maroon silk robe, and his hard brown house slippers that clacked like a horse's hooves as he walked. He led us into the kitchen where we all sat around the table. Meanwhile Daisy, who was in the basement, started to whine and scratch at the basement door.

"Now see what you've done," he said. "I won't know a minute's peace until I let her out of there."

"Sorry," I said.

"Sorry," Abby repeated an instant later.

Doc first looked at me then at Abby. "Is there an echo in here?"

Abby laid the slug on the table in front of Doc. "To get right to it, we need to know what kind of gun this came from."

Doc picked it up and examined it. "There's no way on God's green earth I can tell you that," he said. "Not with what I have here."

"Could you give us your best opinion?" I said.

"Why?"

I told him.

When I finished, he had that old familiar reassuring look on his face that told me, even as a kid, that everything was under control.

"Give me a few minutes," he said. "I'll see what I can do."

He went to the basement door then clacked his way down the basement steps. Evidently Daisy went with him because we didn't hear anything more out of her.

"I love that old man," Abby said.

"Same here."

"When he goes," she glanced around the kitchen with a lost look in her eyes, "I don't know what I'll do."

"He's not going for a long time yet."

She nodded as if she really believed me.

A short while later, Doc came back into the kitchen with Daisy at his heels. She was so glad to see Abby that she nearly knocked Doc over getting to her.

"Spoiled," Doc said as Abby bent over to rub noses with Daisy. "And you can see who the culprit is."

"Well?" Abby said, as she scratched Daisy's ears.

"It's a nine millimeter. I know that for a fact. My best guess is that it came from a German Luger."

Something went off in my head. It sounded a lot like my toy cash register used to when

I'd hit the cash button and the drawer would fly open.

"You're sure?" I said.

"No. I'm not sure, I told you that. You asked for my best opinion, and I gave it to you. Instinct. That's all I'm going on."

World War II. That's what the cash register in my head had rung up.

"Abby, what was it again that Mose Weidner said to you in the ambulance?"

"Bugs Bunny. Tell Bugs Bunny I found it again. Or something to that effect."

"Bugs Bunny. Tell Bugs Bunny I got it back. Isn't that it?"

She nodded. "Yes. That's it. So what's going on?"

I told her.

"I'm going with you," she said.

I shook my head no.

"Why not?"

"Because I can't look out for you and me both."

"I can look out for myself."

We were about to have our first argument, and there wasn't time for it.

"I know you can look out for yourself," I said. "But *I'll* be safer with you here."

Doc said, "What he's saying, Abby, is that you don't march into combat with your love at your side. And he's right, you don't, whether you're a man or a woman."

She looked at Doc then at me. She wasn't happy with either one of us. "Get going, then," she said. "You can't find Elizabeth Ford sitting here."

CHAPTER 21

Dub Bennett's house was only two blocks away, which didn't give me much time to think things through. I hoped I was right about this. If I were wrong, I could end up with more than egg on my face.

Dub and Liddy Bennett lived in a small white frame house along Colburn Road. It had a big shady backyard, a high concrete porch half as big as the house itself, and a giant spirea bush at each end of the porch that, along with a shagbark hickory, took up most of the front yard.

A light was on in the house, and I could hear the report of television gunfire. With Mose and Martin Weidner's blood still on my raincoat, I didn't much care for the sound of it.

I climbed the ten or so steps to the front door and saw Dub Bennett lying on the couch inside. Wearing only boxer shorts and a bib undershirt, he didn't look dressed for company.

Knock, knock. I hated the sound that my fist made against the door. It jarred the stillness of an otherwise quiet night.

Dub Bennett rose from the couch and came to the door. A bear of a man, he had hair, most of it white, growing on nearly every part of him that I could see. Small tufts of it even stuck out from his ears, like the whiskers of a billy goat.

On seeing me at the door, he said, "Get the hell out of here, Ryland. I've got nothing to say to you."

I knew that nothing I said would persuade him to let me inside. So I reached into my pocket, pulled out Mose Weidner's lucky rabbit's foot, and showed it to him.

"Mose said to tell you that he got it back. Just before he died."

The door opened. I went inside.

I didn't recognize the Western that Dub Bennett was watching, but I did recognize a young Gary Cooper and an old character actor whose name I had never bothered to learn. The movie was in black and white, and it wasn't hard to tell the good guys from the bad guys. I had cut my television teeth on Westerns and thought that life would always be that simple. Maybe I should have been reading *Crime and Punishment* instead.

Dub Bennett turned off the television and

sat down on the couch. I moved an afghan and sat down in an overstuffed chair that had a doily on each arm and a larger doily on the headrest. A brass pole lamp with three white shades stood beside me. It was the only light on in the house.

"You say Stick is dead?" Dub Bennett said.

"Stick?"

"That's what all of us in our outfit used to call him. Stick Weidner. He packed about as much weight as a matchstick then."

"Yes. He's dead. Somebody shot him. And slit Martin Weidner's throat."

If he were surprised, Dub didn't let on. "It was bound to happen, I guess. Once he lost his rabbit's foot."

"Where did he lose it, Dub? That's what I'm here to find out."

"What good will that do you now?"

"It might tell me who killed him."

He shook his head. He was absolutely certain of what he was about to say. "That's one thing it won't tell you, Garth. I can guarantee you that."

"Just like you can guarantee me that the painting he stole has no earthly value or anything to do with any of this?"

Dub Bennett looked away. He seemed sorry now that he hadn't left the television on. It

295

would have given him the diversion he needed.

"I don't know what you're talking about, Garth."

"I'm talking about Elizabeth Ford. She's missing, and so is Mose's painting that was last in her possession. So don't lie to me, Dub. Not with her life on the line."

"Describe the painting," he said, certain that I couldn't. "If you know so damn much about it, describe the painting for me."

I told him what I knew about it and hoped that Tom Ford hadn't been lying to me.

He seemed stunned by what I told him. "Damn," he said, as if he couldn't believe that after all the years, it had come back to haunt him. "If I told him once, I told him a hundred times to get rid of that thing. I don't know why he held on to it. For the life of me, I don't."

"Start at the beginning, Dub. And don't leave anything out."

He looked at me and smiled. He hadn't completely lost his sense of humor. "Garth, there's a twenty-four volume set of books on that war. Believe me, you don't want me to start at the beginning."

"The beginning of the end, then."

"I'll buy that. The beginning of the end."

I rested my arms on the top of the doilies and waited.

"We were in what had become Patch's Seventh Army, pushing south across Germany, and kicking hell out of the krauts now that the Rhine was behind us. We came to this village just outside of Stuttgart — I forget its name, if I ever even knew — where we set up camp. Stick and I were on patrol together, looking for snipers and any other stray krauts that might be in the area. It was a nice day, I remember that. Trees budding, birds singing just like at home. We even remarked to each other how pretty and peaceful everything was and how glad we were that this thing was all but over."

Dub's eyes glazed over momentarily. Then they cleared.

"Then this peasant woman comes running out at us. She was damn lucky we didn't shoot her first and ask questions later." He paused, as if wondering if that might not have been the best course of action. " 'Nazi!' she yelled. Then she pointed to a house to show us where."

Again he paused. "We had to go in there," he said, as much to himself as to me. "Here this woman was right in our face screaming Nazi at the top of her lungs."

I waited for him to continue.

"An old man and his wife. That's who was inside the house. Both scared to death. You could see it in their eyes when we kicked in the door. But proud. You've got to give the krauts credit for that. They were a proud bunch of people, even when they might be facing death, like those two were.

" 'Where's the Nazi?' we said.

"They shook their heads and said something in German, like 'No Nazi here.'

"I said to Stick that we should get the hell out of there and leave them alone. Even if there was a Nazi in there, he was probably their son, who had deserted his outfit and gone home, like so many of them were doing by then. But Stick had noticed how the old man's eyes kept going to this painting beside the door. It seemed almost as if the old man was more afraid for the painting than he was for his son — if in fact his son was even around. So Stick struck a bargain, like he's been doing all of his life.

" 'Tell you what, old man,' he said. 'We'll trade you that painting for that Nazi you've got hidden in here. What do you say, old man?'

"Of course the old man didn't say anything because he didn't understand a word Stick had said. But he still kept glancing at the painting, like it was his last great treasure on earth.

" 'That sounds like a yes to me, doesn't it to you, Dub?' Stick said.

"Then he turned his back on the old man and reached for the painting.

" 'Stick!' I yelled, because the old man had charged Stick, intending to throttle him."

Here, Dub Bennett paused again. I didn't hurry him along because I thought I knew what happened next.

"Stick didn't think," Dub finally said. "He just reacted the way any of us would have at that time. And the old man ran into Stick's bayonet." Dub shook his head in amazement. "Even that didn't stop him. He still lunged for Stick's throat and nearly got it."

"Instead he got Stick's rabbit's foot," I said.

Dub nodded. "Stick didn't realize it until we were back in camp and he had the painting cut out and rolled up inside this map case he'd found. You should have seen the look that came over him. I've never seen a man so shook in my life.

"The funny thing is," Dub continued, "we'd both gone from Normandy to the Bulge to there without so much as a scratch on either one of us, and the very next week both of us went down. I told him right then, while we were still there in the field hospital, to get rid of that damn painting, it was bad luck. But he said the damage was already done. He'd lost his luck the moment he'd lost his rabbit's foot."

I leaned my head back on the doily and stared at the ceiling. I now thought I knew who had killed Mose and Martin Weidner and why. But I had to be certain.

"He never even tried to go back after his rabbit's foot?" I asked.

"There wasn't time. We broke camp that night. The next morning we'd crossed a river and were on our way to Munich."

"And the old man that Mose bayoneted?"

"I assume he died. We didn't stay around long enough to find out."

"Did Mose ever have that painting appraised?"

"He tried a couple times once we got home, but nobody would ever put a price on it. One guy said it was priceless. Another guy said it was worthless. You figure it out. I can't."

"And there in the house was the only time you saw the painting?"

"The only time, Garth. That's the God's truth. But I remember it just like it was yesterday."

"Describe it for me in detail, please."

He did but had little to add beyond what Tom Ford had told me.

"Did Mose ever show that painting to Lawrence Hess?"

"He talked about it, but I'm not sure he ever did."

"Do you mind if I use your phone, Dub?"

He pointed to show me. "It's there on the table. Help yourself."

I called Ruth at home and told her what I wanted her to do for me. "Garth, do you realize what time it is?"

"Whatever time it is, Ruth, it might be growing short for Elizabeth Ford. I wouldn't ask if it weren't important."

"I'll see what I can do."

My next call was to Lawrence Hess. I hoped that he was home, but I couldn't be sure he would be.

"Whoever it is," he said on answering, "it's too damn late to be calling. Call me again at a civilized hour." He hung up.

I tried again and got through. "Lawrence, this is Garth. I need to talk to you."

"You need to what?"

"Talk to you."

"I do have office hours, you know."

"Sorry, Lawrence, but I need answers and I need them now."

He yawned, then said, "Speak."

I told him what I knew about the painting, what it looked like, where it had come from and when, everything but the circumstances that surrounded it. "What I need to know is, could it be valuable?"

"To whom?"

"Anybody."

"Things can have value that have no worth, Garth."

"On the market, then."

"I wouldn't know without seeing the painting. But the way you describe it, I don't see how it could be worth a great deal. During the Third Reich, the only paintings that were allowed to be displayed in Germany were those that glorified the Reich. And frankly, Garth, a lot of those paintings of that particular era aren't worth a shit on the market today. There's a warehouse full of them collecting dust. You can't even give them away." He paused, which I hoped meant he was thinking. "But the painting as you describe it doesn't seem to fit that particular school of thought. So it could have come from somewhere else."

"Paris, for example?" I was thinking that it might have been stolen during the German occupation.

"Perhaps. But after stealing it, who then would be foolish enough to hang it on his wall?"

"Thanks, Lawrence. Sorry to disturb you."

"I hope it's the last time for a while."

"With any luck, it will be."

Dub Bennett had turned the television back

on but not the sound. "You leaving?" he asked.

"Yes."

"Is this the end of it?"

"You mean am I coming back? No."

"Good."

I nodded and left.

CHAPTER 22

Amber Utley looked as if she had been crying. Her eyes were red and her cheeks were streaked with mascara. She had answered the door, wearing the same sea-green housecoat that I had last seen her in. It hadn't grown any in my absence.

"Is Tom here?" I asked.

"No. I sent him home. But you're welcome to come in." She took my hand and led me inside, then closed the door behind us.

"I can't stay," I said.

But when I started to explain, she burst into tears, and a moment later I found myself holding her.

"To think," she said between sobs, "I was all ready to run away with that man. If my car hadn't broken down, I would have."

It had begun to heat up in that apartment, with parts of me warmer than others. But when I tried to put some distance between us, she clung to me all the tighter. I hadn't tried as hard to get away as I might have, either.

"Oh, it was great in the beginning, just the two of us," she said. "Tom and me for as long as we wanted each other, it seemed. As soon as my car was fixed, we'd take off and start a new life somewhere else, the way we'd always talked about doing. It was crazy, I know that now, but I found that kind of exciting. Run away to paradise. Have Tom Ford all to myself . . ."

I noticed that she wasn't crying anymore or clinging to me with the ferocity that she once was. I could have released her but didn't. She didn't offer any resistance.

"Then he had to have this. Then he had to have that. Then he had to have his beer, and when that ran out, he got ugly. Not mean ugly. Just ugly. Not any fun to be around at all. And when he drank too much, he wasn't any good in bed. When he stopped drinking, he fell asleep. And he snores. God, how that man snores. I don't know how his wife has stood it all these years."

I could feel the hard tips of her breasts through my raincoat. She no doubt could feel the tip of me through her housecoat.

"Amber, I have to go," I said in a husky voice that I didn't recognize as mine.

"Stay, please. For a little while."

Then she stepped back away from me and loosened the tie on her housecoat. I noticed, among other things, (1) that while she had sent Tom Ford home, the diamond pendant had stayed here, (2) that she was every bit as beautiful as I had imagined she would be, and even more desirable.

Here was my fantasy — no longer in my head, but real, right before my eyes, ripe and ready for the taking. Had Abby Airhart not come into my life, had Elizabeth Ford not been missing, already I would have been out of my clothes.

"I'm sorry, Amber. I can't."

"I won't ask again."

I kissed my finger and touched it to her nose. "You won't need to ask again. Life should be kinder to you in the future."

She reached up and kissed my finger before I drew it away. "I've wanted to anyway, with you. For a long time now."

"Same here," I said, then left before I changed my mind.

I was on my way to Tom Ford's house when Danny Palmer's words came back to haunt me. "You can always have what you don't want."

Amended by me to: you can have what you want, but you don't know it yet, and by the time you learn it, it's too late to do anything about it. Or perhaps a more succinct version: everything having been taken into consideration and all factors being equal, you're screwed, bucko. Which only proved that God, or nature, or the Great Spirit, or the Great Bambini, whoever rolled my dice, had a sense of humor.

As I stood in the mist outside of Tom and Tanya Ford's back door, I was struck by how sad the house looked. It seemed to sag ever lower toward the ground, as if its foundation, which had started giving years ago, now had only its framework to hold it up. Sort of like a lot of things.

Tanya Ford sat at the kitchen table, smoking a cigarette and drinking a cup of coffee. Her ashtray was full to overflowing. Apparently she had been sitting there for some time.

"He's in the living room, Garth. At least he was the last time I looked."

"I haven't found Elizabeth yet."

She took a deep drag on her cigarette, then blew a smoke ring toward the ceiling. Her eyes had gone dead, as had her voice. One woman's loss was another woman's pain.

"I figured you hadn't," she said. "Will you?"

"I hope so."

I went into the living room where Tom Ford

sat at the far end of the couch, staring at a fuzzy television screen. Whatever station he had been watching had gone off the air, but he apparently hadn't noticed, or didn't care. The twelve-pack of Old Milwaukee lay on the floor at his feet. Six dead soldiers stood on the end table beside him. He still wore a handcuff like a large silver bracelet on each wrist.

"She dumped me, Garth," he said while staring straight ahead. "She said to get out and never come back." His voice was thick with emotion. He would have cried, had he allowed himself that luxury. "I loved that girl, Garth. I loved her with all of my heart. I would have done anything in the world for her. Anything . . ." His voice trailed off as he reached down for another beer.

"I need your help, Tom, in finding Elizabeth. Can you forget about your own troubles long enough to give it to me?"

He popped the tab on his beer, took a drink of it, and slammed the can down hard on the end table, rattling the other cans as he did. "Elizabeth. That little sneak. She had that damn painting all along, and what did she do, let me get my ass thrown in jail, that's what she did. Ruined my frigging life, that's what she did."

A shadow crossed the room as Tanya Ford came in to stand in the doorway. "You're miserable, you know that," she said to him. "Your daughter's missing, maybe dead, and all you can think about is yourself. God, I don't know why I ever married you in the first place. I must have been crazy."

He said, "You were crazy, all right. Crazy for what I had. You still are, if you want to know the truth about it."

She jiggled her blouse, then fanned her face as if the thought of him were too hot to handle. "I want you all right. I want you out of here first thing in the morning."

"Yeah, yeah," he said. "And by tomorrow afternoon, you'll be begging me to come home again, just like you always do. So why don't you put a lid on it and save yourself some grief."

She flipped him off then went back into the kitchen.

He just smiled at her and reached for his beer. "She knows who wears the pants in this house," he said. "She knows."

"Later, Tom," I said. "I can see I'm wasting my time."

"What is it that you wanted to know, Garth?" he said after draining his beer.

"When Martin Weidner showed you the painting to make sure you had the right one, where was Dutchman Yoder at the time?"

"Let me think." He reached up to scratch

the dark stubble of his beard, which he had let go for the past few days. "He was standing right behind us when I first noticed him. I didn't see or hear him come up, so I don't know how long he was there."

"Then he saw the painting?"

"I don't see how he could have missed it. Not unless he was blind."

Tom Ford was reaching for another beer when I left the room.

"I mean it, Garth," Tanya said to me on my way through the kitchen. "I'm throwing him out of here the first thing tomorrow morning, and I don't care what he says, I'm not taking him back."

"Then do it."

"I will."

But neither one of us believed her.

One more stop to make. I just hoped that Luella Skiles was still up. Not only up, but watching for me through her bay window. Watching for someone, anyway.

"Any word on Elizabeth?" she said on answering the door.

Luella wore the same baggy cotton pants and flannel shirt that she had been wearing when I last saw her a few hours ago. The same worried look of concern on her face.

"No word yet. But I'm about to go looking for her."

"If anything happens to that child, I'll never forgive myself," she said.

With good reason, I thought.

"You could have told me what you knew," I said. "It might have saved both of us a lot of grief."

"I didn't think it was important. Simply because I didn't think that Dutchman Yoder could be the one to have done what he did. Not until this morning when I went downstairs and smelled him."

"What is that smell, anyway?"

"Horse liniment." My brows must have raised in question because she said, "My father was a blacksmith."

"You smelled it, too, in Monroe Edmonds's house?"

"Earlier. On those nights when Sheriff Roberts and then Sheriff Clark came and no one was there. Not the night that Monroe died. I never went into the house."

"Then why did you go out to Dutchman Yoder's house on Monday to buy butter that you didn't need?"

"Because I saw his wagon parked just down the street Friday, which wasn't unusual because he's always around at garage sales. But when I checked the *Reporter*, I didn't see any garage sales advertised in the neighborhood."

"He could have been making home deliveries," I said. "He does sometimes."

"Not for two hours at a time. So once I had time to think about it, I put the liniment and horses together and came up with Dutchman Yoder." She frowned, disappointed in herself. "But when I drove out there to confront him about it, I couldn't smell a thing on him . . ."

"Lucky for you," I said. "But I couldn't smell a thing on him, either. I think it has to do with atmospheric conditions, how much moisture is in the air, and whether he's inside or out."

She continued unruffled, the way she always did in Sunday school after I had spoken my piece, as if she had never been interrupted in the first place. "So I thought, well, perhaps whoever it is now has what he wants, and things will return to normal. I'm not big on justice, Garth, as you are. But then he had the temerity to come *here*." Her face had hardened, her voice along with it. "*Here*. Into my house. My sanctuary. I want that man arrested, Garth. I want the sun to never shine on his face again."

With any luck, she'd get her wish.

CHAPTER 23

On my way home in Jessie, I met another car. Because of the fog on Jessie's windshield, I couldn't see the driver, but I recognized the bubble light on top. It was Eugene Yuill, out patrolling the streets of Oakalla, facing up to his demons rather than waiting for them to come to him. Somehow that helped give me the courage to face some demons of my own.

Ruth was sitting at the kitchen table when I came in the back door. The kitchen clock read two-thirty. It seemed later. I wondered if, just for the hell of it, Ruth had set it back a few hours.

"You look a mess," she said.

"I imagine I do."

"Abby called a few minutes ago, worried about you. I told her that as of last report, you were all right. She wanted you to call her when you got in."

"You'll have to do that for me, Ruth. If you will?"

She didn't say anything, but I assumed she would.

"Ruth, you can figure out where I'm going. Just don't tell her. I don't want her ending up out there. You, either."

"Somebody needs to know, Garth. If not for your sake, mine."

"Then call the state police. Have them send somebody out."

I thought about what all I ought to take with me and dismissed everything but a flashlight. The odds were that Dutchman Yoder wasn't even there. If he was there, waiting for me, as he had been for Monroe Edmonds, Elizabeth Ford, Mose and Martin Weidner, I didn't see how having a weapon would give me an advantage. What I had to trust, more so than my arsenal, was Dutchman Yoder's integrity. What I had to ignore was that he had already killed three people that I knew of and likely set his sights on another.

"You were right about Dutchman Yoder," Ruth said. "I called my Cousin Agnes, in the Rapids, and she put out the word on what you wanted to know. A friend of a friend works as a teller in the bank across from where we saw Dutchman's horses and wagon parked. She couldn't tell Agnes the details, but she did say a strangely dressed old man converted a whole lot of cash into hundred-dollar bills."

His life savings, no doubt, which he had earned, in the early years of his truck patch and garden, pennies at a time.

"It's sad," I said to Ruth.

"What is?"

"Dutchman Yoder. All these years he's been someone he's not."

"And someone he is."

"That's what's sad. I don't know who he is or who he isn't anymore."

"He killed three people, Garth. That should give you some clue."

I got in Jessie and for the third time that night drove north on Fair Haven Road. Drizzle had gradually changed over to a mist, mist to a dense fog that settled into every bottom and valley, and came and went with every dip in the road. I drove slowly with my head out the window, since I was unable to see a thing through Jessie's windshield. That was why I didn't see her temperature gauge creeping toward red or realize until after it happened that she was about to die on me.

I shifted her into neutral, and we coasted as far as Grandmother Ryland's before I muscled her into the drive and stopped. Nothing to do then but to get out and walk.

Before I ever reached Dutchman Yoder's lane, I could hear his cows bawling. They truly were in agony. I imagined myself with a full bladder, getting fuller, and being unable to urinate. If I lived through this, I would see that relief came in the morning, even if I had to milk each one of them myself.

At the end of the lane, I stopped. The house and barn were both dark, the windmill dead still. Though it was hard to hear above the cows, I thought I heard a noise coming from the barn. It sounded like a door banging.

I went into the barn through the door beside the silo and stood for a moment, while waiting for my eyes to adjust to the dark. I thought I had made a silent entrance. Somewhere above me in the silo, however, a pigeon fluttered uneasily on its perch. Insomnia perhaps. A barn lot full of bawling cows could do that to you. Or perhaps I wasn't alone in the barn.

I heard the banging noise again. Whatever it was, it was coming from the other end of the barn. Outside the barn or inside it? I had to choose which way to go. I chose inside because that seemed the surest way to get there. It turned out to be the wrong choice.

I never saw him coming. He stepped out of a shadow and laid something alongside my ear so gently that I hardly noticed it until my knees buckled and my head hit the floor.

Cold. I was freezing cold, and no matter how hard I hugged myself or into what shape

I bent my body to hold a breath of warmth, I couldn't keep myself from shivering. Then a light stabbed me in the eyes, and I moaned and rolled away from it. For a terrifying instant, when the light had first hit me, it felt as if my head would explode.

"You are awake now, yah?" I heard Dutchman Yoder say.

"Yah," I said, mocking him. "I am awake now."

But I didn't move from where I was. Anything was better than looking into that light again.

"I'll be going now soon," he said. "I had hoped to take your car, but other plans have had to be made."

I was afraid to answer right away. My head hurt, and I still was having a hard time keeping my shivering under control. I felt that if I lost my concentration, if I let either my mind or my arms slip, I would fly to pieces.

"Sorry about the car," I said. "But I probably did you a favor by leaving her home."

I didn't want him to know just how near Jessie was. Not that I would miss her any, but now that she had cooled down, the old rip would probably take him as far as he wanted to go.

"Yah. That one is trouble, you can be sure. But I kind of like the old girl. We are one

317

of a kind, she and I."

I rose to a sitting position then lay back down again. My head wasn't quite ready for vertical yet.

"What did you hit me with?" I said.

"Lead wrapped in leather. It is effective, don't you think?"

"Effective," I said, once again trying to sit up and once again failing.

"Why do you try so hard to get up? You are not going anywhere, you know."

"Because," I gritted my teeth against the pain and forced myself up, "I don't like to be down."

"An admirable trait to be sure."

I didn't say anything. I was having too hard a time holding my head up. Opening my eyes would come next, but that would have to wait.

"You are perhaps wondering why I did what I have done?" he said. "Let me say only this. Vengeance has a long life."

"If you feed it."

"No, my friend. It is better to starve it. Make it hungry like the wolf in winter. Then when its chance comes, it will strike swiftly, without thought. Without mercy. Vengeance fat might grant forgiveness."

I opened my eyes, saw that I was in the corncrib, and closed them again. "God knows we're overrun with forgiveness these days."

"And had it been your papa who was killed? Would you let his death go unpunished?"

I opened my eyes. Success! If I squinted, I could keep them open without blowing off the top of my head.

"No. But I wouldn't have made his death my life's crusade, either."

"I do not agree. Otherwise, you would not be here now, and I would not have been here waiting for you. Like me, you will see things through to the end. It is in our blood. We do not rule it anymore than we do the stars above."

"Don't compare us, Dutchman. We're not the same."

"That's because you think I am a big bad Nazi. But I am not and was not. I was a boy, who at seventeen was already a two-year veteran of the German army. A deserter by then, running for his life, who had come home to his mama and papa and asked them to please hide him." His voice had lost its customary lilt. He, in fact, could hardly speak at all. "Do you know what my papa's last words to me were? 'Heinrich, it appears I played my part too well.' No Nazi either was my papa. But a simple gardener, and a would-be painter, whose last act was to give his life for his son."

I stared at the mound of corn in front of me. It sounded like a rat was stirring somewhere in its midst.

"It was all an act, your father's obsession with the painting?" I said. Perhaps I hadn't heard him right.

"All an act," he said. "Except to me, that painting has no value. It was painted by a friend of my father's when they were students at the Academy of Art in Vienna. My father only hung it because he did not want to hurt his friend's feelings, and like an old shoe that you cannot bear to part with, it stayed on his wall ever since."

"Then why go to all the trouble to get it back?"

"Because it is *mine*, and I am alone. I have no family. I am the only son, the only child, born late in my mama's and papa's life. It is the only thing of me left alive."

Definitely a rat. I could hear him gnawing on the corn. I was having no trouble keeping my eyes open now.

"You count no friends, no family among the people of Oakalla?"

"I count you," he said.

"No one else?"

"No. No one else. To the rest of Oakalla, I was just a curious old Dutchman, who kept them supplied with what they needed at a price they thought fair. Just a trader to them, that's all. But you. You saw into my soul."

"Apparently not far enough."

"If you are talking about Mr. Monroe, that was an accident. I had no desire to kill him, only to search his house without his interference. If you are talking about Mose Weidner, yah, I intended to kill him. But first, I wanted his son to die in his arms, as my papa died in mine."

"You put the rabbit's foot in Martin's hand?"

"Yah. It is home now where it belongs."

If by home, he meant my pocket, then he was right. "And Luella Skiles, didn't you intend on killing her last night?"

"I thought about it, yah. She knew too much, I feared. But once I was there in her house, it did not feel right to me, so I left."

"And went after a twelve-year-old girl instead."

"I know what you are doing. You are trying to shame me. But that twelve-year-old girl has the heart of a lion and the mind of a fox. When I did not find my painting among Mr. Monroe's things, I knew he must have given it to someone else. But who? Who?"

I turned to look at him for the first time, saw something white where his mouth should be, and assumed they were his teeth.

He continued. "Who among that crowd would I trust with something that I thought had great value?" He was shaking his finger at me now. "That's when it paid to be a simple old Dutchman, who could watch all he wanted and not be worried about. People tell on themselves by how they act, yah, when they think no one is watching. That girl, I thought, is the one I would trust."

"Where is she now, Dutchman?" I asked in the hope of catching him off guard.

But he ignored me. "It will be light soon. It is time for me to go."

"Another question or two, since you're the only one who can answer them?"

"If you hurry. Yah."

The rat sounded as if he were having too good a time. I threw an ear of corn his way and silenced him for the moment.

"Are you the one who knocked out Deputy Yuill Sunday night?"

"Yah. I was the one. Forty-eight years now. Forty-eight years, and all I have had is a rabbit's foot, and a name, Oakalla, Wisconsin. Forty-eight years of planning and searching and living the lonely life. Of going from a young man with dreams to an old man with only memories, most of them made in a strange land that was not his home. Bitter memories. Though not all of them. Not all of them. There was some sweetness in my life, sure." Here he paused and smiled, as I had often done of late, as if on the first breath of dawn he could still taste the sweetness. "Forty-eight years of not even knowing if my quest was true, of sticking a pin in the face of doubt whenever it grew too large. Forty-eight years, my good friend. I would not let some stupid man who is not even a fit deputy take that away from me."

"Then Mose and Martin Weidner were in the house?"

"The M and M Boys. I had followed them into town to keep them out of trouble. I did a good job, hey? I had to be sure that Mose was the one who took the painting. When he went to Mr. Monroe's house, I knew for sure."

"They were in a pickup. You were in a horse-drawn wagon. How did you keep up with them?"

"Not in a wagon, no. And I did not keep up with them. I went to where I knew they would go."

"And if you had never found the painting, what would you have done?"

His smile widened. His teeth looked as large as piano keys. "Beside the point, my friend. I found it."

He started in the direction of the house, went a few feet, and stopped, turning back to me. "When you are rescued, will you see that my cows are milked? I will not have time."

"I've already made a note of that."

"I will miss them." He took one last sweeping look at his farm. "I will miss all of them."

As soon as he was out of sight, I stood and got the biggest head rush of my life. Fighting for balance, I slid on an ear of corn and slammed into the side of the corncrib, where I clung, like a monkey to the bars of his cage. Then my head gradually cleared, and I opened my eyes again.

Morning was on its way. Through the slats of the corncrib, I could see a waning moon and a few remaining stars that seemed to dissolve all at once as the sky lightened. I took a step toward the door and had to wait for my head to clear. Getting out of here was going to take longer than I had first thought.

Then I saw Dutchman Yoder walking down the lane that led to his back pasture and the woods beyond. Had Jessie not conked out on me, he would have been driving her instead of walking right now. Food for thought, however I wanted to chew it.

My first attempt at breaking down the door proved futile. All I got for my effort was a sore shoulder and a case of the dizzies that brought on the dry heaves. Sitting back down again, watching the corncrib slowly spin to a stop, I heard the rat munching on another ear of corn. But I didn't have the strength to throw something at him.

Dawn. Almost a blue sky above, almost a white radiance below. Torn patches of mist skulked about the barnyard, as if looking for someplace to hide now that the sun was coming out, and swirled around Dutchman Yoder's herd of brown Jerseys, like surf around a reef. Somewhere to the north a rooster crowed. Somewhere to the west a horse whinnied. The rooster was no doubt one of Mose and Martin Weidner's bantams, announcing a new day. The horse I had to wonder about.

I rose unsteadily and slowly made my way to the door of the corncrib. Like the rest of the corncrib, the door was made of seasoned oak boards about an inch thick and four inches wide and reinforced with two diagonal crosspieces that formed an X, like the arms of a railroad crossing. With a hammer and a pry bar, I might have made it out of there within the hour. With my bare hands, it was going to take me considerably longer.

Then I saw what appeared to be an angel in white running through the mist. Not wanting to miss the last train bound for glory, I yelled at her.

She stopped, turned my way momentarily, and was off again. To say that she ran like a scared rabbit wouldn't do her justice. No rabbit, scared or otherwise, could have kept up with those whirling legs of hers.

"Elizabeth! It's me, Garth Ryland."

She stopped again, but it wouldn't be for long. Wherever she had been, she wasn't going back if she could help it.

"Show yourself," she said, glancing nervously about her as if her head was on a swivel.

"I would if I could, but I'm locked in the corncrib."

"How do I know you are who you say you are?"

"I talked to you Sunday morning after church. You sent your sisters on ahead. You said Miss Utley wasn't really your type."

"Where did you say you are?"

"The corncrib. It's the small building with the slanted roof and the spaces between the boards."

She glanced over her shoulder then around the barn lot. "How do I know *he's* not still around?"

"Because I saw him leave a few minutes ago." Probably more than a few minutes ago by now, but I wasn't keeping track.

She came to the door of the corncrib. She wore the long white nightie that I had seen

her in Saturday morning and that was all —
no shoes, socks, hat, or coat. She peered in
at me, still not sure that she wanted to open
the door. I felt like the star of a freak show.

"It is you," she said at last. Then she unlatched the door.

I started forward then stopped. My head
wasn't quite ready for motion yet.

"What's the matter?" she said, helping me
outside.

"He hit me over the head. I'm still dizzy."

"You probably have a concussion," she said
with authority.

"Probably."

"We'd better get you to a doctor."

"First things first." I felt better now that
I was out of the corncrib.

"Where are you going?"

I had started in the direction that Dutchman
Yoder had taken. "Do you want your painting
back or not?"

"Yes," she said. "But only because Mr. Edmonds gave it to me."

"Then I'm going after it."

"Then I'm going with you."

I started to say no but changed my mind.
She had a right to know what had cost Monroe
Edmonds his life, and if Dutchman Yoder was
going to do either of us any harm, he would
have done it already. Besides, the way I fig-

ured it, Elizabeth had a right to reclaim the picture if she still wanted it. It was free for the taking, since it had already been bought and paid for many times over.

"Come on, then," I said. "If you're going."

CHAPTER 24

The sun ignited the woods ahead just as we entered the lane that would lead us to the back of Dutchman Yoder's property. Four strands of barbed wire nailed to locust posts ran along on either side of us and made the lane seem narrower than it was. The hard-packed ground underfoot felt spongy, almost boglike from all of the rain, and gave me the not-so-pleasant sensation of walking on March ice. Two ankle-deep wagon ruts ran down the center of the lane, as straight and true as railroad tracks. We followed them.

"What happened to you?" I asked. I noticed that Elizabeth Ford was limping.

"He had me locked in the feed bin. I had to kick my way out." She was staring at my raincoat. "What happened to you?"

I told her.

"I guess he was serious, then." Her eyes were in sharp focus, as if she were staring death in the face.

"About what?"

"He said he would kill my two sisters if I didn't give him the painting, then my mother when she came home."

"And you believed him?"

"I didn't have a choice."

"He was waiting there in your room when you went to bed?"

"Yes. He pointed this gun at me and told me to be very still. He didn't have to tell me twice."

We came to the pasture at the end of the lane. Though the walking was more difficult here because of the soft muddy ground, I was glad to put the lane behind us.

"He didn't hurt you in any way, did he?" I said.

"No. He was the perfect gentleman," she said, reading between the lines. "He even apologized for putting me through all of this. But it was necessary, he said, to right a wrong. Or how did he put it, to make all the chickens come home to roost again. Except . . ." There was a gleam in her eye. "A perfect gentleman would not threaten to kill my mother and sisters, yah."

We came to a large multiflora rosebush that had taken over one corner of the pasture. It was there that I saw fresh horse droppings for the first time. Apparently this was where Dutchman Yoder had hidden his horses and wagon when he was through with them the night before.

"It looks like he's headed for the creek," I said.

"Is that bad?"

"It is for us, if he makes it across."

"Then we'd better hurry," she said, wanting to run.

I shook my head and regretted it immediately, as a thousand stars spilled out of it. "No. I'm not up to it."

"I am." She took off running before I could stop her.

I went after her but couldn't keep up. After slowing to a walk, the best that I could do was to keep putting one foot in front of the other.

What stopped her, and what had stopped Dutchman Yoder's wagon, was Hog Run. At its very brim, it churned through the glide of solid bedrock that was once a cattle crossing, defying anyone to cross it.

Dutchman Yoder had tried but apparently had not succeeded. One of his Belgians, either Bill or Bud, stood almost up to his neck in water about halfway across Hog Run, as if anchored there. The other Belgian was still hitched to the wagon.

"Why doesn't he cross?" Elizabeth asked about the horse in the water.

"Maybe he can't swim."

She gave me an unforgiving look, and I saw Elizabeth Ford's only blemish. She had a limited sense of humor.

"Okay," I said. "Maybe the water drops off there, and he's afraid to go on." But I saw no high bank on the other side, which would indicate a drop-off.

"Why doesn't he back up?"

She was asking an equestrian illiterate, whose only knowledge of horses came from Dick Francis novels. "I think horses are pretty much straight-ahead animals, like you and me."

She looked at me and smiled. I was forgiven. "We can't just leave him there. He'll drown."

She was using twelve-year-old logic, true, which came straight from the heart, but she also had a point. It took a heroic effort to stand stock-still against that current, which the horse was doing. In time, it would wear him down, and he probably would drown. I had no great love of horses, but I did of heroic efforts.

"You're right," I said. "We can't let him drown."

After unhitching the other Belgian from the

wagon, I saw that I had an immediate problem. How did I get up on him, and once up, how did I stay on his broad back? The last time I had ridden a horse, which was nearly forty years ago, I had reins, bridle, saddle, and stirrups, and someone to lead me around the ring in the park.

"This isn't going to work," I said, after a couple feeble efforts to mount him failed.

"I'll help you." She bent down and cupped her hands.

"No. That won't work, either." I could already see me sliding off the other side onto my head.

"What will work, then?" A bright girl, she had already guessed that I really didn't want to do this. "Why don't you get up on the wagon, and I'll lead him to you?"

I had already thought of that and dismissed it. It would have taken a far better horseman than I to stay on the horse under any circumstances, let alone in the midst of a raging stream.

"Why don't I walk the horse instead."

"You'll drown," she said.

"Only if I fall."

I grabbed the horse by the bridle. "Come on, Bill," I said.

He didn't move.

I tried again. "Come on, Bud."

He did as I asked. At least now I knew his name.

Positioning Bud upstream to block some of the current, I took my first step into Hog Run and immediately was knocked off my feet. When nineteen, I had almost drowned in a riptide off of Santa Monica Beach. The force of Hog Run felt exactly the same. Without good old Bud there to hang on to, I would have been swept downstream.

"Come back!" Elizabeth yelled at me.

I didn't know how to tell her that I couldn't do that, even if I'd wanted to. Bud had made up his mind that he was going to cross the stream, with me or without me.

"Easy, big fella," I said, feeling for the bottom and finally hitting bedrock. "I can only go so fast."

Smart horse that he was, Bud understood. He adjusted his pace accordingly.

We did fine until we got to the middle of Hog Run where Bill stood. He didn't have the same look in his eye as Bud. A lot of the light had gone out of it. Exhausted from his battle with the cold current, he had started to tremble. It took all of his strength just to maintain his position. The thought of going on really didn't appeal to him.

I hung between the two great horses, one hand on the bridle of one, one hand on the bridle of the other, bouncing in the current, going nowhere.

Bud tried his best, but when he edged forward, and Bill didn't follow, the strain on my arms grew to be too much, as I cried out in pain, "Whoa, Bud!"

He stopped, then backed up a step, as if instinctively he understood my dilemma. I continued to bob in the current, wondering how much longer I could hold on.

"Talk to him, Bud. He won't listen to me."

Bud turned his head my way. What do you expect for free, his look seemed to say. But he did nudge Bill on the chin with his nose, as if to say, "Keep your head up."

"Last chance, Bill," I said. "I'm going with Bud."

Then I remembered what Dutchman Yoder had done so many times in the past.

"Yah, Billy! Yah, Bud!" I yelled at the top of my voice.

In the surge that followed, I was nearly torn in two, but I hung on long enough to reach the opposite shore, where I dropped to the ground as they thundered past. A few minutes later, I caught up to them at a gate. There, I saw the anchor that had been holding Bill to the bedrock of Hog Run. The reins wrapped around his right arm, his left arm cradling a long green cylinder, Dutchman Yoder lay dead at Bill's feet.

CHAPTER 25

"I'll meet you at the bridge," I yelled to Elizabeth Ford across Hog Run.

I carried the Army-green map case in my hand and Dutchman Yoder's money belt around my waist under my raincoat. I hadn't had time to count the money yet, but for whatever I chose to spend it on, it would do nicely.

"Where did you find that?" Elizabeth asked about the map case.

"I'll tell you about it when we get to the bridge."

I had also found a new suit of clothes under Dutchman Yoder's old one and discovered that the last thing he had done before he left home was to shave. It was strange to see him freshly shaved in a new suit of clothes — stranger even than seeing him dead.

"Is he dead?" Elizabeth asked about a half hour later when we finally made our way to the iron bridge just south of Mose and Martin Weidner's house.

"Yes. He's dead."

"I'm sorry."

"Yeah. Me, too."

"He wasn't a bad man. Do you think?"

I looked up the road to the house where the floor was painted with blood. I looked down the road to the farm where Dutchman Yoder had spent forty-some years of his life doing good.

"Don't ask me to judge, Elizabeth. I'm not that smart."

She shivered. Since she still wore only her nightie, I thought it was from the cold.

"You want my raincoat?" I asked.

She shook her head no. "It's just that you think you know somebody, and you don't."

"Ruth and I shared those same thoughts earlier this morning."

"Ruth?"

"My housekeeper, Mrs. Krammes."

"What did she say about Dutchman Yoder?"

"She said he killed three people. That should tell me something."

"Is that how you feel?"

"No. But don't ask me why."

I handed her the map case. I was glad to be rid of it.

"Should I open it?" she said.

"It's up to you. I thought you already had."

"No. Mr. Edmonds said it was my future. But not to open it until I really needed it and then to take it to Mr. Hess to sell it."

"You'd better open it," I said.

She unlatched the top of the map case and withdrew the painting, which was still dry and sound, even after having been submerged in Hog Run. As she unrolled the painting, I saw what appeared to be a French chateau done in watercolors. Tom Ford was right about the painting itself. It was nothing special.

"Turn it over," I said.

She did. As we stood there in the gravel atop the iron bridge, I saw what all the fuss was about. Written in German was the inscription: Fur meinen guten Freund Otto. Hier ist Dein Traumhaus. It was signed: A. Hitler.

"I know him," Elizabeth said. Her voice left no doubt.

"A lot of us do."

She hurriedly rolled up the painting and put it back in the map case, as if suddenly it had become too hot to handle.

"Is it really worth anything?" she asked

once it was safely inside.

"That depends on whom you ask."

"What about to Mr. Hess?"

I thought about Lawrence Hess's room in the turret and the ghosts who seemed to haunt it. Had they been Dutchman Yoder, hungry for a touch of home, or were they something else again, the hounds of hell waiting for their master's call?

"I don't know, Elizabeth. You'll have to ask him."

"What do you think he will offer me?"

I didn't know what Lawrence Hess would offer or what he would do with the painting once he got it. But I knew that he would be fair and pay the going price.

"Enough to buy you a year or two of college," I said. "Beyond that, I can't say."

"That's not much of a future."

"It's a start."

She checked the lid on the map case, making sure that it was secure. Then she tossed the case into Hog Run. The last I saw of it, it had shot a rapids and was still riding high.

"Now I feel like a fool," she said, watching it go.

I put my arm around her and didn't say anything.

A couple minutes later, a Wisconsin State

Police car pulled up on the bridge and stopped beside us. The man driving it was young and obviously lost.

"Could you tell me how to get to . . ." Here he referred to his notes. "Dutchman Yoder's place?"

"I could tell you," I said. "But it won't do you any good. There's no one home."

He studied Elizabeth and me for a moment and understood. "Would you like a ride back to town?"

I looked down at Elizabeth's bare feet, her briar-scratched legs, and bruised heels. "Yes. I believe we would."

CHAPTER 26

The next Saturday morning, Ruth and I sat at the kitchen table, drinking coffee. I had found a home for Dutchman Yoder's Jerseys with Gene Hurst, a local dairyman, who said that while his Holsteins weren't quite sure what to think of them, the Jerseys certainly didn't hurt his butterfat count any. Bill and Bud went to Alfred Thomas, a local logger, who still dragged out hard-to-get logs the old-fashioned way with a team of horses. Mose and Martin Weidner's exotic animals were still fending for themselves, while the county court decided what to do with them.

Monroe Edmonds, Martin and Mose Weidner were buried on the same day in Fair Haven Cemetery. Dutchman Yoder was buried the following day in the pines behind his house. A letter found in the seat box of his wagon, along with a Luger and a bloodstained bayonet, made me the guardian of his estate. A will found in Monroe Edmonds's secretary left all of his estate to the Railroad Widows and Orphans Fund.

"What do you think, Ruth," I said, "did Dutchman Yoder know who had signed that painting or not?"

"What if he did? Would that change anything?"

"I just want your opinion, that's all."

"My opinion is that it doesn't matter one way or another. We all believe what we want to believe. Dutchman Yoder was no exception."

"You don't think his father died trying to save him rather than the painting?"

She gave me a look that said I should know better. "Think about it, Garth. You're living in a country filled with fear, where the next knock on the door might be the last thing you'll ever hear. But there hanging on your wall is your insurance policy, a painting signed by the Führer himself. To a small man, which Dutchman Yoder's father probably was, it would become a giant thing, something to hang on to, no matter what the cost."

"Even your own life?"

"Maybe that was his life, Garth. All that was left of it."

"And Dutchman Yoder? What was the painting to him?"

"Maybe something to look forward to," she

said. "A reason to keep on going. He didn't keep it long, did he, once he got it?"

"You don't think he planned to?"

She shrugged.

I drank the rest of my coffee then looked at my watch. "Time to go," I said.

"You're sure that you want to go through with this?"

"I'm sure, Ruth. It's a good investment."

"If there is such a thing."

At exactly nine A.M. I met Elizabeth Ford in front of the First Farmers Bank of Oakalla. Five minutes later, Eddie Vincent, vice-president in charge of trusts, shook my hand warmly and showed us into his office. At nine-thirty A.M., Elizabeth Ford and I left First Farmers Bank on our way to her house.

"You understand what a trust is?" I said. "You can't touch the money until you're eighteen and only then if you go on to college and stay there through graduation. Otherwise, it reverts to the town of Oakalla to be used to promote local business."

Elizabeth, who wore shorts, sneakers, bobby sox, and the red University of Wisconsin sweatshirt that I had bought her, said, "I understand all that. What I don't understand is why Mr. Edmonds never told me about this?"

"It probably slipped his mind."

344

"Or why he gave me the painting on top of everything else?"

"Insurance."

She wrinkled her nose at me. She didn't believe me but was too polite to call me a liar.

"I only wish I could thank him," she said.

"You can. By fulfilling the promise that he saw in you."

"Really thank him. With a great big hug."

"I haven't had a hug lately. Why don't you give me one, instead."

So we stopped along School Street while she gave me a great big hug. Then we went on.

"Well, here we are," she said, as we stopped at her back door. But she seemed in no hurry to go inside.

"How are things?" I asked.

"About the same as always. Things don't change very much around here."

"You're up to it. Just remember that."

She nodded. She knew that what I said was true, but that still didn't make it any easier on her.

"I just wish . . . sometimes I just wish I had a normal family. But then, I don't know of hardly anyone who does anymore."

"I don't either, Elizabeth. Not the kinds of families we used to have."

"It sure makes things tough on us kids."

"On all of us, Elizabeth."

I gave her what passed for a smile and left.

Luella Skiles waited for me at her door. "Come in, Garth. I thought you might be by one of these days."

"Then you're a mind reader."

She gave me a smug little smile. "Perhaps I am."

We went into the parlor where her grand piano stood. A cool bright sunny day outside, a warm bright sunny day inside the parlor. Had you nothing to do but sit and think, it would be a very easy place to spend your mornings.

I sat down on the couch and rested my arm on the armrest. Beside me on the end table stood the old photograph of Luella Skiles and her four sisters.

"Which one do you think I am?" she asked.

This was too easy. But for her sake, I pretended to study the photograph. "The oldest one," I said, choosing the sternest and most sober.

"Guess again."

I didn't have a second guess, but I made one anyway, choosing the second sternest face I could see. "The middle one."

She shook her head no. I really studied the photograph this time, realizing that I had been had. So I picked the most unlikely of all —

the youngest, who with skinned knees, rumpled dress, and tousled hair, looked like a pot about to boil over.

"Right," she said, with immense satisfaction.

"I don't understand."

"I didn't think you did. As children, I imagine that you and I were very much alike — headstrong, passionate, unwilling to deviate from any path that was not our own. My problem was, and I imagine to a degree that yours was too, that if I didn't get myself under control, I would very likely hurt someone else seriously, or even more likely, destroy myself. So my passion became my discipline, and in time my discipline became my passion. Which is fine if one wants to teach but not if one wants to perform."

"Which you did?"

"With all my heart."

I stared at her without saying anything. "I'm sorry" seemed a woefully inadequate response.

"And Monroe Edmonds, did he have the passion without the discipline?" I asked.

"He had both, damn him, and the talent to go with it. But he wouldn't take himself or his music seriously. All he wanted to do was to play for fun."

"There are worse things."

She smiled at me — a warm, bittersweet smile that carried in it wit and wisdom. "Too late I realized that."

I nodded and understood.

"So that's my life story," she said. "In a nutshell. That is what you came to hear, isn't it?"

"One of the things. The other was to ask you to teach Elizabeth Ford piano. She's willing if you are. You can send the bill to me."

"What makes you think I can?"

"Just a feeling I have. But if you're afraid that you'll ruin her, don't be. She has enough joy in her for both of you."

"Let me think about it."

"What's to think about? You know you can do it. I know you can do it."

"You didn't when you walked in here."

"I was much younger then."

I rose and walked to the door. She followed me there. Before leaving, I took a long look around the place. I doubted that I'd be back any time soon.

"Amateur Night, all those years ago," I said. "What was it that Monroe played?"

" 'Alexander's Ragtime Band.' I thought everyone knew that song, Garth."

"No. The other one. The one he seemed to do just for spite."

"Rachmaninoff's Prelude in G minor. He

knew it was my favorite."

"That man sure could play the piano."

"Yes. He surely could."

At the Marathon, Danny Palmer was at the back of the bay, putting new brakes on someone's blue Chevy pickup. A wrench in his hand, a look of pure concentration on his face, he seemed as content as a man could be.

"Morning, Garth," he said.

"Morning, Danny. I see you got Miss Utley's RX-7 fixed. At least I don't see it anywhere around."

He laid down his wrench and picked up a rag to wipe the grease off his hands. "Yeah, it's fixed. Funny thing was, it wasn't the timing belt after all. She just had it flooded."

I studied him. I had never known an instance when Danny Palmer couldn't tell a flooded engine from a broken timing belt.

"Lucky for her you made that mistake."

"How so?" If he were playing dumb, he was doing a good job of it.

"Rumor has it that she was about to skip town with some no-good lowlife. But by the end of a long weekend with him, she'd changed her mind."

"I hadn't heard that rumor," he said.

"Then I'd just as soon you not repeat it."

He was trying hard not to smile, but a small

one lifted at one corner of his mouth. He knew a lot more than he was telling, but I would never know how much.

"Last week when I was in here, you made the comment that you can always have what you don't want," I said. "Do you really believe that?"

"You mean would I trade my wife and kids for a chance at our favorite teacher? No, Garth. Not in this lifetime."

"I was hoping you'd say that."

He threw the rag aside and picked up his wrench again. "But there's no law that says I can't think about it."

I nodded and left. I'd gotten what I'd come for, which was reassurance that Danny Palmer would not be running off with Amber Utley any time soon.

I made my way south on Perrin Street toward a big white house with thick stone pillars that was directly across the street from the United Methodist Church. Maybe Abby Airhart wouldn't be there, but her Uncle Bill would be, and we would sit down at the kitchen table, drink a cup of coffee together, and plan our next grouse hunt. Then, when Abby finally did come home, I would call her or she would call me. She would tell me how her day went, and I would tell her what we'd planned.

ACB
11-1-2000

X